Francis Espinasse, John Parker Anderson

Life of Voltaire

Francis Espinasse, John Parker Anderson

Life of Voltaire

ISBN/EAN: 9783337333218

Printed in Europe, USA, Canada, Australia, Japan

Cover: Foto ©Raphael Reischuk / pixelio.de

More available books at **www.hansebooks.com**

LIFE

OF

VOLTAIRE.

BY

FRANCIS ESPINASSE.

LONDON:

WALTER SCOTT, Ltd.,

24, WARWICK LANE, PATERNOSTER ROW.

1892.

CONTENTS.

CONTENTS.

———•◦•———

CHAPTER I.

CHAPTER II.

He studies for the bar; is disgusted with the profession; enters the " Society of the Temple," where he is much appreciated; is sent by his father to Caën; gets into disgrace there; is sent to the Hague; falls in love with Mademoiselle Dunoyer; is sent back to Paris at the close of 1713; his father's anger; is condemned to enter the office of an attorney; gains the friendship of Thiériot, a fellow clerk; leaves the office in a few months; competes without

CHAPTER IX.

CHAPTER X.

CHAPTER XI.

CHAPTER XII.

10 *CONTENTS.*

LIFE OF VOLTAIRE.

CHAPTER I.

(1694–1711.)

FRANÇOIS MARIE AROUET, who, in his twenty-fifth year, called himself Voltaire, was born in Paris, November 21, 1694. He came into the world so sickly an infant that for months he was not expected to survive, and though he lived to be eighty-three, he suffered much from ill health throughout his prolonged existence. His only surviving brother, Armand, was by ten years, and his only sister, Marguerite, by nine years, his senior. His father, François Arouet, sprang from a reputable middle-class family of Poitou, whence his grandfather had migrated to Paris, and became a thriving clothier. François Arouet, a man of recognized ability and integrity, belonged for many years to the highest class of Paris notaries, and prospered in a calling the exercise of which included the performance of some of the more important functions of the modern English family solicitor. He was the notary of the Sullis, the Saint-Simons, the

Praslins, and others of the French *noblesse*. His wife, Marguerite d'Aumard, was well born, and, with her husband, found favour in the eyes of members of the great families, whose man of business he was. The Duc de Richelieu (father of Voltaire's Duke) and the Duchesse de Saint-Simon (mother of the writer of the " Mémoires ") had been sponsors to Armand Arouet. A few years before the birth of his second son, M. Arouet sold the notaryship which he had purchased in early life, and some years later he obtained the well-paid and very responsible office of Receiver of Fees and Fines to the Chamber of Accounts (he is sometimes styled its treasurer), an important state department which exercised jurisdiction in all matters appertaining to the complex revenues of the Crown. Besides an official residence in town, he had a country house at Chatenay, a pretty rural suburb of Paris. Madame Arouet was a friend of the famous Ninon de l'Enclos (another of her husband's distinguished clients), who, after having been made love to by three generations of Frenchmen, was in her old age the centre of a rather brilliant circle of free-thinking and free-and-easy persons of both sexes (many of them belonged to the aristocracy), forming a sort of social opposition to the then gloomy and priest-ridden court at Versailles. One of Ninon's most intimate allies, in her later and latest years, was a certain Abbé de Châteauneuf, clever, agreeable, musical, who made some figure in Paris society, and whose brother, the Marquis (M. Arouet had been the notary of both), rose high in the diplomatic service of France. The Abbé became not only a great friend of Madame Arouet, but the godfather of her second son, of whom, as he grew into a bright, intelligent, and inquisitive boy, he made quite a companion. There may be no truth in the statement, scarcely credible, that actually at the age of three the godson was taught by the godfather to repeat the " Moïsade," a long-forgotten metrical effusion in which Moses was treated as a cunning impostor. But it is clear that, in heinous contravention of his vows at the baptismal font, the godfather did instil a premature scepticism into the precocious godson, and taught him to scoff at most of the things regarded throughout Christendom as sacred,—a fact in the child Arouet's upbringing which deserves to be borne in mind as the story of his life is unfolded. Of Madame Arouet nothing more is known than a solitary saying reported by her second son. She knew Boileau (of whom, too, her husband had been the notary), and pronounced him to be "a clever book, but a silly man." She died when her second son was only in his seventh year.

The motherless boy remained under his widowed father's roof until, verging on his tenth year, he entered as a boarder the Collége Louis-le-Grand. This famous seminary was the greatest of all the teaching establishments which the Jesuits had founded throughout France, in order to influence the minds of its youth. There were two classes of boarders—that to which the young Arouet belonged, and a superior one of boys of good family, among them some very highly born, each of whom had a room to himself, and often a valet of his own to wait on him. With several of these the young Arouet formed friendships which proved both lasting and useful, notably with the two D'Argensons, sons of the potent Minister of Police, the elder of whom became Minister of War, and the younger Minister of Foreign Affairs. Some sixty years afterwards Voltaire put into the mouth of an interlocutor in an imaginary dialogue, represented to be an old pupil of the Collége Louis-le-Grand, a scornful denunciation of the insufficiency and general inutility of the education received at it. On leaving it, the diatribe winds up, " I knew some Latin and a parcel of stuff." But in more genial moods Voltaire bore testimony to the merits of his Jesuit teachers, and to the "delicious hours " which he spent when listening to the prelections of the amiable Father Porée, one of his professors of rhetoric. He acquired a tolerable knowledge of Latin, but never wrote it with anything like scholarly correctness, and his acquaintance with Greek was very slender.

There was one talent shown very early by the boy, the development of which his teachers did not fail to encourage. " Just out of my cradle I lisped in verse" (" *Au sortir du berceau j'ai bégayé des vers* "), Voltaire says in a line which calls to mind Pope's well-known boast. Probably it was very soon after his entrance into the college that his gift of versifying became known to his superiors, and that occurred the following incident, told by Voltaire himself. There came to the college an old soldier, who asked one of the masters to indite a few complimentary verses to be presented on the approaching New Year's day to the Dauphin, in whose regiment he had served, and whose purse he hoped thus to open. The master, busy or unwilling, sent him to the little

Arouet, who dashed off the verses wanted, and they produced the desired effect. This feat of the young collegian was talked of, according to Voltaire, even at Versailles, and led the Abbé de Châteauneuf to present to the aged Ninon de l'Enclos his clever little godson. She was so taken with the boy that, again according to Voltaire's own account, she left him a legacy of 2,000 francs (say £80) to buy books with.

Other anecdotes, and they are many, of the boy Arouet, during his seven years' residence in the Collége Louis-le-Grand, are either insignificant or unauthenticated. The most salient of them all would, if true, be significant. The Jesuit fathers encouraged their more advanced pupils to debate questions, sacred and profane, in gatherings presided over by a school authority. At one of these discussions, Father Le Jay, the popular Father Porée's unpopular colleague, is said to have been so irritated by some audaciously heterodox remarks of the youthful Arouet, that he came down from his presidential chair, and seizing the delinquent by the collar, gave him a good shaking with the apostrophe : "Unhappy boy ! you will one day be the standard-bearer " (in Condorcet's version, "the Coryphæus ") "of Deism in France," a prophecy which has a strong look of being manufactured after the event. As it happens, the young Arouet's first appearance in print—and that during his school years—is as the writer of a most devout piece of verse, suggested by an equally devout composition of this very Father Le Jay. The school authorities were so pleased with it that they printed it at the time as "Ode sur Sainte-Geneviève. Imitation d'une Ode latine du R.

P. Le Jay par François Arouet étudiant en rhétorique et pensionnaire du Collége Louis-le-Grand." In it the boy-poet implores St. Genevieve, the tutelary saint of Paris, to succour, as in the legends of yore, France in the hour of her dire distress.

It is a decidedly spirited piece, and much of the patriotic emotion expressed in it may well have been genuine on the part of a clever and susceptive French boy, who, at home, during the long autumnal holidays and otherwise, must have heard of the dangers in which the War of the Spanish Succession was involving his country. With the close of 1708, the date assignable to the composition of the ode, France was overwhelmed by disasters of every kind. After their victory at Oudenarde (July 11, 1708), Marlborough and Eugene captured Lille. Its fall (23rd of October) seemed to open to the allies the road to Paris, which long afterwards Voltaire the man, drawing on the reminiscences of Arouet the boy, described as struck with terror by the news. To what the boy Arouet saw and felt then may be partly ascribed the detestation of war often expressed by Voltaire the man. To the danger from the enemy were added the calamities of a general famine in France. Brown bread was substituted for white on the college trenchers, and a hundred livres were paid by the good M. Arouet to avert from his delicate second son such a change of diet.

In comparatively recent years there were discovered and printed some letters written by the boy Arouet, during his later stay at the Collége Louis-le-Grand, to a young friend who had left it. They furnish some indications, slight, but genuine, of his attitude towards clericalism at 16 and 17, some years after the composition of the ode to St. Genevieve. They are affectionate, extremely polite, and have the negative characteristic of containing very little school gossip. The little that there is of it shows generally contempt for the devotional element in his school-life, and in the aspirations of some of his more orthodox schoolfellows. One letter opens with the intimation, "I have just come out from retreat, wearied to death, and laden with fifty sermons." Again, after reporting a remark made to him that his correspondent and himself thought of becoming clerics, "I replied," he says, "that I was not sufficiently virtuous for that kind of life, and that you had too much intelligence to commit such folly." He goes on to ridicule the adoption, by two of his schoolfellows, of a clerical career, "after they had reflected on the dangers of a world of the charms of which they were ignorant, and on the pleasures of the religious life of which they did not foresee the disagreeables." The only difficulty with these pious young gentlemen had been to decide which ecclesiastical order they would join, "any kind of life appearing to them good, if they could but quit this land of crime, such being the name they give to whatever is not cloister or monkery. Having, in a quarter of an hour, considered every order in succession, each seemed so attractive that they could not fix on any without regretting all the others ; and they would have remained for ever undecided, like Buridan's ass, which died of hunger between the two bundles of hay," when they bethought them of leaving the decision to chance. "Thus,"

the young satirist concludes, "a throw of the dice deter-
mined one to be a Carmelite and the other a Jesuit."

The latest extant of these letters was written at the
yearly breaking up of the college for the autumn holidays.
There was, on the occasion, the usual performance of a
moral or religious play by some of the pupils, which
the rank and fashion of Paris were wont to honour with
their presence. Whatever influence these representations
may have had in stimulating the dramatic instincts of
the young Arouet, he nowhere makes any but the following solitary and episodical reference to them : two monks
who were present at the performance, he tells his correspondent, somehow fell down and "broke each other's
necks—just as if they had come only for our amusement,"
the youthful reporter adds, evidently chuckling at the
catastrophe. To whatever extent the young Arouet may
have learned, in odes and otherwise, to adopt the devotional tone of his Jesuit teachers, he was in all likelihood a decided sceptic when at 17 he left the Collége
Louis-le-Grand.

CHAPTER II.

WHEN the son returned home from college the father wished him to study for the bar, and intended, after he had passed as an *avocat*, to purchase for him admission to a superior class of pleaders. The young gentleman seems accordingly to have attended the prescribed lectures on jurisprudence, but only to be disgusted with the study of the law, as this then stood and was taught in France. "I belong to Paris," Voltaire makes a full-fledged *avocat* say in an imaginary dialogue, written many years afterwards, "and they kept me for three years studying the laws of ancient Rome," and so forth. He passed his time much more congenially as the welcome guest of the so-called "Society of the Temple," to which, when a mere schoolboy, but a precocious one, he is said to have been introduced by his godfather. This was a cluster of epicurean wits, poets, and men of rank, among them the Duc de Sulli, of whom the Anacreontic and free-thinking Abbé de Chaulieu, laden with fat benefices, was the laureate. Their young *protégé* was bright, witty, with distinguished manners, and an unsurpassable gift for throwing off graceful, sympathetic, and flattering verse. He took delight in making himself agreeable to friendly associates far above him in social position. They encouraged him to scoff at old-fashioned ethics and at the sombre pietism of the Court at Versailles, and to join in the worship of the goddess Pleasure, as the one religion for a Frenchman, old or young. His father, distressed by his neglect of law and his laxity of life, sent him to Caën, the " Athens of Normandy," where he was well received, but soon fell into disgrace, by " reciting verses against morality and religion." Old M. Arouet was at his wits' end to know what to do with this scapegrace of a son, when an opportunity was presented for getting him away, with some chance of permanent absence, not only from Paris, but from France. The Treaty of Utrecht (signed April 13, 1713) brought the War of the Spanish Succession to an end so far as England and Holland were concerned. Diplomatic relations between France and Holland were resumed, and the Marquis de Châteauneuf, brother of young Arouet's godfather (who died some years before), was appointed French Ambassador at the Hague. He consented to take his departed brother's godson with him in his suite, and in the autumn of 1713 the young gentleman found himself in the capital of Protestant Holland. But he did not allow a long respite to his father's anxieties about him. Very soon after his arrival at the Hague he fell in love with a Mademoiselle Dunoyer, whose mother, a Frenchwoman, separated from her husband, pandered to the tastes of gossip and scandal-loving readers by writing memoirs and anecdotes of the living, for which she drew largely on her imagination. The daughter—she had previously been engaged to Jean Cavalier, the hero of the revolt in the Cevennes, who seems to have jilted her—gave decided encouragement to her fascinating Parisian admirer, some years her junior. In this case there was no talk of marriage, and if there had been, the lover's position was insignificant and his prospects dubious. Madame Dunoyer forbade him the house. Then followed stolen interviews, the young lady, once at least, in male attire, visiting the young gentleman in his room, to which his chief confined him. Fearing that his subaltern's imprudence might compromise him with the Dutch authorities, the ambassador sent him back to his father and to Paris, where he arrived, after scarcely three months' absence, at the close of 1713.

M. Arouet was a very irascible old gentleman. In the first burst of his anger at having his son thus returned upon his hands, he talked of consigning him to prison under a *lettre de cachet*, a threat which was softened into one of bundling him off to the French West India islands. At last he consented to allow the culprit to remain in Paris, but only on condition that he entered the office of an attorney, with whom he was to board, and who was to train him for that far from brilliant vocation. With the beginning of 1714, young Arouet was duly installed in the household of M. Alain, attorney, of the Rue Pavée St. Bernard. He made use of his opportunities in his new and strange employment to acquire a knowledge of ordinary law-procedure, which he turned to account in the course of his varied career.

Another of his acquisitions was the admiration of one of his fellow-clerks, Thiériot, an idle young fellow, but with some taste for literature, who became his henchman and trumpeter.   His stay under M. Alain's roof did not last beyond a few months apparently.   His father, who was far from implacable, yielded to his pleadings and those of his friends, and he was permitted to abandon the incongruous drudgery of incipient attorneyism. Probably the young gentleman persuaded his father to make him an allowance, and to let him do what he liked with himself.   However this may have been, in the very year of his admission into M. Alain's office, he was making a noise in the Paris world of letters.   He had competed for a prize offered by the French Academy to the writer of the best poem on the new choir at Nôtre Dame.   The ode which he sent in was devotional enough in tone and tenor.   But the prize was awarded to an elderly Abbé, on whom and whose chief patron among the Academicians his disappointed rival took revenge in a stinging satire, "Le Bourbier."   With its appearance its author at once leapt into notoriety, and earned a reputation as a satirist, which stood him in ill stead afterwards.

The young poet was already, however, occupied with a more ambitious literary enterprise.   He had begun his tragedy of "Œdipe," founded on the masterpiece of Sophocles, the Œdipus King, a subject handled by Corneille not with striking success.   He represents the project as having first dawned on him in the course of a connection by which, in more ways than one, his early career was influenced.   It arose out of his introduction to the so-called "Court of Sceaux," presided over by a very high lady, the Duchesse du Maine, a granddaughter of the great Condé, and the wife of the eldest surviving though illegitimate son (by Madame de Montespan) of Louis XIV. A certain accomplished and scholarly M. de Malezieu had been tutor to the Duke, who afterwards presented him with a villa at Chatenay, near Sceaux, where M. Arouet, it will be remembered, had a country house. Malezieu made the acquaintance of his clever young occasional neighbour, and introduced him to the Court of Sceaux. Private theatricals were a favourite amusement of the Duchess, and among the pieces represented at Sceaux were French versions of Greek dramas. At the performance of one of these, the Iphigenia in Tauris of Euripides, young Arouet was present, and then it was, he says, that there came into his head the notion of adapting for the French stage the great Sophoclean tragedy. He may have completed "Œdipe" when, on September 1, 1715, Louis XIV. died, unmourned by his people whose lives and substance he had wasted in disastrous wars. Some time before, Louis had, by edict, both legitimized his illegitimate sons, and vested in them the succession to the throne in the event of the failure of nominally legitimate heirs. The Duc du Maine, as the eldest of these legitimized-illegitimate princes, might thus be one day King of France. In his will Louis constituted his nephew, the Duke of Orleans, head of a council of regency which was to administer the government during the minority of his great-grandson and immediate successor, the boy-king Louis XV. The will gave his favourite son, the Duc du

Maine, a seat in this council, making him also guardian
of the young king, and entrusting to him the control of
the Household troops. Within, however, not many
hours of the death of Louis, the Parliament of Paris, at
the instance of the Regent-Duke of Orleans, cancelled
both of these provisions of the will. The Duc du
Maine himself seems to have taken the matter quietly,
but his Duchess, a clever, ambitious, and intriguing lady,
went at once into opposition to the new *régime*. One
chief mode of political opposition in the France of
that time was the distribution of lampoons against the
ruling powers, and the young Arouet had already shown
himself a master of satire. Very possibly he brought
this weapon into play in the supposed interest of his
patroness, the Duchess du Maine. At all events, to
Arouet was ascribed the authorship of some atrocious
verses on the Regent and the Regent's daughter, who
was every way worthy of her dissolute father, the Duchesse
de Berri. As a consequence, in the first week of May,
1716, was launched a rescript exiling the " Sieur Arouet
fils " to Tulle, a dull town some three hundred miles
from his beloved Paris. Then old M. Arouet indul-
gently intervened. Probably at the expense of truth,
he represented to the authorities that at Sully on the
Loire his son had relatives, who would " correct his
imprudence and temper his vivacity; " so Sully, as the
place of exile, was substituted for Tulle. With or without
relatives in that region, the young gentleman is forthwith
found enjoying himself in the best of company as the
guest of the Duc de Sulli, in the château of the same
name. But impatience of restraint, and a restlessness

which became habitual, soon made him weary of his
new abode. He addressed to the Duke of Orleans, to
whom it was to be communicated by influential friends,
an adulatory epistle in rhyme, with protestations,
sincere or insincere, of his innocence of the particular
misdemeanour with which he had been charged. The
easy-going Regent relented, and in the autumn he was
allowed to return to Paris. This act of grace drew from
old M. Arouet an undoubtedly genuine and interesting
comment, which has been preserved, on the character and
career of his second son. It has escaped the notice of
Voltaire's chief recent biographers that, in a letter addressed by his father (October, 1716) to the President of
the Chamber of Accounts, there occurs this rather touch-
ing and suggestive passage : " Perhaps, *Monseigneur*, even
you may have heard that it has pleased the Regent to
recall my son from his exile. The exile distressed me
much less than does this precipitate recall, which will
complete the ruin of the young man, intoxicated as he is
by the success of his poetry, and by the praises and
welcome bestowed on him by the great, whom, with all
the respect that I owe to them, I must regard as really
poisoning him."

CHAPTER III.

(1716–19.)

AFTER leaving Sully, Arouet is found no longer under his father's roof, but the denizen of a Paris lodging-house. The event proved that old M. Arouet had good reason to fear the consequences of his son's return to Paris. Before the end of 1716 he was having advances made to him by the right-hand man of Charles XII. of Sweden, the Baron de Goertz, then in Paris, who was planning against England a coalition between Charles and Charles's old enemy, the Czar Peter. Goertz appears to have been so struck by the young man's cleverness as to have invited him to accompany him on a European journey in furtherance of his schemes. Nothing came of the invitation, but Goertz's communings with Arouet were doubtless made known to the authorities, who had spies everywhere, and who were keeping a watchful eye on the disaffected and dangerous young poet, apparently more irritated by his exile to Sully than grateful for his recall from it. He must have been much maligned if, during the winter of 1716 and the spring of 1717, he was not busily occupied in lampooning the

Regent, at the instance of the angry Duchesse du Maine. The poet's best modern biographers have doubted whether he was really at that time active in thus aiding and abetting the intrigues of the aspiring Duchess. But researches in the archives of the Bastille, made since they wrote, indicate that Demoulin, a former clerk of old M. Arouet, and then and years afterwards employed in various ways by his second son, was engaged in promoting the illicit printing of pamphlets against, and libels on, the Regent, some of them in all likelihood young Arouet's handiwork.

Fortunately, however, for his fame, Arouet was being led, in the intervals of lampooning, towards a poetic enterprise more worthy of his genius; and it must be remembered that even his "Œdipe," the hero of which had innocently, because unconsciously, married his own mother, was sometimes, though quite wrongly, regarded as glancing at the criminal relations which Parisian scandal talked of as existing between the Regent and his daughter, the Duchesse de Berri. The Lent of 1717 was passed by Arouet in the Château of Saint-Ange, in the Forest of Fontainebleau, as the guest of one of the new friends whom he was always making and fascinating, M. de Caumartin, a very interesting old gentleman. Caumartin had filled high official positions and moved in the best French society of his time. His father had been a confidential friend of the Cardinal de Retz, and he himself had at his fingers' ends all the anecdotal history of the reign of Louis XIV., much of which, poured into a willing ear, was reproduced when, long afterwards, Voltaire came to write the "Siècle de Louis

Quatorze." But, above all things, Caumartin was a worshipper of Henry IV. of France, who, it has been said,
built for his Gabrielle that very Château of Saint-Ange.
The fervour with which the elderly host sang the praises
of his favourite hero, inspired his young guest with a
desire to turn into verse the story of the gallant king's
successful struggle against the anti-Protestant League of
French grandees, aided by the power of Spain and of the
Papacy.

Full of enthusiasm for his new theme, the poet returned to Paris, to find his earlier dramatic project about
to be carried into effect. The players had accepted
"Œdipe." But, as happened more than once in his
career, just when Fortune seemed to smile on him most
graciously, the worst was about to befall him. A pretended friend, one of the Regent's innumerable spies,
Beauregard, an officer in the army, denounced him to
the authorities on the strength of alleged conversations
with him in his Paris lodging just after his return from
Saint-Ange. According to the spy's report, Arouet had
not only grossly abused the Regent and his daughter,
but had boasted of his authorship of a Latin lapidary
inscription (probably accompanying a drawing of a statue
of France) which, circulated from hand to hand, had
made considerable stir in Paris. It catalogued some of
the Regent's crimes and misdemeanours, real or supposed.
"Regnante puero" (the young Louis XV.), "veneno et
incestis famoso administrante" (the Regent) were the
opening words of the inscription, and are quite sufficient
to indicate its tone and tenor. Arouet afterwards declared
that he was not only innocent of the authorship of this

inscription, but that he had never so much as seen it. Unfortunately, in such cases, the mere denials, whether of Arouet the youth or of Voltaire the man, go for nothing. He was arrested and (May, 1717) lodged in the Bastille, where, after a strict examination of him by the police-minister, D'Argenson, father of his old school-fellows, he was left a prisoner for nearly a year.

Little is known with certainty of the treatment which the poet received during his captivity, but this, under any circumstances, must have been very trying to so restless as well as social a being. It is said that he was deprived of pen, ink, and paper, as a punishment for the use which he was supposed to have made of them in freedom. Among the things, however, he asked for and which were granted him a few days after his arrival in the Bastille, were two volumes of Homer, Greek and Latin. One glimpse we have of him dining with the Governor of the Bastille. As the weeks rolled on he may have persuaded that official to allow him writing materials, and the use of other books (some of French history among them)—concessions occasionally allowed, though under stringent conditions. He was soon occupied with the poetic enterprise which happily had been suggested to him at Saint-Ange. His, indeed, was a brain incessantly active and irrepressibly productive. Even during his most troubled hours, he had a singular power of forgetting annoyances in absorbing work. The second canto of "La Ligue," the poem which grew into the famous " Henriade," he is represented as composing in the Bastille in his sleep, say, rather, when awake during the watches of the night. It is the canto in which Henri Quatre, during an imaginary visit to England, tells Queen Elizabeth the gruesome story of the Saint Bartholomew massacre.

At the beginning of 1718 the rigorous D'Argenson was promoted to be Keeper of the Seals. His successor as Lieutenant of Police appears to have been induced to intercede for the poet-prisoner, whose father also took some part in the successful intervention. On April 10, 1718, there was inscribed in the Paris police-registers this entry : " The intention of his Royal Highness," the Regent, " is that the Sieur Arouet *fils*, a prisoner in the Bastille, be set at liberty and relegated to Chatenay near Sceaux, where his father, who has a country-house there, offers to take charge of him." Next day, after nearly eleven months' imprisonment, the Prodigal Son left the Bastille for his father's house at Chatenay, and under the paternal roof, there or in Paris, he appears to have had a home whenever he chose to make use of it, during the remainder of old M. Arouet's life. Successive requests to be allowed to visit Paris, for shorter or longer periods of days and weeks, having been granted, on October 12, 1718, was registered the most welcome "permission for the Sieur Arouet de *Voltaire* to come to Paris as often as he pleases." Among the fruits of his prison reflections on his past life had been the resolve to change his name (as Molière, originally Poquelin, and other celebrities had done before him)—a name under which he had suffered so much and incurred so much odium. The " Arouet " was eliminated by degrees, and in a few months he was known generally as Voltaire, or as M. de Voltaire when addressed, or written of, in more ceremonious fashion.

The origin of the famous pseudonym is still debated.
The dominant theory resolves it into an anagram of
Arouet l.j. (*le jeune*).

With this change in his surname, Voltaire's first great
triumph in public was fast approaching. During a few
weeks after the issue of the order authorizing him to visit
Paris when he pleased, he was fruitfully busy there
among the players and his friends. The performance of
" Œdipe," suspended by his imprisonment in the
Bastille, was fixed for November 18, 1718, at the
Comédie Française. The house was full, and the play,
well acted, was completely and conspicuously successful.
The majority of the audience knew nothing of Sophocles,
and were unfamiliar with Corneille's " Œdipe," so that in
spite of the love intrigue which Voltaire had grafted on
the stern Greek tragedy, the deeply interesting plot, unfolded in impressive and graceful verse, kept curiosity
on the stretch. One of Voltaire's most significant
additions to the original (as he knew it through Dacier's
French translation,) was his expansion of the slight
reference made by the Sophoclean Œdipus to the predictions of the Oracle as the cause of all his seeming,
and only seeming, criminality, followed by Jocasta's
daring protest against the injustice of the gods in dooming
her to unconscious guilt. "In my own despite, and in
blind ignorance," Voltaire makes his Œdipe say, "I
was the slave and tool of an unknown power. This is
my sole offence ; I know no other. O pitiless gods !
yours are my crimes, and yet you punish me for them."
So, too, Jocaste, at the moment of committing suicide ;
"Virtuous I lived : I die without remorse. . . . Amid

the horrors beneath which Destiny crushes me, I have made blush the gods who forced me to crime." All this is very alien to the antique spirit of the original, in which no hint is given that Œdipus and his wife-mother are not righteously punished for crimes committed by them unwittingly, and to the commission of which they were driven in accordance with supernal prescience. In his quite modern treatment of the finale, Voltaire may have had in view the predestinarianism of the Jansenists in general, and of that furious Jansenist, his brother Armand, in particular, which, for no fault of their own, doomed to everlasting punishment so many of the human race. But this is a theory of the closet, not of the boxes and pit of a theatre,—the occupants of which, however, during the first performance of "Œdipe," were ready enough to make a present application of here and there a seemingly suggestive line or distich. Before the catastrophe which made good their sinister predictions, the Sophoclean Œdipus and Jocasta speak slightingly of Oracles. But the audience at the Comédie Française evidently thought that Voltaire was ministering to the then fashionable unbelief, when they applauded loudly the declaration of his Jocaste : " Priests are not what a foolish people think them to be ; their knowledge lies only in our credulity." A curious episode of the performance remains to be mentioned. In one of the scenes in which figures the High Priest of Jupiter (who in " Œdipe " combines with his own part that played by Tiresias in the original), Voltaire, having slipped on a theatrical costume, appeared on the stage, carrying the Pontiff's train, and indulging, it would seem, in some antic gestures very inappropriate to the solemn dialogue. Among the great people present was the Maréchale de Villars, the handsome and much courted wife of the very distinguished and veteran Marshal of France, who had brought to a close the insurrection in the Cevennes, "the hero of Denain," where he was victor in the last conspicuous battle (July 20, 1712) of the War of the Spanish Succession, helping to terminate it by defeating, then and there, the Dutch under Albemarle, and the Imperialists under Prince Eugene. "Who is that young man bent on ruining the piece?" the Maréchale is said to have exclaimed. On being told that it was the author himself, she had him, so Voltaire says, presented to her in her box, and then to the Maréchal himself, a very genial old gentleman with some liking for poetry and drama. It was the beginning of a long intimacy between the ex-notary's son and these two high personages.

"Œdipe" had a run, said to be unprecedented, of forty-five nights, bringing its author a considerable sum. In spite of the sinister rumours previously mentioned, the Regent and the Duchesse de Berri went to see it, and, crowning triumph of all, it was played before the young king at Versailles. About this time, in a rather obsequious letter, Voltaire asked the Regent to listen to some "fragments of an epic"—the "Henriade" that was to be—"on the ancestor whom you most resemble." He signed himself "your very poor" Voltaire, and hinted that he deserved to owe his Royal Highness some other obligation than that of having been "corrected by a year of the Bastille." Probably it was to make use of this opportunity of binding over to

keep the peace the wielder of so dangerous a pen,
that the Regent made him a present, it is alleged, of
a thousand crowns (£330), and certainly bestowed on
him a pension from his privy purse of 1,200 livres (say
£50), which for many a year, and long after the Regent's
death, Voltaire appears to have drawn from the exchequer
of the House of Orleans. Soon after its performance,
"Œdipe" was published and dedicated to the Regent's
wife. Its publication was followed by a host of pamphlets
laudatory and depreciatory. These gave rise to a series
of (printed) letters to a friend, in which Voltaire criticized the "Œdipus Tyrannus" of Sophocles, and his
own and Corneille's "Œdipe." Seneca's and Dryden's
dramas on the same subject he does not seem to have
heard of. With considerable ingenuity, he introduced
incidentally in these letters a statement which was
intended to prove himself entirely innocent of past
political satire. This he attempted by denying most
emphatically—and for once truthfully—the authorship
of a piece which had been attributed to him, while at
the same time he quietly ignored the lampoons for which
mainly he had been punished. Soon after the death of
Louis XIV. there had been circulated a little piece known
as the "J'ai vu," of which almost all of Voltaire's biographers, following Voltaire himself, have made too much.
"During that reign, I have seen this, that, and the other
evil thing done," it ran, enumerating several of them, and
winding up thus : "I have seen the hypocrite honoured,
and, which is saying everything, the Jesuit adored. I
have seen these evils under the fatal rule of a prince
whom once the Wrath Divine granted, as a punishment,

to our ardent wishes. I have seen these evils, and I am not yet twenty." In town and country the "J'ai vu" was attributed to the young Arouet, but quite wrongly, and he succeeded, as he boasts loudly, in proving his innocence of this particular misdemeanour. He had, however, been exiled to Sully eight months, and imprisoned in the Bastille some twenty months, after the appearance of the "I have seen." In any case the "J'ai vu" could not have greatly irritated the Regent, since it dealt with a previous *régime*, for which, at the commencement of his own, he had promised to substitute one much less despotic. The artful apologist breathes not a syllable of the stinging lines on the Regent and his daughter which exiled him to Sully, or of the "Regnante Puero" which sent him to the Bastille. In point of fact, Voltaire was turning over a new leaf, and wished to persuade the world that there was no new leaf to turn over. The eleven months of the Bastille had taught him a severe lesson, and the bounty of the Regent had inspired him with new hopes. Thenceforth, though the audacities of his pen involved him in many troubles, it was wielded no more to assail overtly French royalty or its representatives and associates. On the contrary, whatever his private thoughts, Voltaire usually addressed thrones, principalities, and powers, at home and abroad, in language of the most courtier-like adulation, if mainly with an eye to his own advantage.

CHAPTER IV.

(1719–26.)

WITH the triumph of "Œdipe," Voltaire was more than ever caressed by the great, and for years much of his time was passed in visits to their *châteaux*. He was, however, under the paternal roof in Paris when his father died there, in his seventy-fourth year (January 1, 1722), having just before been succeeded by his eldest son, Armand, in his post at the Chamber of Accounts. M. Arouet's will, made in the preceding August, lay, legible and accessible, for more than a hundred and fifty years, among the papers in the office of his various notarial successors, but its contents were not known even to the most industrious and painstaking of Voltaire's modern biographers, and it was first published in 1874. It is a document interesting in several ways. It opens with the statement that the testator has not very much to leave, and that the precise amount could not be ascertained until his accounts with the Chamber were made up. Whatever his property, it is to be divided equally between his two sons and his only surviving daughter, Madame Mignot, whose husband

was an official of the Chamber of Accounts. But from
the shares of the two sons are first to be deducted, in
favour of their sister, 3,000 livres (£120), paid for his
elder son when entering the Seminary of St. Magloire
(where he was educated for the Church, a career which
he abandoned after the persecution of his brother
Jansenists by the Jesuits), and 4,000 livres (£160), a
larger sum then than now, paid for Voltaire's debts.
Unlike his brother and sister, Voltaire is to have only
a life-interest in the money to which he may be entitled,
the principal being left, in the event of his death, to
his legitimate children, and in default of any such, to
his brother and sister. "Nevertheless," the thoughtful
testator, strict, but not unkind, proceeds to say—

" if it should happen that my son de Volterre (*sic*), on completing
his thirty-fifth year, has adopted the regular course of life to pursue
which I could have much desired to lead him—in such a case, as I
make this settlement only from a just fear that he will otherwise
dissipate his slender patrimony and fall into want, I humbly beg the
First President of the Chamber of Accounts to be good enough to
accept the paternal power and authority which I now give him, to
destroy and cancel the said settlement in the event of my said son
de Volterre adopting a regular course of life—just as I myself would
do were it possible for me to survive these my last wishes."

Noticeable, too, is the closing monition of the will :—

" To the utmost of my power I exhort my two sons to remember
the advice which I have given them more than once, and by which
it seems to me they have profited but little, namely, that good sense
desires and commands us to accommodate ourselves to the capacity
of those to whom we think ourselves superior in intelligence and
knowledge, and that we ought never to make them feel that
superiority."

Still more noticeable is it that in a sort of codicil dated December 26, 1721, less than a week before his death, M. Arouet revoked the clause in his will restricting to a life-interest Voltaire's share ; but the document was left unsigned. This intended revocation may have been simply in accordance with M. Arouet's habit of relenting when his second son was concerned, or because in the interval between the execution of the will and the drawing up of the codicil, Voltaire had shown that he was not so thriftless as he was thought to be, by depositing with his father the scrip of three shares in the French East India Company, and bank-notes for 5,000 francs (£200), which were undoubtedly in M. Arouet's keeping when he died. More hereafter of the results of the will, which Voltaire contested in the courts of law. As it happened, very soon after his father's death he received, at the Regent's recommendation, a royal pension of 2,000 livres (£80), which, with the former one of 1,200 from the Regent's privy purse, made in all 3,200 livres, or about £130 a year, his only regular income for the time being, and equivalent perhaps to, £400 a year now. It was a very tolerable income for a man under thirty, without encumbrances ; but then ambition and luxurious tastes had been developed in Voltaire by the society of the great. He had nothing definite to expect from the theatre, since the tragedy of "Artémire" (1720), from which he hoped for a second success on the stage, had been a failure. From literature he might expect something from the publication, by subscription, of his poem on Henry IV. ; but both permission to print it, and subscribers for it, had still to be obtained.

His father's death leaving him without a home, Voltaire procured one of some kind, through a question-able intimacy which he formed with a Madame de Bernières—a lady of five-and-thirty. Her husband, a Marquis—the pair lived together, and had financial interests in common, otherwise they went their several ways—was a Law-President at Rouen, with a country house in its neighbourhood, and a town house in Paris. By and by Voltaire is found entering into an agreement with them, for a specified sum, to board and lodge him-self and Thiériot, his former fellow-clerk at M. Alain's, and now his factotum. His host and hostess were a speculative couple, and they made use of Voltaire and his nascent influence at Court to try and obtain conces-sions, financial and fiscal, in the profits of which, of course, he was to participate. Business of this kind took him often to Versailles, where the Court was. On one of these visits he found, admitted to the intimacy of the Minister of War, the very Beauregard, the spy, whose denunciation of him as the writer of the " Regnante Puero" had consigned him to the Bastille. In the presence of Beauregard and the Minister, Voltaire ex-claimed with natural indignation: "I knew very well that spies were paid, but I did not know until now that their reward was to dine at the table of a Minister." The taunt cost him dear, for Beauregard, watching his opportunity, stopped at the Bridge of Sèvres the vehicle in which he was being driven, made him descend from it, and caned him so severely as to leave a mark on the unfortunate poet's face. The incident is worth mentioning, were it only for the way in which it was talked about in Paris, where, to judge from contemporary comments, nothing seems to have been thought more natural than that poets in general, and Voltaire in particular, should be chastised when they offended with tongue or pen, whatever the provocation received. From some of these comments, moreover, it is clear that, intoxicated, as his father said, by the caresses of the great, Voltaire held his head rather high, and made too free with his tongue, thus increasing the dislike for him which his success had created among his envious brethren of the pen. To an actor with whom about this time he had an altercation, and who challenged him, he is credibly reported to have haughtily replied, that it was not for "a person of his consideration" to fight a duel with a player !

Other efforts at self-advancement, besides applying at Court for financial or fiscal concessions, were made by Voltaire after his father's death. The earliest was an overture to Jean Baptiste Rousseau, to whom he had been introduced, as a distinguished pupil, at the Collége Louis-le-Grand, and whom he knew to have spoken admiringly of "Œdipe." Rousseau was then at Vienna, where he had been treated most munificently by Prince Eugene, who not only admired "Œdipe," but was reported to have said that its author would be welcome at Vienna. Voltaire threw out a hint, in a letter to Rousseau, that he would gladly visit Vienna if the expenses of his journey were paid, but the hint was ineffective. Bent on a visit to Vienna free of cost, Voltaire turned with adulatory verses to the infamous Dubois, now a Cardinal, the good Fénelon's successor in the archbishopric of Cambrai, and virtually Prime Minister to the Regent. He proposed to Dubois (one of the least creditable epi- sodes of Voltaire's career) to undertake a spy mission to Vienna, the French Government being desirous of accurate information respecting the Emperor's in- tentions. This particular scheme came to nothing. Taking leave before he started of Dubois, and writing to him an amusing, free-and-easy, but rather servile, letter from Cambrai, where a congress was then assem- bled, Voltaire is next found travelling to Holland in the company of an attractive and coquettish widow, who had been in her youth one of the ladies-in-waiting to the Regent's daughter, the dissolute Duchesse de Berri. Madame de Rupelmonde belonged to the numerous class of persons who wish to believe, but are harassed by doubts, and she confided her spiritual perplexities to the agreeable young philosopher as well as poet, her travelling companion. The result was the "Épître à Uranie," the "Pour et le Contre," the "For and Against"—a poem noticeable as Voltaire's earliest extant confession of Faith and Unfaith. He paints in it a lurid picture of that section of the creed of Pascal and his own brother Armand, according to which the Deity creates men to condemn them to everlasting torments. He scoffs at the Incarnation and the imperfect results of the Atonement. This is "The Against." "The For" is a brief but glowing passage on the divine morality taught, and the consolations offered, by the Founder of Christianity, by whom, "if he builds the doctrine upon imposture, it is still happiness to be deceived." But there is another creed into which no deception enters, and this it is that he recommends to the acceptance of his fair companion :—

" Believe that the eternal wisdom of the Most High
Has graven with his hand, in the depths of thy heart,
The Religion of Nature.
Believe that thy soul, in its candid simplicity,
Will not be the object of his undying hatred.
Believe that before his throne, at all times, in all places,
The heart of the just is precious.
Believe that a modest bonze, a charitable dervish,
Will find more favour in his eyes
Than a pitiless Jansenist,
Or an ambitious pontiff.
Ah! what indeed matters the name under which we pray to him?
He receives every homage, but by none is he honoured.
A God does not need our assiduous services.
If he can be offended, it is by unjust deeds.
By our virtues he judges us, not by our sacrifices."

Voltaire and his lady friend were on their way to the Hague, whither Madame was bound on family affairs, and Monsieur on practical literary business. This was to arrange for the printing and issue by subscription, there, in Paris, and other capitals, of Voltaire's poem on Henry IV. While the arrangement was being negotiated he had time to look about him in the country which he had left in disgrace, and which he re-visited famous and caressed. The liberty, political and religious, enjoyed in Holland exhilarated him. All forms of creed were tolerated, and if the opera at the Hague was " detestable," he could discuss theology, as he gleefully reported, with " ministers of religion of every kind, Calvinists, Arminians, Socinians, Rabbis, Ana-

baptists." Busy and industrious Amsterdam, too—what
a contrast to frivolous Paris and courtier-crowded
Versailles! In its population of half a million, "there
is not," he wrote home, "a single trace of idleness, of
poverty, of coxcombry, of insolence. We meet the
Pensionary" (the chief magistrate of the Republic) "on
foot, without lackeys, in the midst of the multitude.
Nobody is to be seen there who has to pay his court
to anybody else. There people do not form a line to
look at a prince passing,"—sentences which help us to
estimate the true value of Voltaire's homage to French
royalty. On his way back to Paris he paid a visit to
La Source, near Orleans, the château where resided the
exiled Bolingbroke, who had read and admired "Œdipe."
Voltaire was enchanted with the conversation of the
famous Englishman, who "combines," he wrote, "all
the erudition of his own country with all the politeness
of ours," and who became, in his correspondence,
"Pericles-Bolingbroke," though in his later years he
said of Bolingbroke's works, that they contained more
leaves than fruit. As a matter of course the MS. of the
poem on Henry IV. was shown to Bolingbroke, who, to
Voltaire's delight, praised it to the skies. But all the
praises of admirers, and all the influence which Voltaire
could bring to bear on its behalf, availed nothing to
the unfortunate poem. He returned to Paris early in
1723, and soon afterwards found that, far from receiving the coveted *privilége* which secured copyright,
he was refused even the official *approbation* which was
necessary to the circulation of any book in France.
Voltaire had done much to soften passages which might

offend the bigots. He had even gone the length of representing his hero's interested conversion to the creed of Rome as the victory of religious truth over error. But enough was left to induce the persons in authority, or of influence, to condemn the poem as unfit for publication. After all excisions and modifications there remained the choice of a champion of Protestantism as its hero, the praises of Queen Elizabeth of England, the unflattering picture of the Papal Court, the ever-recurring protests against bigotry and fanaticism, the denunciations of sanguinary persecutions in general and of the massacre of St. Bartholomew in particular. The subscriptions were returned to those who had paid them, and Voltaire's efforts for years to produce a national epic, with a stirring period in his country's history for its theme, seemed to have been thrown away. It is easy to imagine his feelings towards the Church and the ecclesiastical system which had done him this great wrong.

Bitterly disappointed, but not to be wholly baffled, Voltaire resolved on having his poem secretly printed and circulated. For the place of printing he pitched upon Rouen, from its proximity to La Rivière-Bourdet, the country seat of the De Bernières couple. He was soon at Rouen, where he arranged for the printing and binding, both of them on a modest scale. With the opening of 1724 a number of bound copies of "La Ligue ou Henri le Grand. Poème Épique par M. de Voltaire," a small, thin octavo, packed in a furniture van, accompanying the carriage in which Madame de Bernières was coming to town, were handed over to a trusty recipient at the Boulogne of the famous Bois, and by him successfully smuggled into Paris. Such was the contraband fashion in which the only poem in print that can claim to be called a French national epic, reached its earliest readers. The edition consisted of 2,000 copies, and the little volume was soon circulated, to be admired wherever it was read. For many readers the passages which had made the authorities refuse their sanction to it, constituted its principal charm.

Meanwhile had occurred (December 2, 1723) the death of the Duke of Orleans, a few months after that of Dubois. The new Prime Minister was the Duc de Bourbon, the head of the House of Condé, a very stupid as well as ugly man, who was governed by his mistress, the Marquise de Prie, one of the prettiest Frenchwomen of her time. Voltaire was presented to her, and with flattering verses and otherwise, made such way in her good graces that she gave him quarters in her residence at Fontainebleau, just when the young King was to be married there to Marie Leczinska, an amiable simple-minded princess, daughter of Stanislaus, ex-king of Poland. The wedding took place September 4, 1725, and Voltaire had several friends among those around her person, two of her ladies of the bed-chamber being the Maréchale de Villars and the Madame de Rupelmonde of the journey to the Hague. He succeeded in having " Œdipe," his tragedy " Mariamne," and his pleasant little comedy " L'Indiscret" played before the Queen, who, he reported delightedly, wept at "Mariamne" and laughed at the "Indiscret." A rhymed epistle of his own incomparable kind accompanied the copy of "Œdipe" which he presented to the virtuous Queen. This was soon followed by a dedication of "L'Indiscret," in verse the most graceful, to the far from virtuous Madame de Prie. The Queen conversed graciously with him, calling him "my poor Voltaire," an epithet the application of which was soon appropriately followed by a pension to him from her privy purse of 1,500 livres (some £60). Finding favour in the eyes of the actual and the virtual queens of France, Voltaire felt almost certain at last of obtaining some secure and lucrative post about Court. Once again his hopes, just when they were highest, were to be blasted, and the direst catastrophe of his life was about to befall him.

When the disaster occurred, Voltaire was in Paris, and doubtless, after his successes at Court, carrying his head higher than ever. There are various versions of the story now to be told in a condensed form, but they agree in essentials. In December, 1725, probably at the opera, and in the box of Adrienne Lecouvreur, with whom Voltaire was growing very intimate, something in his tone or talk irritated a certain Chevalier de Rohan-Chabot, a scion of the great house of Rohan, who was also there, and who may have been a competitor with him for Adrienne's good graces. "Monsieur de Voltaire, Monsieur Arouet, what is your name?" the Chevalier asked, contemptuously. According to one account, Voltaire replied, "I do not drag a great name" in the mud, as it were, the Chevalier being suspected of practising usury; "but I know how to honour the name

which I do bear." According to another of several
accounts : "I am beginning my name; you are ending
yours." The Chevalier, it is said, lifted his cane, and
Voltaire's hand was making for his sword, when Adrienne
fainted, and the scene closed. But from a hint dropped
by a Paris diarist of the time, it would seem that the
scene was followed by the circulation of deadly epi-
grams (*épigrammes assassines*), doubtless Voltaire's, on
the Chevalier de Rohan. However this may have
been, a few days afterwards Voltaire is dining at the
Duc de Sulli's, when he is told that he is wanted
below. He leaves the party, and is asked at the door
to step into a hackney coach standing in front of it,
where he will find the person who wishes to speak to
him. No sooner has he placed his foot in it than he
is seized, pulled back, and held firmly from behind,
while blows are showered upon his shoulders—six,
according to his own account, being the number of his
assailants. The Chevalier de Rohan, in another vehicle
at some distance, directs the chivalrous operation.
Frantic with rage, Voltaire rushes back to the dinner-
table, and, telling his story, calls on the Duc de Sulli
to accompany him to a commissary of police, and join
him, as the Duke's outraged guest, in making a
deposition of the facts. The Duke refuses to meddle
in the matter, and Voltaire rushes to the opera to tell
his story to Madame de Prie. She is sympathetic, but
all her influence with the Duc de Bourbon will not induce him to order the prosecution of a Rohan for having
perpetrated a foul outrage on a poet. The authorities
did, however, issue, though not until the 5th of February

(1726), an order for the discovery of the actual assailants, and for their arrest; but even this was to be effected very quietly, and not in the house of their ruffianly employer. Meanwhile Voltaire took lessons in fencing, with a view to a challenge and a duel. The upshot of what appear to have been his stormy sayings and doings for weeks and months—and the police were instructed to keep a watchful eye on him—was that, on the 17th of April, he found himself a second time in the Bastille. Friends, however, were allowed to visit him, and his request to be allowed to go to England was granted.

There the law protected the humblest plebeian not less than the highest patrician. There he would find a welcome from Bolingbroke and Bolingbroke's circle. Bolingbroke was in opposition to the powers that were, but Voltaire was recommended to them also. Sir Robert Walpole was then supreme in England, and Sir Robert's brother, Horatio Walpole, was English ambassador in Paris. Incited thereto by the Comte de Morville, Minister of Foreign Affairs, a well-wisher of Voltaire, Horatio Walpole wrote recommending him to the notice of the Duke of Newcastle, of Bubb Dodington, and in all likelihood of Sir Robert himself. In the letter to Dodington nothing was said of Voltaire's enforced exile. The foreign visitor was introduced as "Mr. Voltaire, a French poet, who has wrote several pieces with great success here, being gone for England in order to print by subscription an excellent poem, called Henry IV., which, on account of some bold strokes in it against persecution and the priests, cannot be printed here." Dodington (Pope's Bufo—afterwards

his Bubo—" fed with soft dedication all day long,")
was asked to promote the laudable enterprise. These
letters followed Voltaire to England, the soil of which
he touched for the first time, probably on May 30, 1726.

CHAPTER V.

(1726-29.)

IN a new country, where very few knew of the incident, Voltaire could not easily forget the brutal outrage which had driven him from France. For this and for another reason, some of the saddest letters in all his correspondence were written during the early months of his residence in England. Soon after his arrival he heard of the death of his only sister, Madame Mignot, to whom he was sincerely attached. To the letter in which a lady-friend of the family informed him of the event, he replied in this pathetic strain: "What can I say to you, Mademoiselle, of my sister's death but that it would have been better for my family and myself if I had been taken away in her stead?" But there was much in the present to prevent him from brooding too long on the past. He had a new language to learn, English literature, philosophy, and science to study, and the acquaintance of distinguished persons to make. Some mastery of English was indispensable, and at once he devoted himself to acquire it. He fixed his headquarters at Wandsworth, where he resided with

Everard, afterwards Sir Everard Fawkener, or as Voltaire spells the name, Falkener, a Turkey merchant apparently, who rose to be English ambassador at Constantinople among other official elevations. The origin of their acquaintance is obscure, but it ripened into cordial intimacy, Fawkener being a man of considerable culture and of a philosophic turn of mind. Some little knowledge of English Voltaire seems to have acquired before his arrival, and in a few months he could write it intelligibly; but he never wrote it with the correctness of a native. From Wandsworth he paid flying visits to London and elsewhere, and sometimes his French correspondents were asked to address their letters to him at "Lord Bolingbroke's house in London." Bolingbroke, "half restored" from exile, allowed to remain in England, but not to resume his seat in the House of Peers, then lived chiefly at Dawley, in Middlesex—not far from his friend Pope at Twickenham—where he played rather ostentatiously the part of a gentleman-farmer. Voltaire received a welcome from him, and still more from his French wife, but some time before, a hint of Voltaire's that he intended to dedicate the " Henriade " to Bolingbroke having come to nothing, the Englishman had spoken of himself as not being the dupe of his French admirer's "verbiage." A flattering letter from Voltaire to Pope, six months after his arrival in England, written in English, and doubtless corrected by another hand, reads as if he had already made the personal acquaintance of the great man at Twickenham, on whose "Essay on Criticism" and "Rape of the Lock," he is found about the same time lavishing the warmest

praise. With two other friends of Pope he became
more or less intimate. He was the guest for some time
of Peterborough at Parson's Green, and there he met
Swift, who had just published "Gulliver," and whose
last visit to England was paid in 1727. When in
that year Swift thought of visiting France, Voltaire
sent him letters of introduction to the Count de
Morville. Gay showed him the "Beggar's Opera"
before it was performed. Then there are the visit and
famous reply to the veteran Congreve, who, having interrupted the compliments of his French admirer by
asking to be looked on, not as an author, but as a gentleman, was told that if he had had the misfortune to be
simply a gentleman, Voltaire would not have troubled
himself to wait on him—an anecdote expunged from the
later editions of Voltaire's "Letters on the English," in
which it first appeared. Thomson, whose "Winter"
was published in 1726, and who in 1727 dedicated his
"Summer" to Bubb Dodington, he knew sufficiently
to admire the "simplicity" of his character. With
Young, afterwards of the "Night Thoughts," then
issuing his Satires, Voltaire was the fellow guest at East-
bury, the Dorsetshire seat of Bubb Dodington, to whom
one of those satires was dedicated. To this visit
belongs the well-known and perhaps apocryphal epigram
attributed to Young, and said to have been produced
after a warm discussion in which he defended the episode
of Death and Sin in "Paradise Lost" against Voltaire's
trenchant criticism :—

> " You are so witty, profligate, and thin,
>   At once we think thee Milton, Death and Sin."

Yet when, years afterwards, Young dedicated his "Sea-Piece," in most cordial language, to Voltaire, it was thus that he referred to the incident :—

> " On Dorset downs when Milton's page,
> With Sin and Death provoked thy rage,
> Thy rage provok'd, who soothed with gentle rhymes?
> Who kindly couch'd the censurer's eye,
> And gave thee clearly to descry
> Sound judgment giving law to fancy strong?"

The epigram can scarcely be called either "gentle" or "kind," and was not likely to "soothe" the irritable Voltaire.

Sir Isaac Newton was on the brink of the grave when Voltaire arrived in England, and he died March 20, 1727. But Voltaire sought and made the acquaintance of his niece, the beautiful and gifted Mrs. Conduitt, the Catherine Barton whom Swift admired, and from her he learned the story of the apple and gravitation which was first told in print by Voltaire. With Newton's champion and expositor, the metaphysical theologian, Samuel Clarke, Voltaire conversed and discussed philosophy and theology. He found his way to the old Duchess of Marlborough, and heard her confirm in detail the impression that Queen Anne wished ardently her brother, the Old Pretender, to succeed her on the throne, if he would but become a Protestant. He dined with Lord Chesterfield, and became intimate with the Herveys, Pope's Lord Fanny and his wife, "the beautiful Molly Lepel," addressing to the lady two amatory stanzas in not intolerable English verse. By Lady

Sandon, George II.'s mistress, his flattery was graciously
received, and he found favour in the eyes of Queen
Caroline, George II.'s wife. It does not appear what
precisely the introduction to the Duke of Newcastle did
for him, or whether he had more than one interview with
Sir Robert Walpole, neither of them a patron of literature. But never before surely had a foreign visitor to
England been on at least speaking terms, and in not
a few cases intimate, with so many of its distinguished
denizens.

Meanwhile the chief practical object of his English
visit was not forgotten. To push on and superintend
the issue of the "Henriade" by subscription, he appears to have migrated from Wandsworth to London
towards the close of 1727. There is a letter of his in
the December of that year, from "Maiden Lane at the
White Peruke," asking Swift to use his influence in
Ireland to procure subscriptions for the poem, at a
guinea each, and forwarding to the Dean a volume just
issued by Voltaire as a precursor and advertisement of
the "Henriade." It consisted of an essay on the civil
wars of France, which was in fact a sketch of the career
of Henri Quatre, and another on the epic poetry of all
nations from Homer to Milton, some fractions of which
are pleasant reading even now. Both of these are
written in English, no doubt made correct by a competent
reviser. In altering and expanding "La Ligue" for the
English edition, now entitled the "Henriade," Voltaire did
not, as is generally said, out of resentment for the Duc
de Sulli's behaviour to him after the Rohan-Chabot
affair, expunge from the poem the name of the Duke's

illustrious ancestor, Henry IV.'s Sully. Certainly in the
first canto Duplessis-Mornay was substituted for Sully as
the hero's companion in the purely imaginary visit to
Queen Elizabeth, in the account of which the praises of
England in " La Ligue " were considerably heightened in
the " Henriade," out of compliment to Voltaire's English
hosts. But in the eighth canto mention remained of
Sully as Henry's comrade at the battle of Ivry, and in
one of the prose-notes to it full justice is done to his
character and career. At last, in March, 1728, the sub-
scription-edition of the " Henriade " was issued, an
illustrated quarto. The king and queen (in the preceding June George II. had succeeded George I.) and
many of the " nobility and gentry," were among the
three hundred and fifty-four subscribers. It was dedicated to Queen Caroline, the only royal personage of the
Hanoverian connection in that age who respected and
favoured intellect. " Our Descartes," Voltaire said, in
a graceful English dedication, " the greatest philosopher
in Europe, before Sir Isaac Newton appeared, dedicated
his ' Principles ' to the celebrated Princess Palatine
Elizabeth, not, he said, because she was a princess
(for true philosophers respect princes and never flatter
them); but because of all his readers she understood
him the best and loved truth the most. I beg leave,
Madam (without comparing myself to Descartes), to
dedicate the ' Henriade ' to your Majesty upon the
like account, not only as the protectress of all arts
and sciences, but as the best judge of them." In
spite of Voltaire's persistent efforts to procure subscribers—he sent a bale of copies to the cultivated and

accomplished Carteret, then Irish Viceroy, to be disposed of in Ireland—and in spite of the accredited statement that his large gains from the sale of the "Henriade" in England laid the foundation of his fortune, they appear to have been really inconsiderable.

For another year after the publication of the "Henriade," Voltaire remained in England, employed mainly in collecting material for his "History of Charles XII.," and then, having reaped a rich harvest of multifarious knowledge, he left it never to return. Many of the impressions made on him by his English visit are recorded, and much of the influence which it exerted on him is disclosed, in his bright little book, the "Lettres Philosophiques, ou Lettres sur les Anglais," which was not published until some years after his return to France, but the greater portion of which was either composed or thought out in England. In writing it he had in view two objects mainly. One was to make his countrymen acquainted with what appeared to him most interesting, important, and striking in the thought, science, literature, politics, and social aspects of England. The other was to bring out, as far as he dared, sometimes directly, oftener indirectly, the contrast between what he admired in free England and what repelled him in despotic France, with its oppressive administration and intolerant Church. If priority in the list of subjects treated indicated Voltaire's estimate of their interest, he was most impressed by Quakerism and the Quakers, since to them the opening letters on the English are devoted. With his curiosity piqued by what he had heard of them, he made his way to a certain Andrew Pitt, a wealthy Quaker,

living at Hampstead, and was cordially welcomed as the
first Frenchman whom he had found desirous of information about the sect. "He received me," Voltaire says,
"with his hat on, and came towards me without the
slightest inclination of the body; but there was more
politeness in his frank and benevolent countenance than
in our fashion of drawing one leg behind the other and
carrying in the hand what was made to cover the head."
Like a modern interviewer, Voltaire put, concerning
the doctrines and singularities of the sect, questions
which were duly answered; the inquiring Frenchman
expressing, at least so he pretends, the astonishment
which would have been natural in an orthodox
Catholic. He even accompanied his Hampstead
friend to a Quaker's meeting near the Monument.
"They had already assembled," he says, "when I
entered with my guide. There were about four hundred men in the meeting-house, and three hundred
women. The women concealed their faces, and
the men wore their broad-brimmed hats. All were
seated and profoundly silent. I passed through the
midst of them without one of them raising his eyes to
look at me." Voltaire at a Quaker's meeting might
furnish a painter with a subject! "This silence continued for a quarter of an hour. At last one of them
rose, took off his hat, and after a few sighs, gave forth,
half with his lips, half through his nose, some balderdash,
which neither he nor any one else understood in the
least." But in spite of this, Voltaire was evidently
delighted with Quakerism from its minimum of dogma,
its rejection of a priesthood and of litigation, its con-

tempt for titles, and last not least, its abhorrence of war. Yet after sketching sympathetically the career of William Penn and the history of his Pennsylvania, Voltaire thus concluded his account of what was, to him, a most estimable sect :—

"I cannot conjecture what will be the fate in America of the religion of the Quakers, but I see that it is dying out in London. In every country the dominant religion, if it does not persecute, swallows up, in the long run, all the others. Quakers cannot become members of Parliament, or occupy any official post, because they would have to take an oath, and this they will not do. They are reduced to the necessity of making money by trade and commerce. Their children, enriched by the industry of their parents, wish to enjoy, along with honours, buttons and ruffles. They are ashamed to be called Quakers, and become Churchmen to be in the fashion."

From Quakerism to the general subject of religion in England the transition was an easy one.

" England," he begins his dissertation, "is the country of sects. ' In my father's house are many mansions.' An Englishman as befits a freeman, goes to heaven by any road he pleases. . . . The Anglican clergy have retained many of the Catholic ceremonies, and above all that of receiving their tithes with very scrupulous care. They have also the pious ambition of wishing to be masters, for what village curate would not desire to be a pope ? " But a stop has been put to the sittings of Convocation, and though " in spite of the Whigs " the bishops still have seats in the House of Lords, " there is in the oath which they take to the State a clause which much exercises these gentlemen's patience. They promise in it to be of the Church as by law established. There is scarcely a bishop, dean, or priest who does not consider himself such by right divine, and thus it is a great subject of mortification for them to be obliged to confess that they der've all that they are from a miserable law made by pagan laymen."

In regard to morals, the Anglican clergy "lead more regular lives than the French." One cause of it is that—

"every cleric is brought up in the university either of Oxford or of Cambridge, far from the corruption of the capital. . . . Besides, priests are almost all of them married men. . . . That undefinable being, neither clerical nor secular, whom we call an abbé, is a species unknown in England, where all ecclesiastics are reserved, and almost all of them pedants. When they are told that in France young fellows, notorious for their debauchery, and raised to bishoprics by feminine intrigues, make love in public, amuse themselves by composing amatory songs, daily give long and sumptuous supper-parties, and going thence to implore the illumination of the Holy Ghost, call themselves boldly successors of the apostles, they thank God that they are Protestants."

After a sketch of Scotch Presbyterianism, to the influence of which Voltaire attributes the Puritanical observance of Sunday in England—

"although," he says, "the Episcopalians and the Presbyterians are the two dominant sects in Great Britain, all the others are welcomed there, and live together very fairly, whilst most of the preachers hate each other almost as cordially as a Jansenist damns a Jesuit. Enter the London Exchange, a place much more worthy of respect than most Courts, and you see assembled for the benefit of mankind representatives of all nations. There the Jew, the Mahometan, and the Christian deal with each other as if they were of the same religion, and call infidels only those who become bankrupts. There the Presbyterian trusts the Anabaptist, and the Anabaptist relies on the promise of the Quaker. On leaving these free and peaceful assemblies, some proceed to the synagogue, others to the tavern. One goes to have himself baptized in the name of the Father, through the Son, and to the Holy Ghost; another to have his son circumcised, and some words in Hebrew, which he does not understand, muttered over the infant; while a third betakes himself to his meeting-house to wait

for the inspiration of God, with his hat on his head—and all are content. If in England there were only one religion, its despotism
would be to be dreaded; if there were only two, their followers
would cut each other's throats; but there are thirty of them, and
they live in peace and happiness."

In his sketch of the political history of England and
of British institutions, Voltaire admires the evolution
of freedom from rebellion and civil war.

"No doubt the establishment of liberty in England has been
costly; it is in seas of blood that the idol of despotic power has
been drowned; but the English do not think that they have paid
too high a price for their laws. Other nations have not had fewer
troubles, have not poured out less blood; but the blood which they
have shed in the cause of liberty has only served to cement their
slavery. . . . You do not in England hear of one kind of justice for
the higher class, a second for the middle, and a third for the
lowest; nor of the right to pursue game on the land of a citizen who
is not allowed to fire a shot in his own fields. Because he is a
nobleman or an ecclesiastic, an Englishman is not exempt from
paying certain taxes; all imposts are regulated by the House
of Commons, which though only second in dignity, is first in
authority. . . . The peasant's feet are not lacerated by wooden
shoes; he eats wheaten bread; he is well clad; he is not afraid to
increase the number of his cattle, or to cover his roof with tiles, lest
his taxes should be raised the year afterwards. You see in England
many peasants"—or rather yeomen—"who have nearly five or six
hundred pounds a year, and who are not above continuing to cul-
tivate the soil which has enriched them, and on which they live
as free men."

In all these respects what a contrast, though Voltaire
does not dare to say so bluntly, between England and
France! Great, too, is the contrast between the feelings
with which Frenchmen and Englishmen regard one
principal form of modern industry.

"Milord Townshend, a minister of State," Sir Robert Walpole's brother-in-law; "has a brother who is content to be a merchant in the City. At the time when Milord Oxford governed England, his younger brother was a factor at Aleppo, whence he did not care to return, and where he died. . . . In France, whoever pleases is a marquis, and whoever arrives in Paris from the depths of the provinces, with money to spend and a name ending in 'ac' or 'ille' may talk of 'a man like me,' 'a man of my quality,' and look down with sovereign disdain on a trader. The trader himself hears so often his vocation spoken of contemptuously that he is foolish enough to blush for it. Yet I know which of the two is most useful to a state, a carefully-powdered nobleman who can tell at what hour precisely the king gets up, at what hour he goes to bed, and who gives himself the airs of a great man while performing the part of a slave in the ante-chamber of a minister; or a trader, who enriches his country, gives from his desk orders for Surat and Cairo, and contributes to the welfare of the world."

Sentiments little calculated to please in the latitude of Versailles. Voltaire's study of English literature during his residence in England appears to have been chiefly one of poetry and the drama. He boasted afterwards that he had been the first to make Milton and Shakespeare known to his countrymen. In both cases his expression of admiration was combined with great severity of fault-finding. In the "Essay on Epic Poetry" he speaks with enthusiasm of Milton's description of the spousal loves of Adam and Eve. "In other poems love is regarded as a weakness, in Milton alone it is a virtue: nowhere else is there anything like such love, or the poetry which describes it;" but, on the other hand, the episode of Death and Sin is a "disgusting and abominable story." Shakespeare is a semi-barbarous writer with many beauties; and in the "English Letters" there is a French translation of "To be or not to be," but nothing can be more nonsensical, Voltaire declares, than the talk of the grave-diggers in the play from which he took the famous soliloquy.   There are fine things in Dryden, but in a general way English tragic writers are "barbarous," and the sole exception is Addison's "rational" Cato.   As to comedy, Wycherly is too indecent for the French, Vanbrugh has gaiety, and Congreve's plays possess, among other merits, that of a rigid conformity to the rules of the drama.   In poetry, samples in French rhyme are given of Waller and Rochester, and, what is more striking, of "Hudibras;" while Voltaire reserves his highest praise for Pope, "the most elegant, the most correct, and the most harmonious of English poets."

Towards Newton and Locke, however it may be with our poets and dramatists, Voltaire's feeling is almost wholly one of enthusiastic admiration.   Pemberton's "View of Sir Isaac Newton's Philosophy" was published while Voltaire was in England, and he mastered it sufficiently to enable him to give in the "Letters" a lucid and lively summary of Newton's discoveries and of their results, foremost among these being the annihilation of the *vortices* of Descartes.   With Samuel Clarke, the Arian Rector of St. James's, whose consciousness of heterodoxy was just effective enough to prevent him from accepting a bishopric, he conversed on natural theology (in which Clarke took "the high *à priori* road") and metaphysics.   For a time Voltaire was dazzled by Clarke's speculations, and long afterwards spoke of the reverence

with which Clarke pronounced the name of God. But
his chief teacher in metaphysics became, and remained,
Locke, whom Voltaire considered to have destroyed the
innate ideas of Descartes, just as Descartes's *vortices* had
been destroyed by Newton. A hint, almost casually
thrown out by Locke, that the Creator may have conferred on mere matter a capacity for both thinking and
feeling, often re-appears in Voltaire's writings as not
much less than a positive dogma. He looked on it as a
satisfactory confutation of the belief in spirit as something
altogether distinct from, while associated with, matter.

Certain other English writings Voltaire must have read
eagerly and assiduously during his residence in England,
but he did not dare to hazard an account of them in his
"Letters on the English." The controversy between
Deism and Orthodoxy had been waged vigorously, if
fitfully, in England before Voltaire's visit, and numerous
references to them in his works testify to his familiarity
with such writers as Toland and Tindal, Collins and
Chubb. But never was that controversy prosecuted
more briskly than while Voltaire was in England, through
the publication of most of the now forgotten Woolston's
"Discourses on the Miracles." The audacity, and the then
unparalleled scurrility, of Woolston's assault on much of
the scriptural account of the Founder of Christianity,
threw into the shade the generally decorous argumenta-
tion of Woolston's deistical predecessors and contemporaries, and provoked replies from a legion of orthodox
apologists, Sherlock among them. Woolston's scoffing
irreverence left a deep impression on Voltaire. Many
years afterwards, when he could write and print more

freely than at the time of the publication of the " English Letters," he gave (in the "Dictionnaire Philosophique," art. " Miracles "), citing chapter and verse, some of the most outrageous of Woolston's comments on the Gospel narrative. Much impressed, too, he was by the comparative "liberty of unlicensed printing " in England, where three editions of "20,000 copies " each (at least, this is Voltaire's statement) of Woolston's discourses were rapidly disposed of. But if Bolingbroke's talk, and the writings of the English Deists, contributed to his armoury some new weapons for use in his long war against what he was never wearied of denouncing as " superstition," nothing that Voltaire read or heard during his English visit can have much strengthened the firm conviction which he brought with him of the falsity of the old theology.

CHAPTER VI.

(1729-39.)

VOLTAIRE had powerful friends both in and out of the French Ministry, and after an exile of not far from three years, he received permission to return to France in the early spring of 1729. The entry into Paris, which was at first forbidden him, was in a few weeks conceded, and once more he was afloat in French society, among friends both old and new. He took with him, among the manuscript fruits of his exile, the tragedy of "Brutus," his "History of Charles XII.," and the "Letters on the English," more or less advanced towards completion. He was now in his thirty-fifth year, and without a definite position. He had known to his cost the uncertainties of dependence on the great; and beginning life again, as it were, he was more intent than ever on becoming independent of them, and of the capricious favour of the theatre-going public. Soon after his arrival in Paris an opportunity presented itself for making a financial *coup*, and he availed himself of it with what became a habitual dexterity in the financial sphere of things. The French Controller-General had brought

5

out, in order to liquidate a portion of the public debt, a lottery scheme, so unskilfully planned that if a single speculator, or an association of speculators, bought all the tickets, he or they would gain a million livres—say £40,000. A hint that this would be the result of such an operation was dropped, at a supper party, in Voltaire's hearing, by La Condamine, the distinguished mathematician. Voltaire forthwith formed a syndicate, as it would now be called, which, acting on La Condamine's hint, gained, to the great disgust of the Minister, the sum anticipated, a very considerable portion of it being pocketed by Voltaire. This successful speculation, much more than the supposed profits of the English subscription for the "Henriade," appears to have partly formed the basis on which Voltaire reared what, for an eighteenth-century man of letters, was a colossal fortune. It preceded, and doubtless in some measure produced, another financial triumph of Voltaire's, not recorded by his previous biographers. In November, 1729, he had completed his thirty-fifth year, the period fixed in his father's will at which the limitations imposed on his enjoyment of his inheritance were to cease, should he then be leading a regular life (*ante* p. 37). On March 1, 1730, the President of the Chamber of Accounts, in the presence of notaries, formally annulled those limitations, "being well and duly informed" that Voltaire, "far from wasting his substance and incurring debts, has up till now augmented it, and he"—the President— "hopes that he"—Voltaire—"will make no other than a good use of it." It is said that old M. Arouet had deposited with the Chamber of Accounts the large sum of 240,000 livres, about £10,000, as security for his dealings with the monies officially entrusted to him, and that in pursuance of obscure arrangements for returning it to his heirs, 90,000 francs of this, £3,600, fell to Voltaire's share.

Some of the literary results of Voltaire's exile in England were now to be presented to the public. His tragedy, "Brutus," was played (December 11, 1730), with only a first night's success, and was soon withdrawn. The first volume of "Charles XII." had been printed (January, 1731), when the edition was seized and suppressed by the authorities, ostensibly on account of passages which might have wounded the feelings of Augustus II., King of Poland, of whom Charles had been the implacable foe. Then, as in the case of "La Ligue," Voltaire had "Charles XII." surreptitiously printed at Rouen, whither he repaired incognito to superintend the operation. At the beginning of 1732 it was smuggled into Paris, and was soon eagerly read in reprints throughout cultivated Europe. *Habent sua fata libelli.* The "Henriade" and "Charles XII.," the issue of which powerful governments thought it necessary to oppose, have dwindled into harmless school-books. "Eryphile," a drama composed by Voltaire in his seclusion at Rouen, and performed March 7, 1732, failed so signally, that his friends advised him to give up writing for the stage. The indefatigable and indomitable man replied by writing "Zaïre," perhaps the most effective of all his dramas, which, played (August 13) in the same year, was a striking success, his first of the kind since "Œdipe." In the spring of 1733 appeared his "Temple du Goût" (perhaps suggested by Pope's "Temple of Fame"), which, with its lively hits at Voltaire's literary enemies, made a great, if transient, sensation in Paris. In the May of the same year Voltaire is found, after several changes of residence, domiciled in an obscure quarter of Paris, under the roof of a corn merchant, whom he made use of in a new and serious speculation, a traffic in cereals, in which he invested a portion of his fortune. Among his visitors here was one fair lady with whom he formed an intimacy which became as close as it could be, and which exerted a long and peculiar influence on his career. This was Madame du Châtelet, the "divine Émilie" of so much of his prose and verse, whom he had known as a child when he visited her father, the Baron de Breteuil, a nobleman of very ancient family, and holding a considerable position at Court. Madame du Châtelet was twenty-seven, and Voltaire thirty-nine, when they were again thrown together, with the result which has just been foreshadowed. She had then been eight years the wife of the Marquis du Châtelet, an officer in the French army, an insignificant, and apparently good-natured man, for whom his wife cared little, and who allowed her to do very much what she pleased. Madame, tall, rather thin, bony, and a brunette, was not handsome, but her eyes were beautiful, her face intelligent and expressive, her forehead spacious. She was fond of dress and dissipation, and her *liaison* with Voltaire was by no means the first in her matrimonial career. To him she was passionately attached, and he was strongly attracted to her, as a woman of cultivated intellect, devoted, in the intervals of pleasure, to literature and science, who in early girlhood was a good Latin and Italian scholar, and had begun at fifteen a translation of Virgil.

Voltaire's speculations in exporting grain from Barbary were going on successfully, when, in 1733, the war of the Polish succession broke out, and a French army entered Italy. An old friend of Voltaire's, a great financier of those days, Pâris-Duverney, had the war-commissariat in his hands, and gave him a share in the contracts for provisioning the army, the profits of which brought him, according to some accounts, £20,000. Then he had, and throughout life continued to have, a large interest in a commercial house at Cadiz, and thus in a number of vessels employed in the American trade. Speculations of many other kinds, from dabbling in government loans, at home and abroad, to picture-buying and selling, brought grist to his mill. His gains he invested skilfully, one of his favourite operations being to lend money, mostly to *grands Seigneurs*—some of them, like the Duc de Richelieu, personal friends—bargaining in return to receive annuities on his own life, which yielded him a high rate of interest. In twenty years after his return from his exile in England, Voltaire was enjoying an income, it is computed, of between three and four thousand pounds a year, equivalent perhaps to some £10,000 now, a considerable revenue for a Frenchman of any class, and more especially for a French man of letters. As he kept his expenditure well under his income, with every year he had fresh savings to invest.

By 1733, when Voltaire began to execute his profitable contract for the supply of provisions to the French army in Italy, he had put the last touch to his "Letters on the

English," trying to soften them down in order to conciliate French orthodoxy in religion and politics; but, as
has been partly seen, there was enough left to prevent
the attempt from being successful. In the summer of
1733, the English translation of the book appeared in
London, before the publication of the original in France,
which was being secretly printed at Rouen. In the
French edition there were added to the letters some
remarks on the Pensées of Pascal, that "giant," Voltaire,
calls him. In his comments Voltaire substituted for the
world of gloom and misery depicted by the noble-minded
pietist and ascetic, a very tolerable state of existence, in
which there was much to be enjoyed, and which, if not
all that could be wished, might have been a good deal
worse than it is.

"Contemplating," Pascal said of humanity unenlightened by
religion, "the blindness and the misery of man, the marvellous
contradictions which his nature discloses, and beholding the whole
universe dumb, and man without light to guide him, straying aim-
lessly in this nook of the universe, without knowing who placed
him there, what he has come there to do, and what will become of
him when he dies, I am terror-struck, just as a man would be who,
if brought asleep into a frightful desert island, should, on awaking,
not know where he is, or how he can escape from it; and then
I wonder that such a miserable condition does not drive us to
despair."

To which plaintive outburst, Voltaire replies—

"For my part, when I contemplate Paris or London, I see no
reason for being driven to the despair of which Monsieur Pascal
speaks. I see a city which does not in the least resemble a desert
island; on the contrary, it is populous, opulent, well-policed, and men
enjoy in it as much happiness as is consistent with human nature.

What wise man would be full of despair because he is ignorant of the nature of his thinking faculty, because he knows only some of the attributes of matter, because God has not revealed to him his secrets ? He might as well despair because he has not four feet and two wings. Why should we view our existence with horror ? It is not so unhappy as they would have us believe. To look on the universe as a dungeon, and on all men as criminals about to be executed, is the notion of a fanatic. To believe that the world is an abode of bliss where we are only to enjoy ourselves, is the dream of a sybarite. To think that the earth, men, and animals are what they are intended to be in the order of Providence, is in my belief the opinion of a wise man."

Comments there were too on Pascal's religious faith, which, though politely expressed, were of unmistakable heterodoxy.

The printing of the Letters in French was finished at Rouen, and Voltaire had given strict orders to keep them out of circulation until he thought the moment favourable for publication. He was in the country with Madame du Châtelet, assisting at the *fêtes* which accompanied the marriage (a very unhappy one) of his dissolute friend and debtor, the Duc de Richelieu, when he heard, to his dismay, that an edition of the Letters, with the remarks on Pascal, was being surreptitiously published in Paris. The authorities were enraged at the issue of a book containing so much dangerous matter, and unmistakably intended to contrast the reign of liberty and justice in a great and flourishing neighbouring country, with the slavery, political, ecclesiastical, and social, in which France lay enchained. Punishment followed quickly on the publicity given to the crime. The book was condemned by the Parlia-

ment of Paris, and after being torn in pieces was
burned (June 10, 1734), by the public executioner, "as
scandalous, as contrary to religion, to morality, and to
the respect due to authority." An order was issued for
the arrest of the author. But before it could be executed, the bird had flown. After a month's wandering,
Voltaire found himself permitted to remain unmolested
at Cirey, a new domicile which was to be his headquarters for many years. Madame du Châtelet and he
appear to have some little time before thought of with-
drawing from the frivolities of Paris, to live and study
together in solitude; and now circumstances precipitated
the consummation of their wish.

Cirey, in Champagne, and what is now the department
of the Haute-Marne, was then a tumble-down château,
belonging to the Marquis du Châtelet and pretty far
from the busy hum of men—"nine miles from
a lemon," as Voltaire phrased it. On one side of it
rose a high hill, and between this and the house
stretched a little meadow through which a tiny stream
meandered. Voltaire advanced the Marquis 40,000
livres (£1,600) for repairs, and was to receive for the
loan an annuity of 2,000 livres (£80), which he never
did receive. Madame and he furnished sumptuously
suites of apartments for themselves, oases in a wilderness
of dilapidation. The husband, when not with his
regiment, lounged at Cirey, where Voltaire was the
real lord and master. Before joining him permanently
at Cirey, Madame had communed sympathetically with
such men as Maupertuis and Clairault, and been
smitten with a love of geometry, algebra, and physics,

making in them, according to unexceptionable testimony very considerable progress. In a general way, the life led at Cirey was monotonously regular. Most of the day was passed by Voltaire and Madame at the desk, and, by her, much of the night. The great meal was supper at nine, one of a *recherché* kind, at which Voltaire, dragging himself with difficulty from his desk, was generally three quarters of an hour too late. When he was seated, his valet stood fixed behind his chair, and footmen (who, like Madame's other servants, were fed scantily, and irregularly paid) presented the dishes to him, "as pages did to the gentlemen of the King's household." "Let Madame have every attention," followed his slightest order for himself. The Marquis, when not eating, went to sleep, and amiably withdrew after the table was cleared. Then, if Voltaire was not absorbed in thought, and was in a good humour, especially if congenial guests were present, he poured forth a stream of sparkling talk before rushing impatiently to his desk again. But Voltaire was not always in a good humour. Madame insisted on having her own way with him in trifles, and Voltaire often sulked under the infliction. Sometimes there were altercations, fortunately for ear-witnesses conducted in English, which Voltaire had taught the lady. Occasionally there were scenes more or less violent. But to the outside world "Émilie" was always represented by Voltaire as perfection itself. She repaid him by pleading for him with persons in authority, whose hostility, moreover, she did her best to avert by trying, too often in vain, to check the imprudences of his pen.

She lamented the extreme sensitiveness which allowed the criticisms of the smaller fry of authors in Paris to drive him into fits of ignoble rage; but, none the less, she did battle for him with them. Jealousy of her own sex, which, indeed, Voltaire does not appear at any time to have provoked, she never exhibited. But she could not bear him to be from her side for any length of time, and vented unreasonable reproaches if, when absent on tour or trip, he was not constantly writing to her. He became a little weary at last of her exacting ways, but for years remained strongly bound to her by ties of admiration, affection, and gratitude. He was now verging on forty, and almost for the first time since he quitted his father's house, he found at Cirey something that could be called a home.

For recreation Madame took rides on her mare, *Hirondelle*, and, for the sake of his digestion, Voltaire, in due sportsman's costume, with proper appurtenances, went hunting the deer in the neighbouring woods. Cirey was at its gayest when there were guests of a less serious turn than such occasional visitors as Maupertuis and Clairault. Then the little theatre, in which a stage of a few boards rested on empty barrels, was brought into requisition, and host, hostess, and some of the guests acted tragedies and comedies, mainly Voltaire's own. Madame was an excellent musician, and sometimes would sing a whole opera through. Sometimes, too, there were puppet shows, or Voltaire would work a magic-lantern, and with the accent of a Savoyard showman, make his little audience laugh at his satirical descriptions of friends and foes. And though he was far from Paris, constant correspondence with friends there kept him cognizant of its sayings and doings, which he professed to despise, but in which he took an interest only too keen for his own happiness. One of his most assiduous correspondences was with the Abbé Moussinot, a new financier and general factotum in Paris, where he much needed some one to look after his multifarious speculations and investments. Among the most delicate of the duties of the zealous and trustworthy Abbé was to press Voltaire's debtors among *grands Seigneurs* for the payment of arrears. When rhetoric failed, the law had to be set in motion, and Voltaire's dues to be wrung from tenants on estates the rents of which had been made his security for the payment of the life annuities charged on them. Much more pleasant items in his letters to the worthy Abbé, are frequent instructions to make presents of little sums of money to struggling men of letters, especially the young and promising among them, which were too often repaid by ingratitude.

At Cirey, Voltaire's pen was incessantly and variedly productive. At the time of his first settlement there, the publication of Pope's "Essay on Man" had been completed, and suggested to him a series of metrical dissertations on Man, "Discours en vers sur l'homme," melodious and felicitous. Some of Pope's ideas are borrowed and expanded in them, but Voltaire's aim is more modest than that of his old acquaintance at Twickenham. Not "to justify the ways of God to man," but to make man contented with his destined lot, is the object of Voltaire's musical verse. There is unhappiness everywhere, but everywhere there is happiness. Let us be thankful to God for what happiness he has bestowed on us. Above all, avoid vainly inquiring why man and nature are what they are. These are mysteries which faculties are not given us to penetrate. The universe was not made for man, but both universe and man for God, and so forth. In a treatise on metaphysics, written by him in the early years at Cirey, but not printed until long afterwards, Voltaire shows himself, as usual when dealing with the deepest subjects, a man speaking to men, not a professional philosopher to professional philosophers. He examines the question of the existence of God, and this is the conclusion which he comes to: "In the belief that there is a God there are difficulties, in the contrary belief there are absurdities." One composition only of this period involved him in trouble with the authorities, and, apart from its character, through no fault of his own. In "Le Mondain," a poem which Goethe greatly admired, Voltaire waxed satirically eloquent in a contrast between the good old times with their frugality and simplicity, and his own civilized age, which he much preferred, with its enjoyments and luxuries. The garden of Eden, and our first parents supping on water and acorns, are painted in any but Miltonic hues, and Voltaire, thanking his stars that he was born now and not in an imaginary golden age, sings the delights of a day in modern Paris. He had sent a copy of the rather irreverent poem to a worldly French prelate, among whose papers it was found after his death. Copies of it were circulated among profane sympathizers, and reached the authorities. Voltaire was warned that he might expect the worst, and he fled incognito to Holland, grumbling that "to speak of Adam as having long nails has been made a crime, and treated seriously as heresy." Before long he was back at Cirey, full of fresh indignation at his devout persecutors in Paris, and, to put them off the scent, giving out that he had gone to England, and even shamming death.

Voltaire at Cirey was, as at all times and in all places, faithful to his first love—the drama. "Alzire," "L'Enfant Prodigue," "Mahomet," and "Mérope," which last some English critics consider his masterpiece, were written during the first decade of his stay at Cirey. Great progress was made, too, with the most disgraceful of all Voltaire's writings, the scandalous "Pucelle." Better employment than licentiously burlesquing the story of a noble French heroine and a spirit-stirring episode in French history, Voltaire was busy also with his "Siècle de Louis Quatorze," and laying the foundation of his historical *opus maximum*, the "Mœurs et Esprit des Nations." This last work was begun ostensibly for the benefit of Madame du Châtelet, who despised the "old almanack" histories then current, for which Voltaire aimed at substituting something more profitable to the modern man and woman. Moreover, Madame cared little for poetry and the drama, and was devoted to science, mathematical and physical. With her as his companion, Voltaire breathed an atmosphere of science ; science, too, was becoming fashionable in high French circles, and he was not the man to lag behind the culture of his age. When preparing for the press his "Letters on

the English," Voltaire had consulted Maupertuis, one of
the few Newtonians then in France, on some doubts
which he harboured on points in the theories of Sir
Isaac Newton, and Maupertuis removed them. In 1735
there came on a visit to Cirey, a young Italian, Frederick
the Great's Algarotti, who read to his host and hostess
chapters of what became his "Newtonianismo per le
dame." This book, written in dialogue-form, was to
popularise Newton's astronomy and physics for Italians
in general, and Italian ladies in particular, just as Fonte-
nelle had popularized, in his dialogues on the "Plurality
of Worlds," the Copernico-Cartesian astronomy, then,
and so late as the time of Algarotti's visit to Cirey, all
but universally accepted in France. Why not, thought
Voltaire, do for France what Algarotti is doing for Italy,
and become the French apostle of the Newtonian religion, into which, as he said, he had been "baptized"
by Maupertuis? Forthwith he set to work, and in 1736
his "Elements of Newton's Philosophy" ("Éléments de
la Philosophie de Newton") was ready for the press. But
scientific bigotry was too much for him. Cartesianism
was dominant in France, and here was this Voltaire, a
man suspect, convicted of flagrant heterodoxy, religious
and political, audaciously coming forward with proposals
to substitute for the recognized doctrine of the great and
orthodox Des Cartes, the new-fangled and far-fetched
theories of a native of semi-republican and heretic
England, Voltaire's book on which, teeming with praises
of the English and of their Newton, had been burned
by the public executioner. Even the upright and fearless
Chancellor D'Aguesseau refused the authorization needed

for the publication of the "Elements" in France. An unauthorized edition of the work, not all of it Voltaire's, was printed in Holland (1738), and eagerly bought. It was not until 1741 that Voltaire's own authorized edition was issued. Now that all the world is Newtonian, Voltaire's work is forgotten or neglected. It appears that he had not mastered the "Principia" itself, but his general accuracy, as well as lucidity of exposition, have been vouched for in England and Germany by eminent and impartial scientific authorities. Its intrinsic merits, and Voltaire's name and fame, gave it currency in France and on the Continent. To have popularized for Europe Newton's discoveries was not the least of Voltaire's many shining achievements, and one to which no possible exception can anywhere be taken.

General physics and chemistry also occupied Voltaire at Cirey. He had a gallery stored with philosophical instruments, and a laboratory with retorts and crucibles, where for a time a chemist assisted him in his experiments. An impetus was given to his experimenting when, in 1737, the French Academy of Sciences offered a prize for the best disquisition on the nature and propagation of fire. Voltaire threw himself ardently into the competition. Cirey was in a district of iron-stone, of foundries, and forges, and Voltaire set to work to fuse iron and make it red-hot, weighing the same mass at all degrees of temperature. He found, as most people have found, that its weight was increased on cooling. Some scientific authorities bear strong testimony to his patient industry in these and other experiments, and to his determination, thus exhibited, to take nothing for granted, but to submit other men's theories to the test of experiment. Not only so, they assert that he might have, had he persevered, been a scientific discoverer. They generously represent him as even having been on the verge of anticipating Priestley in the discovery of oxygen, because he came to the conclusion that the increased weight of the iron on cooling was due to its absorption of something in the air. "*Il est très possible,*" are his words, "*que cette augmentation de poids soit venue de la matière répandue dans l'atmosphère.*" Meanwhile, Madame du Châtelet, fired by an interesting spirit of emulation, resolved to compete, without Voltaire's knowledge, for the same prize. Naturally she read what he had written, and ventured to combat in her essay most of his theories. She had to hide frcm him what she was doing, and on each of eight nights, successively, she slept for only a single hour, writing during the rest of it, and keeping herself awake by such devices as plunging her hands into iced water. Voltaire's and her papers were among five selected out of many as the best, but the prize was divided among three other of the foremost competitors, Euler being one of them. It was only when this result was made known, that Madame told her secret to Monsieur, and was agreeably disappointed to find him much pleased—not, as she had expected, displeased with her scientific audacity. Both papers were printed by the Academy, with honourable mention of "a lady of high rank, Madame du Châtelet," as the writer of one of them.

Memorable in Voltaire's stay at Cirey was the formation of his much talked of, and much written of, intimacy with Frederick, afterwards the Great, who was then, as Crown Prince of Prussia, leading a happy life at Reinsberg. Frederick's culture was almost entirely French. One of his chief pleasures was to read French authors, and to try to write French verses; and, above all other French authors, and all other French verses, he prized Voltaire and Voltaire's. He, too, was a sceptic, and his admiration for Voltaire was far from being purely literary. Voltaire the philosopher, who combated "superstition" and preached toleration, was as dear to him as Voltaire the writer of incomparable verse. In his first letter to Voltaire (August 8, 1736) the enthusiastic young prince of 24 lavished praise on Voltaire's writings of every kind,·and begged, as the most precious of favours, that there might be communicated to him, in confidence, any of them which Voltaire might have by him, and did not dare to print. When Frederick said that never before Voltaire had metaphysics been made rhythmic, he had evidently read some of the "Discours sur l'Homme." Since Voltaire loved "philosophy," the Prince sent him a translation, which he had ordered to be executed, of both a statement and refutation of the charges made against the German metaphysician Wolf, who had been "cruelly accused of irreligion and atheism." Voltaire was naturally delighted with such a letter from such a prince, and his response to it was in his best style, grateful and respectful, without adulation. Frederick had said that if destiny did not favour him to the point of being able to "possess" Voltaire—an expression which may have a little alarmed Madame du Châtelet—he hoped one day to "see him whom he had so long

6

admired from such a distance." Voltaire replies that
he will consider it a very precious boon to pay his court
to his Royal Highness. "But," with the fear of Madame
before his eyes, he adds, "the friendship which retains
me in my present retreat does not allow me to leave it."
More important than all these amenities is a passage in
Voltaire's reply, which deserves to be quoted, because
the thought which animates it was often present to him
when he reflected on the results of metaphysical inquiry,
and, in one or another form, frequently appears in his
writings :—

"I cannot," he said, "thank your Royal Highness too much for
your kindness in sending me the little work relating to Monsieur Wolf.
I look on his metaphysical ideas as doing honour to the human mind.
They are flashes of lightning in the midst of a profound night, and
this is all, in my opinion, that can be hoped for from metaphysics.
It does not appear that the first principles of things will ever be
properly known. The mice that inhabit some little crannies of a
vast building do not know whether that building is eternal, or what
its architect, or why he built it. They try to preserve their own
existence, to people their crannies, and to escape from the destructive
animals that pursue them. We are such mice, and the divine architect who built this universe has not yet, so far as I know, told his
secret to any of us."

The correspondence between poet-philosopher and
prince, thus pleasantly and promisingly begun, went
on with much regularity. Voltaire sends Frederick his
prose and verse, published and unpublished, and they
are welcomed with outbursts of rapturous admiration.
By and by Frederick gains courage to send Voltaire speci-
mens of his own French verse. Voltaire exhausts himself
in praising them and their author, but, at the same time,

after a delicate hint that dots must be put upon i's, he points out in them sundry little defects of orthography, idiom, and rhyme, his corrections of which are graciously and gratefully received by his royal pupil. Sometimes, and generally *à propos* of the lucubrations of "le sieur Wolf," the pair indulge in serious, but always friendly, metaphysical debate. Early in their correspondence occurs one lengthy controversy on fate, free-will, fore-knowledge absolute, conducted with considerable dialectic skill on either side, Frederick pronouncing for necessarianism, Voltaire for the freedom of the will, and both of them showing themselves decided theists. Agreeable episodes in their commune is the despatch of an envoy and presents from Reinsberg to Cirey, a bust of Socrates, a portrait of Frederick, and so forth. Frederick pays in his epistles pretty compliments to "Émilie," and a friendly correspondence is struck up between the lady and the prince.

CHAPTER VII.

(1739-44.)

IN the spring of 1739 Voltaire and Madame du Châtelet migrated from Cirey to Brussels, then the capital of the Austrian Netherlands. The Marquis du Châtelet had on his hands a family lawsuit of eighty years' standing, an active prosecution of which was made desirable by circumstances. The burden of it fell of course on his clever and energetic wife. As it was before the Austrian tribunals at Brussels that it dragged its slow length along, thither she had to repair. While at Brussels Voltaire's hands were, as usual, full of multifarious authorship, and his connection with Frederick was in course of full development. Frederick was projecting, at his own cost, a sumptuous edition of the "Henriade." Voltaire was commissioned to superintend for him the publication of Frederick's first book, the "Anti-Machiavel," teeming with the most admirable sentiments on the paternal duties of kings to their subjects, and with declamations on the iniquity and absurdity of seeking glory through conquest, with its accompanying "horrors of war." Voltaire arranged for its publication with a bookseller at the Hague, and some of the sheets were printed, when, May 31, 1730, Frederick's father died, and Frederick found himself King of Prussia. After this no more is heard of the royal edition of the "Henriade." In one of his letters, quite as friendly and familiar as ever, written a few weeks after his accession, Frederick tells Voltaire that he is revivifying the Berlin Academy of Science, and has secured for it Maupertuis and Wolf, but at the same time that he has considerably increased his army, winding up with the apostrophe—"For God's sake buy up the whole edition of the 'Anti-Machiavel.'" Circumstances had altered, and there were remarks in the book on European sovereigns which might give offence now that they came from one of themselves. And at last Frederick's long-cherished wish was to be gratified; he and Voltaire were to meet, but without the presence of Madame. At this stage in the intimacy of king and poet is seen prefigured a struggle of many years between Frederick and Madame du Châtelet, he longing for the acquisition, she bent on the retention of Voltaire. There was a compromise possible, to which Voltaire would have cheerfully assented, but every suggestion of which Frederick steadily declined to accept. Voltaire would have settled at Berlin if Madame had been allowed to settle there with him, and though she never had the chance given her, the arrangement would have been doubtless welcomed by her. But leading, though a husband, a bachelor's life, Frederick did not care to have women about his court, and would have Voltaire by himself, or not at all. Once or twice Voltaire thought for a moment of accepting Frederick's brilliant offers, and of leaving the lady in the lurch, but it was only for a moment. If his affection for her cooled, and he grew a little wearied of her temper, her algebra, and her devotion to physics and metaphysics, gratitude to the lady who had done and given up so much for him, outweighed in the long run all other considerations. In one or another sense he was Madame du Châtelet's to her dying day.

In the autumn of 1740, and the first month of his kingship, Frederick was making a rather extensive tour, and talked of paying, in the course of it, a visit incognito to Voltaire and Madame at Brussels. But to her great disappointment the visit did not come off. On the road he had an attack of fever, and instead of his coming to Voltaire, Voltaire had to go to him at his little castle of Moyland, six miles from Cleves. It was not among royal splendours that the King and the poet-philosopher met on that night of September, 1740.

"I was conducted to his Majesty's apartment," Voltaire long afterwards thus described the scene. "Only the four walls were there. By the light of a candle I perceived in a closet a small truckle-bed two and a half feet wide" (what a memory for detail!) "in which was a little man covered up in a dressing-gown of coarse blue cloth, perspiring and shivering under a miserable blanket, and in a violent fit of fever. I made him my obeisance, and began the acquaintance by feeling his pulse, as if I had been his physician-in-chief. The fit over, he dressed himself, and sat down to table."

Maupertuis and Algarotti were among Voltaire's fellow-guests at the supper-table, and during the conversation there was a profound discussion on the immor-

tality of the soul, free-will, and the androgynes of Plato.
The vigilant Carlyle discovered that there were, in fact,
three suppers, the conversations at which Voltaire rolled
into one. During his stay of two days and two more
nights, Voltaire recited his "Mahomet" to the delighted
king, and even wrote for him a defence of his claims
on the Prince-Bishop of Liége, whom Frederick was
threatening with 2,000 soldiers—"2,000 arguments,"
Voltaire called them. King and poet-philosopher parted
enchanted with each other.

Little more than a month after the first meeting of
Frederick and Voltaire, the Emperor, Charles VI., died
at Vienna (October 20, 1740), and Maria Theresa
reigned in his stead. Forthwith the royal denouncer
of Machiavelli, and declaimer against the military
ambition of kings, resolved to seize on Silesia, commu-
nicating his design to only one or two of his most
trusted confidants. But there was the stir of preparation in the Prussian arsenals; troops were mustered and
marched hither and thither, and everything indicated
the approach of a campaign on a considerable scale.
What were Frederick's designs nobody knew, and everybody wished to know, nor was hardly any one more
curious on the subject than the Prime Minister of
France, Cardinal Fleury, an old acquaintance of
Voltaire. From the days of his youth when he offered
to do spy-work for Cardinal Dubois, Voltaire had been,
and for years to come he was to be, possessed by the
ambition to enter public life, to "serve his King and
country," to be something more than an author of works
which brought him reputation, indeed, but were pub-

lished at his peril, arousing suspicion and displeasure
in high places, driving him from Paris, making him live
in perpetual fear of imprisonment or exile, and inciting
a rabble of Parisian critics, he complained, to defame
him "at least once a week." Even as it was, for some
reason or other, old or new, he was under a ban, forbidden to return to France, and Madame du Châtelet
had gone off to Fontainebleau to plead, not unsuccessfully, for its removal. Madame absent, he could easily
pay a visit to Frederick, who was always ready to
welcome him. If he could extract from his royal
friend and admirer the secret of those military preparations, what a feather it would be in his cap, what a
promising introduction to a possible political career!
He sounded Fleury on the subject by letter, and as the
French envoy at Berlin could discover nothing of
Frederick's intentions, Fleury approved of Voltaire's
visit and its object. When Voltaire dropped a hint of
coming, Frederick promised to receive him with open
arms, and he kept his promise. He fêted and caressed
Voltaire (November, 1741), whom he describes to a
correspondent as "sparkling with new beauties," but
not a whisper would he breathe of the great secret.
They parted exchanging in rhyme some half-bantering,
half-serious reproaches. The object of Frederick's
military preparations was soon disclosed, and in the
middle of December, some weeks after Voltaire's second
visit, he and his army were in Maria Theresa's Silesia,
giving the signal for a general European war, which was
to last, with a few intermissions, for more than twenty
years.

The du Châtelet lawsuit was taking a somewhat favourable turn, so that Voltaire and Madame could indulge in various trips, among others to and from Paris, where they spent several months in 1742, and where, on the 9th of August of that year, the much talked of Mahomet, " Fanaticism, or Mahomet the Prophet," was performed. It is one of the most vigorously written of Voltaire's dramas, for he threw his whole soul into the description of the Prophet as a self-conscious and unscrupulous impostor, founding, by sheer force of intellect and will, a successful religion, and inspiring honest dupes with a fanaticism which made them commit horrible crimes in the belief that they were pleasing God. But all religion was thought by the suspicious orthodox to be glanced at in this delineation of the founder of the youngest of Semitic religions. The clamour against "Mahomet" was such that, after three representations, and on a hint from the authorities, the drama was withdrawn, and Voltaire, disgusted, returned with Madame to Brussels. Frederick had made in June and July, a separate peace with Austria, and the French thought that he had left them in the lurch, for they did not know that Fleury had previously made overtures at Vienna for a peace of the same kind between France and Austria. Receiving an invitation from Frederick to come and see him at Aix-la-Chapelle, Voltaire communicated with Fleury, and set off cheerfully to visit his royal friend, and report what there was to be reported. It was not much. He spent a pleasant week of September (1742) with Frederick, whose renewed offers of a brilliant settlement at Berlin, he declined once more. Back again in Paris, where the old Cardinal Fleury died (January 27, 1743), he was somewhat consoled for the enforced withdrawal of "Mahomet," by the triumph of "Mérope" (February 20, 1743). For the first time, it is said, in French theatrical history, the pit shouted and re-shouted for the appearance of the author on the stage.

Voltaire had long and unsuccessfully aimed at being admitted to the French Academy, and he became, with hopes encouraged by the triumph of "Mérope," a candidate for the seat in it vacant through Fleury's death. The reigning mistress, the Châteauroux, it appears, had been gained over to his side by his friend the Duc de Richelieu. The chief obstacle was the opposition of the orthodox, especially of Boyer, Bishop of Mirepoix, the tutor of the Dauphin, the adviser of the King in the disposal of benefices, and in the administration of ecclesiastical affairs generally. Boyer, in view of Voltaire's notorious heterodoxy, declared it to be impossible to allow him to succeed a cardinal, and pronounce on him the usual panegyric. Voltaire's attempt to conciliate this bigot is one of the strangest episodes in his career. In a long series of falsehoods, from his youth upwards, he had disavowed the author-ship of writings which were unquestionably his, but which brought him into collision with the authorities. He capped them now by inditing letters vindicating his own orthodoxy. "In the presence of God who hears me," he said in the one of these precious epistles which was addressed specifically to Boyer, "I affirm that I am a good citizen and a true Catholic, and I say this simply because I have always been so in my heart. I have never written a page which does not breathe a spirit of humanity, and I have written many which are hallowed by religion." His "calumniators" brought against him his authorship of those " Letters on the English " which were burned by the Parliament of Paris. To this charge he had the audacity to reply: "Most of those which arc printed with my name are not by me, and I have proofs which demonstrate it." Great was the effect produced in Paris by the publicity given to these and similar declarations, but it was not the effect which Voltaire had hoped for. They deceived no one, least of all those whom they were intended to deceive. By a unanimous vote a bishop was elected Fleury's successor in the Academy. Voltaire had to submit to be reproached for his hypocrisy by Frederick himself, who was generally given to remonstrate with him on the imprudence of his attacks on orthodoxy.

The mortification suffered by Voltaire gave delight to Frederick, who hoped that it would drive him from France to seek a final refuge at Berlin. To promote this consummation, he had recourse, in the year of Voltaire's rejection by the Academy, to one of the trickiest of stratagems, which, were it not recorded in his own letters, would be almost incredible. To embroil Voltaire still further with Boyer, Frederick sent his envoy in Paris extracts from letters to himself, in which, in prose and verse, Voltaire had spoken his mind very freely about Boyer. These extracts the envoy was to get in some underhand way conveyed to Boyer, whose enmity to Voltaire being thus made more bitter, Voltaire, Frederick expected, would find France too hot to hold him. As it happened, this very Frederick-like proceeding was inopportune. Boyer, indeed, was hostile, but Amelot, Minister of Foreign Affairs after Fleury's death, was favourable to Voltaire, and among the other ministers were the two D'Argensons, his old schoolfellows and allies. In this way, and through Frederick's known friendship for him, Voltaire was entrusted with more of a diplomatic mission than had ever before been given him, while Boyer's hostility to him was assigned as the reason for his departure from France. Taking the Hague by the way, Voltaire was to proceed to Berlin and sound Frederick, then at peace with all the world, on the feasibility of a renewal of his alliance with France. France was in desperate straits, and her army in Germany suffered a disastrous defeat at Dettingen (June 27, 1743) before Voltaire, in the following September, arrived in Berlin, where, as usual, he was a welcome guest of Frederick, who, at first, little suspected that his French friend had come to sound him, and not to recruit after his maltreatment by his enemies in Paris. Frederick soon found out the truth, however, and though, for good reasons of his own, meditating an alliance with France, he dropped no hint of it to Voltaire. This was the last, for many years, of Voltaire's attempts to become a political personage through his friendship with Frederick. On leaving Berlin he spent a few weeks in Paris, and after another sojourn at Brussels, Voltaire, firmly clutched by Madame du Châtelet, in the spring of 1744 returned once more to home, and Cirey.

CHAPTER VIII.

(1744–50.)

VOLTAIRE was soon busy at Cirey, with a task of a kind unattempted by him for nearly twenty years, when he was basking in the sunshine of Court favour, just before the catastrophe which produced his exile to England. The Dauphin (afterwards father of Louis XVI.) was to be married to a Spanish infanta, and splendid pageants of every kind were to accompany the wedding. The Duc de Richelieu, as first gentleman of the bed-chamber, had control of the arrangements, and he commissioned Voltaire to compose a theatrical piece, with spectacular, Terpsichorean, and musical effects, suited to the great occasion. Voltaire set cheerfully and diligently to work on the "Princesse de Navarre," and spent far more time and trouble on it than on almost any of his elaborate tragedies. He and Madame du Châtelet passed the winter of 1744–5 in Paris, and on February 23, 1745, his wedding-piece was played before the Court, the King, though he never liked Voltaire, signifying his gracious approval of it. On the 1st of April following, his high friends aiding the fulfilment of

a wish which he had expressed, Voltaire was appointed
royal historiographer, with a salary of 2,000 francs (£80).
He had not long to wait for an opportunity to show
what a poet could do as a historiographer. On the
11th of May, the King and Dauphin were present at
the battle gained by the French over the Duke of
Cumberland and the English, the victory of Fontenoy,
which threw the French into ecstasy. Voltaire celebrated it in a poem which went through five editions in
ten days. The King returned to the scene of warfare,
leaving behind him the lady who, as First Mistress, was
to succeed the Châteauroux (dead the previous year),
and who in July was created Marquise de Pompadour.
Voltaire, who before this consummation, was in her good
graces, paid his court to her assiduously, in person and
with pen, during the summer, and for some time she was
his friend, of course one very valuable. At the same
time, bent on checkmating his enemy Boyer, and the
devout party at Court, he was making up to a very
different potentate, no less a personage than the Pope.
Benedict XIV. was a good-natured, easy-going, worldly
pontiff, not the least of a bigot. Voltaire, a French abbé
in Rome helping him in his manœuvres, contrived to
ingratiate himself with the Pope, who sent him medals
and accepted a flattering distich (in French-Latin) from
Voltaire for his portrait. Further, he allowed Voltaire
to dedicate to him, as " the head of the true religion,"
his " Mahomet," as a piece written " against the founder
of a false religion." The Pontiff responded (September 19,
1745) most benignantly, bestowing his " apostolic benediction " on his " dear son," who was not to doubt "the

singular esteem which merit so recognized " as Voltaire's,
had "inspired" in the Holy Father ! By this unparalleled
stroke of diplomacy Voltaire completely baffled Boyer
and his bishops. Which of them could now denounce
"Mahomet" and Voltaire, when the Head of their
Church had expressed his admiration of the piece, and
blessed his "dear son," its author? While among the
archives of the War Office, presided over by the younger
of his two friends, the brothers D'Argenson, Voltaire was
busy collecting material for the history of the war, at the
same time he was employed by the elder of them, then
Minister of Foreign Affairs, to write for him important
State papers. In December, at Versailles, was performed
Voltaire's operatic " Temple de la Gloire," in which Louis
was glorified as Trajan. Grave doubts have been thrown
on the truth of the famous story of Voltaire's inquiring
apostrophe to Louis, " Trajan—est il content? " and of
the contemptuous glance and glacial silence which, it has
been said, was the King's only reply. But if the King
did not like him personally, he was not altogether
insensible to Voltaire's adulation in verse and prose, and
the still friendly Pompadour's influence was supreme.
Thanks to her chiefly, he grasped at last the prize which
he had long coveted in vain. On April 25, 1746, he was
unanimously elected a member of the French Academy.
Earlier in the year the project of a descent on England
by a French army under Richelieu, to co-operate
with the young Pretender was confided to him, and he
wrote the manifesto which Richelieu was to issue on
landing. The defeat of Charles Edward at Culloden
(April 16, 1746) annihilated the project, and made

waste-paper of Voltaire's grandiose manifesto. But the
year 1746 closed in one way gloriously for him. At
last there was fulfilled an old promise that, on the first
vacancy, he should be appointed a gentleman-in-ordinary
to the King, a position which conferred on him some
legal as well as social privileges. When, however,
Voltaire took his seat at the table spread at the royal
expense for the gentlemen of the bed-chamber, they
appear to have looked rather askance at him as a
parvenu. And much as he boasted to others of his
various elevations, he knew in his heart that they were
not the rewards of what he had really done to deserve
reward. "My 'Henri Quatre,' my 'Zaïre,' and my
American ' Alzire,'" he sighed in rhyme, "never gained
me a single glance from the King. With very little glory
I had a thousand enemies. At last honours are showered
on me for a farce of the Fair,"[1] the " Princesse de
Navarre," to wit.

Throughout his career disgraces, too often due to
Voltaire's imprudences of tongue or pen, alternate
with triumphs, and two of the former, more or less
notable, belong to 1747. One evening, in the early
winter of that year, the Court, Voltaire and Madame du
Châtelet with it, being at Fontainebleau, there was high
play at the Queen's table. Madame du Châtelet lost
and continued to lose, until she owed—pay there and

---

[1] The minor Theatres of the Fair (*La· Foire*) were thus called
from being first opened during the chief annual fairs of Paris.
Le Sage, the author of " Gil Blas," wrote a good deal for them,
but the pieces performed at them were generally of the flimsiest
kind.

then such a sum she could not—no less than 84,000 francs (£3,360). In his indignation, and though the other gamblers were some of the greatest people in the land, Voltaire told her aloud that only her excitement had prevented her from seeing that she was playing with knaves. With a touch of discretion he had spoken in English, but it was evident from the angry buzz around them that he had been only too well understood. Foreseeing a storm about to burst on them, Voltaire and Madame withdrew, and that very night they were being driven to an old friend and a place—both of them familiar to him in early youth—the Duchesse du Maine and her château of Sceaux. They had been her guests not long before, and the great lady, alienated from the Court, welcomed the pair and cheerfully harboured the culprit. For security's sake the shutters of his room were closed by day as well as night, and, at work as usual, he wrote by candle-light while it was daylight outside. Every night when the household had gone to rest, and the Duchess retired to her room, on a table by her bedside a dainty little supper was laid for Voltaire, who, emerging from his hiding-place, read aloud what he had been writing for her during the day. It was well worth such an audience, for he had composed, to amuse the Duchess and himself, "Zadig," "Babouc," and "Memnon"—the earliest of those sparkling and inimitably piquant Oriental tales which are still popular, while the "Henriade" and "Charles XII." have been relegated to the schoolroom, and Voltaire's tragedies, once found so thrilling, are, at least out of France, read only by the studious. In the meantime Madame du

Châtelet had raised money to pay her gambling debt, and her creditor pocketed the insult with it. Voltaire's shutters were no longer closed during the day, and he joined in the miscellaneous gaieties which followed the reappearance of Madame du Châtelet at Sceaux. At the request of his hostess Voltaire read his new tales to his assembled fellow-guests, who were enchanted with them. Publication followed by degrees. As entertaining as the "Arabian Nights," and, to French readers, as suggestive as the "Letters on the English" of much that was rotten in the state of France, they were read with avidity by all the world.

Another and grave misadventure, in its consequences very serious for Voltaire, befell him in the early weeks of January, 1748, on returning to Paris from his sojourn at Sceaux. Madame de Pompadour, who still smiled on him, had procured a private performance before the King of Voltaire's "Enfant Prodigue," and had herself played in it, some of the highest of *grands Seigneurs* and *grandes Dames* also taking parts. Such an honour Voltaire thought it incumbent on him to repay with some verses in his best style, addressed to the Pompadour. After the usual burst of lavish flattery, came the wish, "May peace return with Louis to our fields! Be both of you without enemies, and do both of you retain your conquests!" No longer well affected as of yore to Voltaire, now more than suspected of free-thinking, the devout queen and the great ladies who attended her were indignant at this close to verses which Voltaire, not suspecting that they would give offence, had taken care to circulate, and which had been shown

by the Pompadour herself, who was anything but displeased with them. "What," was the cry, "compare
the glorious conquests of the King in Flanders with
those which made such a woman as the Pompadour
mistress of his person!" The King might have cared
little for the dignified reproaches of his wife, but she
brought into play those of his three daughters, of whom
he was very fond, and whom he visited every day. The
Pompadour bowed to the storm, and did not intercede
for her laureate. A decree actually exiling him had, it
is said, been signed, when Voltaire, not waiting to
receive it, hurried off, with Madame du Châtelet, to
Cirey.

In a few weeks Voltaire, with Madame, found himself
in safety at Lunéville, the guests of that amiable old
gentleman, Stanislaus, titular King of Poland, Duke of
Lorraine for life, and father of the Queen of France.
He was glad to have them, especially Voltaire, as
adding lustre to his agreeable little Court. The Marquis
du Châtelet belonging to an ancient house of Lorraine,
Madame wished to procure him an appointment in
the Court of Stanislaus, and her wish was before long
fulfilled. Voltaire, on the other hand, was gratified to
be made much of by the father of the Queen, to whose
displeasure Paris rumour ascribed his absence. Life at
Lunéville was free and easy, and full of gaiety. Things
might have gone on pretty smoothly with the illustrious
pair had not Madame du Châtelet fallen over head and
ears in love. The hero of this attachment was a M. de
Saint-Lambert, who had just been appointed to a company in Stanislaus's regiment of Guards. Madame was

forty-two ; he was thirty-one—handsome, clever, poetical, and could make himself very agreeable when he chose. It was Madame, apparently, who first made love to him, and all along the love was much more on her side than on his. However, he was flattered by being the object of the affection of so famous a lady, so very intimate a friend of the great Voltaire, and he played his part only too well in some respects. There were secret correspondences, stolen interviews, and so forth, the letters from the lady to him, still preserved, showing a passionate devotion on her part. When Voltaire found out what was going on, he was very angry. But he gave in after the rather matter-of-fact explanation from the lady that, as he had grown cool towards her—he was fifty-four—she required some one to love her, and had found that some one in Saint-Lambert. What was at first indignation became a sort of regretful approval, as when, in encouraging verses to Saint-Lambert, Voltaire said, "Thine is the hand that gathers the roses, and for me are only the thorns." More interesting to him soon became the fate of his tragedy "Semiramis," which he wrote because the veteran Crébillon had many years before produced one on the same subject, and Crébillon was now being patronized by the Pompadour and Louis. Voltaire was in Paris at the first performance of his "Semiramis" (August 28, 1748). He had prepared for the hostile reception threatened it by the partizans of Crébillon and his own many enemies. For the first time on record he packed the pit. But the enemy contrived to find admission, and "Semiramis" was not a shining success. The winter of 1749 found Voltaire again in Paris, after the Pompadour and the King had patronized with their presence the first performance of Crébillon's "Catiline," which again Voltaire resolved to efface by a tragedy of his own on the same subject, "Rome Sauveé." It is a symptom of Voltaire's consciousness of the permanence of the royal disfavour that, in the May of this year, he resigned his office of gentleman-in-ordinary to the King, who allowed him, however, to retain the designation ; and if he thus relaxed his official connection with the Court, he made, he boasts, 60,000 livres (£2,400) by selling the post to a successor. And now was approaching the *dénouement* of the drama which Madame du Châtelet and Saint-Lambert had been enacting. She knew in April (1749) that she was to become a mother. The poor lady had a presentiment of her fate, and when in Paris worked hard with Clairault at her version of Newton's "Principia," for, after having been perverted for a time to Leibnitzism, she had returned to the true Newtonian faith. She arranged all her papers in sealed packets, with the names of the persons to whom they were to be delivered. In expectation of the *accouchement*, which was at Lunéville, the Marquis du Châtelet and Saint-Lambert, with Voltaire, of course, were in attendance. A little daughter arrived suddenly on the 4th of September, while Madame, pen in hand, was working at her book on Newton. "The mother," Voltaire wrote gaily to his friends, "arranged her papers, returned to bed, and at the time I am writing, all that (*tout cela*) is asleep like a dormouse." Six days after the birth Madame du Châtelet breathed her last (September 10, 1749).

Voltaire was at first inconsolable. But business had

to be attended to. He wound up accounts with the Marquis du Châtelet, to whom he behaved very generously, and whose tedious lawsuit he had previously ended by negotiating a compromise which brought the du Châtelets 200,000 livres, money down, say £80,000. He despatched from Cirey to Paris what belonged to him, and at Christmas, with his niece, Madame Denis, now a widow, as mistress of the establishment, he was installed in the mansion at Paris, formerly his and Madame du Châtelet's domicile. Voltaire's income at this time was about £3,400 a year, perhaps equal to thrice as much now. He was fifty-five, and, being in indifferent health, he might have taken a little rest. But the favour which Crébillon had found in the eyes of the King and the Pompadour was as a thorn in his flesh. The King, the Court, and the Paris public had to be shown that as a dramatist he was nothing to Voltaire. The very subjects which Crébillon had treated in his dramas, Voltaire would treat one after another, so that the contest might be complete. Crébillon had written a "Semiramis"; Voltaire, as has been seen, wrote another, and produced it on the stage. A "Catiline" of Crébillon had been applauded by the King and the Pompadour; in a "Rome Sauvée" Voltaire dealt with the same episode in Roman history. To Crébillon's "Electra" Voltaire opposed an "Oreste." Play-going Paris was divided into two camps, the genuine admirers of Crébillon being recruited by Voltaire's enemies, of whom he had many. "Oreste" was performed January 12, 1750, when Voltaire was again said to have packed the pit, and the piece was played amid the contending

noises of friends and foes. Once, when the hisses pre-
dominated, Voltaire rushed from his coign of vantage to
the front of his box, and shouted reproachfully, "Barba-
rians! it is Sophocles whom you are hissing!" ·The
actors of the Comédie Française having, he thought,
behaved to him rather cavalierly since the patronage of
Crébillon by royalty, Voltaire opened in his Paris
mansion a private theatre of his own, chiefly for the
performance of his new dramas. In the list of the
persons who were present at the first performance there
of "Rome Sauvée," occur the names of "Messieurs
D'Alembert, Diderot, and Marmontel"—to the last of
whom Voltaire had been the kindest of friends and bene-
factors. At subsequent representations Voltaire himself
played the part of Cicero, with vigour and fire in abund-
ance and superabundance.

With the death of Madame du Châtelet Frederick
naturally began to reckon on a visit of some duration
from Voltaire. Voltaire himself thought of visiting his
royal friend in the summer of 1750, and of then making
a tour in Italy. Meanwhile, during the winter of
1749–50, the post of Paris correspondent to Frederick
had been procured by Voltaire for a certain vain and
idle young versifier, Baculard d'Arnaud, whom, from of
old, he had assisted occasionally with little presents of
money. Frederick took a fancy to D'Arnaud, and
invited him to Berlin in some verses in which the young
man's scribble was lauded so extravagantly as to produce
the impression that the King was at his stratagems again,
and wished, by making Voltaire jealous of D'Arnaud,
to bring him more quickly to Berlin. "D'Arnaud,"

Frederick said or sang, "come! and by your fine genius
revive us with new fire. . . . Before long, winging your
flight to the skies, you will succeed in equalling Voltaire.
. . . Already the Apollo of France is wending towards
his decline.   Come, and in your turn shine.   Rise if he
is still descending.   Thus the setting of a beautiful day
promises a still more , beautiful dawn."   These verses
were written in the December of 1749, and it seems odd
that they were not with malice prepense made known to
Voltaire until the June of 1750, when he was corre-
sponding with Frederick about the cost of a journey to
Berlin, already, apparently, decided upon. It is Marmontel
who tells the story, and, to add to the confusion which
surrounds it, he misquotes Frederick's verses.   According
to him, Voltaire, in bed when he read them, jumped
from it in a rage, exclaiming, " Voltaire is the setting
sun, and Baculard is the rising one I   I shall go ; yes, I
shall go and give him "—Frederick—"a lesson in the
knowledge of men."   Whatever the amount of truth in the
anecdote, Voltaire was on the 26th of June at Compiègne
to ask Louis XV.'s permission for his historiographer and
the titular gentleman of his bed-chamber to leave France
for Prussia.   According to tradition the King told him
stiffly that he might start as soon as he pleased.   Whether
tradition be right or wrong, on July 10, 1750, Voltaire
found himself Frederick's guest at Berlin.

CHAPTER IX.

(1750–53.)

FREDERICK had at last his Voltaire, and did his utmost to retain possession of him. His French visitor was granted a pension of 20,000 francs a year (£800), the office (and gold key) of Chamberlain, the cross of the Order *pour le Mérite*, and board and lodging always in one or other of the royal palaces. Madame Denis was offered an annuity of 4,000 francs (£160) for life if she would come to Berlin and take care of her valetudinarian uncle, but she preferred freedom and flirtation in Paris, where she did as she pleased, with a fixed allowance from Voltaire. His welcome from all and sundry was the warmest imaginable. The princes, Frederick's brothers, and their sister, Princess Amelia, acted with him in his own dramas, in which he himself took the elderly parts, Cicero in " Rome Sauvée," Lusignan in " Zaïre," and so forth. Grandees, courtiers, ministers, all did homage to the King's chief favourite. His office of Chamberlain was a sinecure, and he had ample leisure in which to ply his never-resting pen. His duties resolved themselves into

dining, or, at least, supping with the King, and correcting
and criticising verse and prose submitted to him by
Frederick as a pupil submits his exercises to a teacher.
The King's dinners were somewhat formal, but the
suppers were free and easy, accompanied by the feast of
reason and the flow of soul. Frederick's talk was vivid,
and Voltaire's brilliant. "This is the paradise of
Philosophes," Voltaire wrote in one of the early months
of his stay. "Language fails to express what it is. It
is Cæsar, it is Marcus Aurelius, it is Julian, it is sometimes the Abbé de Chaulieu," the sceptical French
Anacreon of Voltaire's youth, "with whom we sup. Here,"
at Potsdam, where there was a royal palace, with Sans
Souci close by, "there is the charm of retirement, there is
the freedom of country life, with all the little comforts
which the host of a château, who is also a king, can
procure for his very humble guests." With the more
intimate French favourites of the King, his reader
D'Arget, the witty Marquis d'Argens, the madcap
La Mettrie—these two last primarily befriended by
Frederick, mainly for their audacious scepticism—Voltaire
was on excellent terms. The one cloud in the sunshine
of his new life was Baculard d'Arnaud, who committed
the unpardonable sin of writing spiteful things about him
to Paris, and was soon, at Voltaire's instance, sent about
his business. With Frederick, D'Arnaud had served his
turn, and "the rising sun" of a few months before disap-
peared from the Berlin horizon. Voltaire's satisfaction
at the discomfiture of his former rival was not, however,
unmixed. He bethought him that if Frederick could
so easily turn adrift one whom he had so recently

belauded and pensioned, this was not a king a continu-
ance of whose favour could be so very confidently relied
on.

But it rested with Voltaire himself to be, for an in-
definite period, as happy as it was possible for him to be
with health very indifferent, and bodily ailments coming
upon him, though not so grievous as he wished his friends
to think them. For Frederick's first coolness to him he
had only to thank himself, and his insatiable cupidity.
With an ample fortune of his own, a handsome pension,
and all the necessaries and comforts of life furnished
him free of cost, he might for a time, at least, have been
content, and avoided questionable financial speculations,
especially at Berlin itself, watched as he was there by
jealous and envious eyes. The first great scrape in which
he was involved during his visit to Frederick, arose out
of a connection, at first perhaps innocent enough, with
Hirsch, a cunning and unscrupulous Berlin Jew, who traf-
ficked in precious stones among other things, and from
whom Voltaire was in the habit of borrowing, or
partly buying on credit, jewellery with which to adorn
his person when taking part in Court theatricals.
The two were soon engaged in an illicit transaction,
which, Voltaire declared, Hirsch had suggested to him,
and which, he also declared, he himself had backed out of
as soon as he found it to be illicit ; Hirsch, on the other
hand, maintaining that the suggestion came from Voltaire. The Saxon Government, which had been allied
with Austria against Frederick in the second Silesian
war, had, in its financial straits, issued inconvertible
paper-money, *Steuer-Scheine.* These fell considerably

below par, and at the peace of Dresden (1745), Frederick made it a stipulation that when the *Steuer-Scheine* were held by Prussian subjects, they should be paid, after presentation, at par. Of course they began to be dealt with in Prussia. They were bought in Saxony at their depreciated price, and then sent to Prussia to be presented for payment at par by Prussian subjects. To put an end to this traffic, Frederick issued in 1748 a severe rescript forbidding such transactions. Whatever Voltaire's denials, it was generally believed that he sent Hirsch to Dresden to buy *Steuer-Scheine* for him at a considerable discount, to be afterwards presented for payment at par. For one reason or other, the *Steuer-Scheine* were not bought. Hirsch came back from Dresden empty-handed. When Voltaire found that this was to be the result of the Jew's mission, he protested a bill on Paris for 40,000 livres (£1,600), which, he asserted, he had given Hirsch for the purpose of buying, not *Steuer-Scheine*, but furs and jewellery in Saxony. Hirsch then demanded compensation for his time and trouble, and for the injury done to his credit by the protest of the bill which had been cashed for him at Dresden, where he, of course, had to refund the money received for it. When sending Hirsch to Dresden, Voltaire had kept in his hands, as security both for the bill and for money advanced to Hirsch to make purchases which he did not make, a quantity of jewellery borrowed from Hirsch for stage purposes. These he now proposed to take from Hirsch in payment of Hirsch's debt to him. The transactions closed with the signature by Hirsch of a document which purported to be a final settlement of accounts. But then a new and desperate controversy broke out. Voltaire asserted that he had been cheated, because the jewels were not worth nearly as much as Hirsch had valued them at. Instead of putting up with some loss rather than drag the whole affair before the public, he brought a lawsuit against Hirsch. Hirsch, as defendant, asserted that some of the jewels furnished had been changed by Voltaire for others of less value, and he denied that the signature appended to the document intended to be final was his. The signature was undoubtedly his, but it was very much doubted whether Voltaire had not, after Hirsch signed, interpolated the document in his own interest. The gist of the judgment was that the jewels should be valued by sworn experts, that Hirsch, if he could prove that they, or any of them, had been changed, might bring an action in which he should be plaintiff and Voltaire defendant. As to Voltaire's alleged fraudulent interpolations, he was to be called on to swear that he was innocent of them. This he declared himself ready to do, while Hirsch, as a Jew, was not allowed to take an oath in the dominions of even the sceptical Frederick, who ostensibly tolerated all religions, and granted equal rights to his subjects of every creed. Hirsch was further fined ten thalers—thirty shillings—for denying his signature. Voltaire, it appears, did not take the oath after all, nor did Hirsch go on with the new trial. Probably influenced by the bad impression which the suit had visibly produced, and by the reproaches which Frederick addressed to him, Voltaire compromised matters, and accepted in almost every instance Hirsch's valuation of the jewels. The legal proceedings had lasted from December 30, 1750, to February 26, 1751. There is a carefully detailed account of the affair in Carlyle's "Frederick," Carlyle pronouncing decidedly against Voltaire, both as regards his denial of a persistent attempt to purchase *Steuer-Scheine*, and of a fraudulent interpolation of the document signed by Hirsch. What can be said in Voltaire's favour will be found in the elaborate biography of him by Gustave Desnoiresterres, by far the best and most complete French work of its kind which has appeared, or is likely for long to appear.

Voltaire tried hard to persuade his correspondents, with such slender aid as he could derive from the trifling fine imposed upon Hirsch, that he had come off victorious ; but neutral observers, to say nothing of his enemies, looked on his victory as a disgraceful defeat. Frederick himself was very and naturally angry, to find his guide, philosopher, and friend exhibited to the world in so sorry a light. He kept aloof from Voltaire while the lawsuit was proceeding, and told his sister Wilhelmina, a staunch ally of the culprit, that Voltaire's behaviour had been that of "a rogue trying to cheat a pickpocket." Two days before the compromise, he wrote Voltaire an indignant letter, in which he reproached his French friend with other and minor misdemeanours, among them his vindictive conduct to D'Arnaud, and his gossiping with the Russian minister "about things with which you had no business to meddle." "You have on hand the most disgraceful affair possible with the Jew. You have caused a frightful scandal throughout the town. The affair of the Saxon bonds is so notorious in

Saxony, that I have received serious complaints about it. I preserved peace in my house until your arrival, and I warn you, that if you have a passion for intriguing and caballing you have come to the wrong place," and so forth. Voltaire was fairly frightened, and sent a penitent reply. Frederick's wrath did not last long, or at least did not show itself long, and the strange pair were soon, to all appearance, on the old footing again. Voltaire continued to correct the King's prose and verse, and, on returning each batch of either, accompanied it with transcendant laudations of the King's literary skill. Frederick, on his part, came to look, or tried to look, on Voltaire as not one man but two. There was. Voltaire, the prince of poets and prose writers, the enlightened philosopher, who had trampled on "superstition," whose genius he had worshipped since his youth, whose presence shed lustre on his Court—the charming and brilliant companion, who, moreover, was very useful to him, and very diligent and painstaking as a corrector of his compositions. Then there was the other Voltaire, greedy, tricky, jealous, vindictive, ever ready to quarrel with his brethren, and bent on persecuting to the uttermost all with whom he quarrelled. Frederick could not have the society of Voltaire the angel, whom he loved, without that of Voltaire the demon, whom he detested; so he put up with the demon for the sake of the angel. But after the Hirsch affair, whatever their apparent cordiality, the King was readier than before to hear evil spoken of Voltaire, and Voltaire grew doubtful of the sincerity of the King's attachment to him. Frederick was fond of bantering rather coarsely, even

those of his friends for whom he had an unadulterated
liking, of playing practical jokes on them, and of requiring
them to be constantly within call.   After a time, wearied
of their barrack life, the faithful D'Arget left him, and
the loyal Marquis D'Argens and the gallant Chasot.
Even La Mettrie, whom he allowed to take liberties with
him that he would tolerate from no one else, was bent
on flying back to France.   In the autumn of 1751, Voltaire was urging the Duc de Richelieu to facilitate La
Mettrie's return to his fatherland, and the two were on
very intimate terms.   Great was Voltaire's horror, when
La Mettrie told him at this time, that in a conversation
with the King on the favour shown to Voltaire, and the
jealousy which it excited, Frederick replied, " I shall
need him for another year at least.   We squeeze the
orange and throw away the rind."   The speech haunted
him during the remainder of his Prussian visit.   Time
after time he attempted, but in vain, to extort from La
Mettrie an admission that it was an invention of the
reporter.   All hope of the kind was extinguished, when
without having made any such admission, La Mettrie
died a few months afterwards of a surfeit, Voltaire
lamenting that he had not cross-examined the mischief-
maker when in *articulo mortis*.   Nor were tale-bearers
wanting to irritate Frederick against Voltaire by repeating
sharp things said of King by poet.   Voltaire was busy
or otherwise, one day in those months, when there
arrived a packet of the King's verses for him to correct.
" Will he never be tired," the imprudent poet said, or
was said to have said, " of sending me his dirty linen to
wash ? "   Maupertuis, Voltaire believed, had circulated

this saying, so that it might reach the King's ears. Maupertuis welcomed Voltaire to Berlin, but gradually became very cool, being jealous, no doubt, of the favour shown to the poet by the King, which he thus tried to diminish. There had been sundry passages of arms between the two, and now this of the dirty linen was added to the Perpetual President's misdemeanours. If there came an opportunity for revenge Voltaire was not the man to neglect it.

Whatever Voltaire's troubles, and among them are to be reckoned an attack of erysipelas and other maladies which made him often speak of himself as on the point of death, he was always busy with his pen. Soon after Voltaire's arrival in Berlin, Frederick had applied on his behalf to Louis XV. for permanent leave of absence. It was granted, but at the same time Voltaire was deprived of his office of historiographer of France, while allowed to retain his titular dignity of gentleman-in-ordinary of Louis's bed-chamber. Voltaire took the deprivation more philosophically than usual, since it gave him more freedom than he might otherwise have enjoyed in preparing for the press his "Siècle de Louis Quatorze." He had brought with him to Berlin material for it, collected orally and from books during many, many years, onward from the time when in his youth he had hung on the lips of M. de Caumartin at Saint-Ange. It was published at the end of 1751, and, living in security in Berlin, Voltaire had not been tempted to soften it down as he might have been had he finished it in France. There it was a prohibited book, but none the less was it reproduced in Paris and generally read in

France, while editions of it were issued in Holland, Germany, and Great Britain. The age of Louis XIV. was as interesting to the Europe of that day as the age of the first Napoleon to the Europe of the last generation, and no modern historian had before treated a great period with Voltaire's brilliancy, good sense, and, on the whole, impartiality.

Once more in Voltaire's career a triumph achieved was to be followed by a disaster, due partly to Maupertuis. The Perpetual President of Frederick's Academy of Sciences had promulgated a theory that, in motion, Nature works according to a law of thrift, and employs, in every movement, a minimum of action. This theory was controverted by König, a meritorious mathematician and physicist, who, like Maupertuis himself, had been a science teacher of Madame du Châtelet. In the course of controverting it, König quoted a passage from a letter written by Leibnitz, in which that sage declared himself to have "remarked that, in the modification of motion, the action becomes usually a maximum *or* a minimum." If Leibnitz said this, and was right in saying it, Maupertuis's theory was only half true, and even in propounding what was half true in it, he had been anticipated by Leibnitz, to say nothing of the blow dealt to "the Law of Thrift," announced by him as a great discovery of his, and an important contribution to natural theology, since such a law involved the existence of a law-giver. It seems strange nowadays that the doubt thus thrown on a metaphysico-mathematical theory, should have provoked Maupertuis to take dire revenge on König. But the Perpetual President was

not accustomed to contradiction, and being regarded
with reverence by the members of his Academy, who
were mainly of his own appointing, he had a high idea
of his own importance and omniscience. He could not
brook being criticized, and having his new argument for
the existence of a God refuted in the face of his own
Academy, and before the scientific world, by the comparatively unknown König. He demanded the production of the original letter of Leibnitz, which König had
quoted. After due search by König, the original was not
to be found. So at last, Maupertuis not present but
pulling the strings of his puppets, the Academy, in con-
clave assembled, solemnly and formally pronounced the
alleged extract to be a forgery, leaving it to be implied
that poor König was the forger. This decision was come
to in April, 1752. In the following year König resigned
his seat in the Academy, and in September issued an
appeal to the public. Meanwhile Voltaire had been
looking into the rights and wrongs of the matter. Partly
out of sympathy with the maltreated König, partly out
of an accumulated antipathy to Maupertuis, he wrote,
in the true Voltairean style, a brief but stinging letter,
defending the former, and attacking the latter, in what
purported to be "A Reply from a Berlin to a Paris
Academician," who was supposed to have asked to be
informed of the ins and outs of the controversy.

" Here," it began, " is the exact truth asked for. M. Moreau de
Maupertuis, in a pamphlet entitled ' Essai de Cosmologie,' asserted
that the only proof of the existence of a God is $AR + nBB$, which
is bound to be a minimum. He alleges that in every possible case
action is always a minimum, which has been proved to be false, and

he says that this law of the minimum was discovered by him, which
is not less false."

Then follows a history of the controversy, and of the
harsh sentence which Maupertuis "forced some members of the Academy, who are pensioned and who
depend on him," to pronounce on König. In conclusion, according to the Berlin academician,

"the Sieur Moreau de Maupertuis has been convicted in the
face of scientific Europe, not only of plagiarism and of blundering, but of having abused his position to deprive men of letters
(*gens de lettres*) of their freedom, and to persecute an honest man
whose only crime was that of not being of his opinion. Several
members of the Academy have protested against conduct so
revolting (*conduite si criante*), and would quit the Academy, over
which Maupertuis tyrannizes, and which he dishonours, were it not
for a fear of displeasing the King who protects it."

This pretended letter of an academician of Berlin,
printed in a respectable periodical, was anonymous, but
it was soon known to be Voltaire's, and it threw Frederick
into a genuine passion. For Maupertuis personally, with
all his faults—vanity the chief of them—he had a great
regard. Maupertuis had exiled himself to become the
President of the Berlin Academy, and had drawn to it
Euler, and other, though minor, scientific notabilities.
Not only Maupertuis, but the members of the Academy,
which Frederick had reorganized and·was proud of, were
as a body being vilified by Voltaire, and held up to
general contempt, as a collection of sordid and timorous
satellites of their harsh and unscrupulous President.
So Frederick took pen in hand, and launched a " Reply,"

from another pretended academician of Berlin to another imaginary academician in Paris. In this rather absurd, as well as frantic and most unkingly effusion, he did not touch on the pros and cons of the controversy respecting the genuineness of the Leibnitz fragment, and its bearing on the law of the minimum. Ignored, likewise, were the statements of König in his defence, nor was there any inquiry made into the justice or injustice of the verdict pronounced on him by the Berlin Academy. But Maupertuis was deluged with ludicrously exaggerated laudation, and Voltaire, though of course not by name, was denounced as the paltriest and most malignant of libellers. Maupertuis, Frederick said, "enjoys during his life the glory which fell to Homer long after his death (!); Berlin and St. Malo"—his birthplace—"dispute which shall claim him for its own." In short, "we look upon his character as the model of that of an honest man, and a genuine philosopher." The assailant of the man whose "glory" is compared to that of Homer, is "a wretch," the author of an "infamous libel," the "despicable enemy of a man of rare merit," one of those writers "whose malignity blinds them to the extent of betraying at once their frivolity, their rascality, and their ignorance." The appearance at Berlin of a second edition of this furious epistle, with the Prussian eagle and other royal insignia engraved on its title-page, soon disclosed its anonymous author, and Voltaire was on the alert to avenge himself. Meanwhile—we have now arrived at October, 1752—he joined as usual the King's supper-parties, where no allusion was made to the controversy waged under the mask of anonymity, and host and guest kept up an outward show of amity. On one occasion the conversation turned on some criticisms which had appeared on Bolingbroke and his scepticism (he died in December, 1751), and Voltaire proposed to write a defence of him, the printing of which in Berlin the King cheerfully sanctioned. When he signed the royal permission required, he little suspected the use which the artful Frenchman was to make of it.

Maupertuis himself supplied just the opportunity that was wanted for Voltaire to revenge himself on the King, through his beloved President, to whom—he was very ill (from taking too much alcohol, his malicious enemy insinuated)—Frederick was writing affectionate letters and paying visits of sympathy. About the time when the King, as an academician of Berlin, was reviling Voltaire in print, Maupertuis issued a volume of "Lettres," on which his enemy pounced as a famished cat might pounce on a plump mouse. The book contained soaring *quasi*-scientific projects which provoked ridicule, while, by an assiduous search in the previously published works of the President, Voltaire collected other notions quite worthy of keeping company with those in the "Lettres." Foremost among the absurdities gravely propounded by Maupertuis, was the suggestion—luckily for him made long before the rise of the anti-vivisection movement—that light might be thrown on the mysterious union of soul and body by operating surgically on the brains of living men. Criminals, he calmly added, might rightly be made the subjects of the delightful experiment; nor should this proposal be thought to smack of cruelty: "A man is nothing compared with the human race; a criminal is even less than nothing." Specially promising would be the dissection of the brains of giants ten or twelve feet high, whose heads would offer a large area for investigation by a commission sent out to Patagonia. Even as things were, the soul of man might, by the action of opium, be so exalted as to predict the future. Still more wonderful, the span of human life could be indefinitely extended by checking the development of the frame, "as we preserve eggs by preventing them from being hatched." The improvement of education is not forgotten. Latin is at once slowly and imperfectly acquired in schools and colleges. Why not build a Latin town, where nothing but Latin should be spoken, even in the pulpit or on the stage? The youth of many countries would flock to it, Maupertuis opined, and learn more Latin in a year than in five or six under the present system. Then, as we know little of the contents of the globe, let us have a hole dug to its centre—and we shall see what we shall see. With these and other fooleries for his raw material, Voltaire elaborated his far-famed "Diatribe of Dr. Akakia, Physician to the Pope," which Macaulay and Carlyle (agreeing for once) regarded as the per- fection of malicious satire. Sooth to say, however, their estimate will appear to some readers of it rather ex- aggerated, the projects broached by Maupertuis being so ridiculous as to make ridicule of them easy. The form of Voltaire's satire was ingeniously conceived. Perhaps because medicine had in his case done little more than lighten his purse for the payment of doctors' bills,

Maupertuis ran full tilt against the Faculty, and insisted that a physician should be paid only when he has effected a cure. This naturally roused the ire of Dr. Akakia, who, in revenge, submits to the Holy Inquisition a report which begins thus :—

"Nothing is more common nowadays than to meet with young men who issue under well-known names works little worthy of them. There are quacks of every kind. Here is one who has taken the name of the president of a very illustrious academy, under which to dispense rather singular drugs. It is demonstrable that it is not the respectable president who is the author of the works attributed to him, for that admirable philosopher, who has discovered that Nature always acts through the simplest laws, and who adds so wisely that she always works in the most sparing way, would certainly have spared the few readers capable of reading it the trouble of reading the same thing twice, first in the book entitled his ' Œuvres,' and then in that called his 'Lettres.' At least the third of the one volume is copied into the other. That great man, so far removed from being a quack, would not have given the public letters which were written to nobody, and assuredly he would not have fallen into certain little errors which are only pardonable in a young man."

After this not very scathing exordium, Dr. Akakia runs through and ridicules the president's various remarks on physic and physicians, winding up in the following strain :—

" It will be seen, from the report which we have given, that if these imaginary letters were written by a president, he can only be a President of Bedlam, and that they are, as we have said, incontestably the work of a young man who desired to decorate himself with the name of a sage, respected, as is well known, throughout Europe, and who has consented to be pronounced "—by Frederick ?—"a great man. We have sometimes seen at the Carnival, in Italy, Harlequin disguised as an archbishop, but he was soon distinguished from the real prelate by the style in which he gave the benediction. Sooner or later a pretender is recognized. One is reminded of La Fontaine's fable" (the ass in the lion's skin): "'A little bit of ear unfortunately protruding discloses the imposture.' Here the whole of both ears is visible. Everything considered, we commend to the Holy Inquisition the work imputed to the president, and refer it to the judgment of that erudite body, in whom, it is well known, physicians believe so thoroughly."

Of the decree of the Inquisition one specimen will suffice, it being premised that his "Cosmology" was the work in which Maupertuis first promulgated with emphasis the great law of the minimum.

"Specially and particularly do we anathematize the essay on 'Cosmology,' since its unknown author, blinded by the principles of the sons of Belial, and accustomed to find everything to be bad, insinuates, contrary to the language of Scripture, that Providence is in fault because flies are caught by cobwebs (page 9), and since in the aforesaid 'Cosmology' the author afterwards gives it to be understood (page 45) that the only proof of the existence of a God is in $Z = B C$ divided by A *plus* B. Now, as these characters are taken from a book of magic, and are visibly diabolical, we declare them to be an attack on the authority of the Holy See."

Iteration and reiteration of the President's absurdities form one of the mischievous Voltaire's favourite devices for tormenting his victim. The inquisitors send "the letters of the young author in the disguise of a President to be examined by the Professors of the College of Wisdom (*Sapience*)," and from their lengthy report one or two extracts may be given. Item No. 10 of it is that the young author :

"May rest assured that it will be difficult for him to bore a hole, as he proposes, to the centre of the earth (where apparently he wishes to hide, ashamed of himself for having advanced such things). Such a hole would require the excavation of three or four hundred leagues of land, which might derange the system of the balance of Europe."

In conclusion, M. le Docteur Akakia, having been requested to prescribe cooling and refreshing dietetic drinks to the young author, who is exhorted to study at some University, and to show himself modest there, the Professors of the College of Wisdom address indirectly to Maupertuis a string of admonitions, one of which may stand for all. Let him learn that

"in a miserable dispute on dynamics it is not right, by an academic intrigue, to summon a professor to put in an appearance within a month, to have him condemned for non-appearance, as having made an attack on his "—the young author's—" glory, and as a forger and falsifier of letters ; above all, when it is evident that letters of Leibnitz are letters of Leibnitz, and it is proved that the letters purporting to be by a President have been no more received by his correspondents than read by the public."

It was of the book mainly dealt with by Voltaire in this satirically contumelious fashion that Frederick wrote to its author: "I have read your 'Letters,' which in spite of your critics are well done and very profound. I repeat what I have already said to you—Keep your mind easy, my dear Maupertuis, and don't trouble yourself about the buzzings of insects of the air."

And now came into play the "privilege," which Frederick had given Voltaire for printing the "Defence of Bolingbroke," an insignificant piece. By one of the most ingenious and least scrupulous of the many manœuvres of a long life, he substituted at the Berlin printing-office the "Diatribe" for the "Defence;" and the privilege granted for an apology of Bolingbroke served to sanction the attack on Maupertuis! When Frederick heard the trick that had been played him, he was furious. He sent Voltaire a wrathful letter, and the whole edition was consigned to the flames, in the presence of the King and of the author of the "Diatribe" himself. But Voltaire had taken care to supply his bow with two strings. He had sent either MS. or proof-sheets to Dresden, to be printed there in a separate edition, copies of which were soon being circulated in Berlin. Frederick was more furious than ever. Voltaire, foreseeing the storm about to burst on him, had come from the King's palace at Potsdam to stay with a friend in Berlin, and on the Christmas eve of 1752, in accordance with Frederick's orders, a copy of the Dresden edition was burnt by the public executioner, in the street next to that in which Voltaire was domiciled. He had for some time been deciding on departure, and had converted his money investments at Berlin into annuities secured on the French estates of the Duke of Wurtemberg, so that he had nothing to fear on that score from Frederick's wrath. The public and ignominious burning of the "Diatribe" strengthened his intention of migrating from Prussia. On the New Year's Day of 1753 he enclosed in a packet, with some lines meant to be pathetic, his chamberlain's key, and the Cross of the Order *pour le Mérite*, and sent them to the King.

Frederick returned them the same afternoon, and even
invited Voltaire to join him at Potsdam on the 30th of
January. But Voltaire pleaded ill-health, and lingered on
in Berlin, preparing for departure, with or without leave.
He applied more than once for permission to go and
drink the waters at Plombières. At last came Frederick's
letter of reply, the gist of which lies in the opening
sentences : " There was no necessity to make a pretext
of the need which, you say, you feel for the waters of
Plombières, in order to ask me for your *congé*. You can
quit my service when you please, but before you go let
me have the contract of your engagement, the key, the
cross, and the volume of poetry which I confided to
you." Voltaire saw things more calmly now than when
he was in a state of passionate indignation after the
ignominious burning of " Akakia." He was resolved to
go, but to start without more ado after returning the
things asked for by the King, would be a tacit admission
that he left in disgrace. He wrote for a final interview
with Frederick : " If I do not throw myself at the King's
feet, the waters of Plombières will kill me." The King
granted the interview. As the hour of parting came,
Frederick's heart softened once more towards the man
whose genius had fascinated him so long, and perhaps he
feared to let loose on the world one who might be as
dangerous when away from him as he was troublesome
when with him. Voltaire, on his part, was ready to say
or to promise anything that would ensure his departure,
and at the same time allow him to tell the world that he
was not dismissed, but retained the favour of the King.
He arrived at Potsdam in the evening, and next day was

closeted for two hours with Frederick. For six days more Voltaire remained at Potsdam, the King's guest, fêted and caressed by him for the last time. From a letter written to him by the King some time afterwards, it can be gathered, not only that they made up their feud, but that they parted intending to meet again, and that Voltaire was to remain ostensibly in the King's service, on the understanding that he would never write another word against Maupertuis. This would explain why Voltaire was not then asked to return the contract of engagement, the chamberlain's key, the cross, and the volume of poetry. On March 26, 1753, Voltaire and Frederick parted ; and they never met again.

Voltaire was in such hot haste to leave Prussia behind him, that after taking leave of the King, he did not bid good-bye to any of his old friends at Potsdam. Stepping forthwith into a carriage with four post-horses, he was driven off to Leipzig and its printing-presses. The promise given to Frederick not to attack Maupertuis was quickly broken, as when giving it he doubtless intended it to be. The world was soon laughing over refurbished satirical pleasantries discharged at the President and his scientific castles in the air. Frederick, however, did not laugh when he found that he had been duped, and that Voltaire had never meant to return to him. It was known at Potsdam that Voltaire had despatched sundry packages to Frankfort, where they were to await his arrival. The King therefore sent written orders to his resident at Frankfort, instructing him as soon as Voltaire arrived there, to procure from him the chamberlain's key, the cross, and the volume of poetry among other things.

Knowing nothing of these orders, the runaway, after a stay of rather more than three weeks at Leipzig, proceeded to visit at Gotha the Duke, and more especially the charming Duchess, of Saxe-Gotha. They received him with open arms, and made him for five weeks the happiest of men. At the suggestion of the Duchess he began at Gotha his " Annales de l'Empire," from Charlemagne to Charles VI., whose death had been followed by Frederick's invasion of Silesia—a book which cost him far more trouble than it proved to be worth.

A sad contrast to those delightful five weeks at Gotha were the five which he passed at Frankfort, where he arrived on the 31st of May, pitching his tent at an inn, " The Golden Lion." Freytag, Frederick's resident, was with him next day, and there was a long examination of his papers and effects. Among them was not to be found the volume of poetry, which the King was most anxious should be restored him, since there were stinging reflections in it on living princes and potentates. It was in a packing-case expected from Leipzig, and Voltaire gave his word of honour that until its arrival he would remain where he was. In a fortnight or so he was joined by his niece Madame Denis. While awaiting the arrival of the case, he wrote plaintive and indignant letters to all and sundry, and what was equally characteristic and less futile, he worked steadily at the " Annales de l'Empire." At last, on the 18th of June, the case arrived. But Freytag refused to open it just then. He had been puzzled by one of the original orders, which was that he should seize any writings of the King's found among Voltaire's papers. This instruction he could not obey, since he did not know the King's handwriting when he saw it, and so he waited for further illumination from Berlin. Unfortunately Frederick was at this time in a distant part of his dominions, and the official whom he had left in charge of the Voltaire business, told Freytag to do nothing until the King returned. Voltaire, after three weeks of detention, completely lost patience, although if he had waited, as he was asked, only three days more, when Freytag expected a final order from the King himself, who had at last returned to Berlin, the crowning catastrophe of his stay at Frankfort might have been averted. On the 20th of June, leaving Madame Denis to look after his effects, Voltaire with his secretary Collini tried to escape. In a vehicle of some kind they were just leaving Frankfort behind them, when they were overtaken by Freytag, who arrested them with the help of the city guard. Frankfort was a free town, but King Frederick's name was a tower of strength in it, and the municipal authorities supported Freytag. Not only Voltaire, but Collini, and, what enraged him most of all, Madame Denis, were treated as prisoners of war, and soldiers were told off to guard them. Next day arrived orders from Frederick to let Voltaire depart in peace, on the very easy condition that he would formally promise, on the word of an honest man, to return the volume of poetry without making a copy of it, and to engage in advance that, if he broke this promise, he would consider himself a prisoner of Frederick's in whatever country he might be. From this point Freytag kept blundering and needlessly detaining Voltaire, partly on the ground that the order to let him go had been given

when the King did not know that Voltaire had attempted
to escape. At last, after various explosions, not merely
oral and epistolary, for Voltaire once presented a pistol
at an emissary of Freytag's, he and Collini shook the
dust of Frankfort from off their feet, and were driven
without let or hindrance to Mayence, leaving Madame
Denis to pack and follow them. So ended the affair of
Frankfort. Voltaire made it world-famous for a time by
his account of it in the "Vie privée," written by him
years afterwards to avenge himself on Frederick, whom
he never forgave for the arrest at Frankfort and its ignominious sequel. The narrative is one of the most
amusing pieces that ever came from Voltaire's pen, but
much of it is as imaginary as any of his professed
fictions. This was made clear when the official documents connected with his detention at Frankfort were
published, and compared with his own account of it.
What did really happen then and there is told minutely in
Carlyle's History of Frederick, and more favourably to
Voltaire by Desnoiresterres.

CHAPTER X.

(1753-62.)

SELF-EXCLUDED from Prussia, and with Paris forbidden him, Voltaire had no definite goal when he left Frankfort behind him. He was bent on finishing, however, the " Annales de l'Empire," and in intervals of roaming he pitched his tent at Colmar, in Alsace, where he could consult jurists learned in the laws of the empire, and have his book printed. Early in 1754, he sent a copy of the first volume of it to Frederick, with overtures not merely for a reconciliation, but for a return. The King declined them, reminding him of the promise which he had given, and broken, to write no more against Maupertuis. His fresh attempts to make his peace with the French Court and authorities, were defeated by the issue of piratical and surreptitious extracts from the " Essai sur les Mœurs," and of editions of the " Pucelle," with falsifications and interpolations, so Voltaire asserted, of a kind to irritate the powers that were in France. In quest of a home of his own, he bethought . him of free and republican Switzerland. Some time before, a firm of booksellers and printers at Geneva

9

had suggested to him that, by settling in that region, he would enjoy the comparative liberty of printing allowed there. He went, he saw, he was satisfied. The clergy of Geneva, where Calvin had burned Servetus, were partly Socinianized, though they did not like to have this said of them, and the Consistory still maintained the old standard of Calvinistic morals to the extent of denouncing the theatre. Another attraction was the presence in Geneva of the famous physician, Tronchin, and Voltaire's health was really infirm. In theory, Roman Catholics—and Voltaire always called himself one—were not allowed to settle in the territory of Geneva, or in any of the Protestant cantons, but the local authorities had, as may be supposed, no great faith in Voltaire's sincerity in this respect, and threw no obstacles in his way. In the spring of 1755 he was the leaseholder of a house and little domain in the vicinity of Geneva, which he christened the Délices. Soon afterwards he was the similar possessor of Monrion, close to Lausanne, a town in which there was even less of clericalism than in Geneva, and Monrion being not so cold in winter as the Délices, he called this his winter and that his summer palace.

" The house "—he is speaking of the Délices—" is pretty and convenient. Its charming aspect surprises and never wearies. On one side is the Lake of Geneva, on the other the town. From the lake the Rhone rushes in a torrent, forming a channel at the bottom of my garden. The river Arve, which flows down from Savoy, throws itself into the Rhone ; a little further off another river is seen. A hundred country-houses, a hundred smiling gardens, embellish the banks of the lake and of the streams. In the distance soar the

Alps, and beyond their precipices are discerned twenty leagues of mountains covered with eternal snow. At Lausanne, I have a still finer house and a more extensive view; but my house at Geneva is much the more agreeable. I have in these two domiciles what kings do not give, or rather what they take away—freedom and repose. Mine are all the conveniences of life, in furniture, in equipages, and in good cheer. Pleasant and intellectual society fills up the moments left me by study, and by the care of my health."

Voltaire was forthwith busily occupied, building, gardening, planting, laying out poultry-yards, and forming a dairy. Over his establishment, that of an opulent country gentleman, his niece, Madame Denis, presided, for better or for worse. Tourists from all parts of Europe, visiting Switzerland, made a point of calling at Les Délices, and were cordially received by the host. Theatricals were forbidden there, but at Lausanne Voltaire indulged to any extent in his favourite amusement. Gibbon, then a young man, has left a stately record of the pleasure given him, during his first stay at Lausanne, by the performances of "a company of gentlemen," formed by Voltaire, and especially by "the uncommon circumstance of hearing a great poet declaim his own productions on the stage." " His declamation," according to Gibbon, "was fashioned to the pomp and cadence of the old stage, and he expressed the enthusiasm of poetry rather than the feelings of nature." With Voltaire, from first to last, the drama was a passion. Whatever other work he was engaged in, he had always a play of some kind on the anvil. In the months of wandering which followed his flight from Frankfort, he diversified his laborious researches into the history of the Empire by composing " L'Orphelin de la Chine," of which Genghis Khan was the central figure. While its author was in virtual exile it was played with great success in Paris, during the first year of his stay in Switzerland—August 25, 1755. Successes of this kind he prized, not merely because they flattered his vanity, but as keeping his high friends at Court in mind of him, for he still cherished the hope of being allowed to return to his beloved Paris.

A few weeks later, the civilized world was horrorstruck by the news of the terrible earthquake of Lisbon (November 1, 1755). Strictly considered, this frightful catastrophe was only, on a large scale, what, on a smaller, was, and is, happening every day. A vessel founders at sea, a house or theatre is on fire : the just and unjust alike, parents and innocent children, perish in the waves or in the flames, and there is weeping and wailing in many a home. But the colossal magnitude of the appalling disaster at Lisbon made transcendently more intense that feeling of the problematic in human destiny, which is aroused more or less, in susceptive minds, by the vicissitudes of daily life. Goethe, then a boy of six, was as much perplexed as the sexagenarian Voltaire how to reconcile the goodness of the Deity with the seemingly aimless cruelty of what he had permitted, or ordained, to happen at Lisbon. The " whatever is is right," the " all partial evil universal good," of Pope's famous essay, so much admired by Voltaire, who translated them into the pithy formula : " All is well " (*tout est bien*), were now pronounced by him unsatisfactory. He had opposed a sort of optimism of his own to Pascal's pessimism, and in " Le Mondain " had sung of the pleasures enjoyed by cultivated and civilized man. But he now struck his lyre to a very different tune in his " Poem on the Disaster at Lisbon ; or, an Examination of the Axiom, All is Well "—to which he opposed a gloomy catalogue of all the ills that flesh is heir to. To one edition of it he prefixed a prose introduction, a passage of which summarizes the piece in quite an orthodox strain :—

" He," its author, " owns with all mankind that there is evil as well as good on the earth ; that no philosopher has ever been able to explain the origin of moral and physical evil; that there is as much that is feeble in the intelligence of man as there is misery in his life. He gives in a few words an exposition of all the systems of philosophers. He says that Revelation alone can disentangle the knot of which all the philosophers have made a tangle. He says that the hope of a new development of our being, in a new order of things, can alone console us for present misfortunes, and that the goodness of Providence is the only refuge to which man can have recourse in the darkness enshrouding his reason, and in the calamities of his feeble and mortal nature."

Was Voltaire sincere in offering this consolation ? Or was there not more sincerity in one of the closing passages of " Candide," which, though not printed until some years later, was begun soon after the Lisbon earthquake ? The philosophic and Leibnitzian Pangloss and his friends, domiciled in the vicinity of Constantinople, having been made miserable by destiny in what he had been celebrating as the best of all possible worlds, they resolved to visit in their mental perplexity, "a very famous dervish, who passed for being the best philosopher

in Turkey. They consulted him accordingly. Pangloss
began the conversation by saying, 'Master, we come to
beg of you to tell us why so strange an animal as man
was made.' 'Why do you trouble yourself about it,'
replied the dervish, 'is it any business of yours?'
'But, my reverend father,' said Candide, 'evil abounds
horribly on earth.' 'What does it matter,' said the
dervish, 'whether there is good or evil ? When his
Highness'—the Sultan—'sends a vessel to Egypt, does
he trouble himself as to whether the mice in it are at
their ease or not?' 'What then is one to do?' said
Pangloss. 'To hold one's tongue,' said the dervish. 'I
flattered myself,' said Pangloss, 'that we should have a
little argument together on cause and effect, the best of
possible worlds, the origin of evil, the nature of the soul,
and pre-established harmony.' The dervish replied by
shutting the door in their faces."

In the year after the earthquake at Lisbon, England
declared war against France (May, 1756), and in the
following month, to Voltaire's great delight, his steadfast
friend, the Duc de Richelieu, captured Minorca from the
English, after Admiral Byng's failure to relieve the garrison. Richelieu appears to have written to Voltaire that
Byng had done his best, and when Byng, whom Voltaire
had known slightly during his English exile, was lying
under sentence of death, Voltaire good-naturedly sent
him a formal and detailed justification of his conduct by
Richelieu, to be made use of with the authorities in
England. It was, as is well known, of no effect, and
Byng was shot (March 14, 1757), having previously sent
his thanks to Richelieu and Voltaire for their interven-

tion. The Byng tragedy was commemorated in a passage of "Candide," one phrase in which is familiar to every one. Candide and Martin, his philosophic or phlegmatic *protégé*, are on board a Dutch vessel, which is nearing the English coast.

" ' What is that crowd on shore ? ' said Candide. ' Something very mad and very abominable,' replied Martin. 'You are acquainted with England ; are people as mad there as in France ? ' 'It is a different kind of madness. You must know that these two nations are at war about a few acres of snow in the direction of Canada, and that they are spending on this beautiful war much more than all Canada is worth. My feeble intellect does not permit me to tell you whether there are more people who ought to have on strait waistcoats in one country than in another. I only know that the people we are about to visit are very atrabilious.' Chatting thus they came close to Portsmouth. On the shore were a number of people, looking attentively at a tolerably bulky man, on his knees, with his eyes bandaged, on the deck of one of the vessels of the fleet. Four soldiers were posted in front of him, each of whom sent, in the most peaceful manner possible, three bullets into his skull, and the whole assemblage broke up, extremely satisfied. 'What is all this?' said Candide, ' and who is the demon that sways the world every-where?' He asked who the stout man was that had just been killed thus ceremoniously. ' 'Tis an admiral,' was the answer. 'And why should this admiral be killed?' ' Because,' was the reply, ' he did not kill people enough. He offered fight to a French admiral, and it was thought that he was not close enough to him.' ' But,' said Candide, ' the French admiral was as far from the English admiral as the English admiral was from him ? ' ' That is indispu-table,' was the rejoinder ; ' but in this country it is well from time to time to kill an admiral, by way of encouraging the others ! ' "

The war for "a few acres of snow," thus lightly spoken of, was to decide whether the North American continent was to be French or to be English.

In September, 1756, Frederick invaded Saxony and occupied Dresden. Then began the Seven Years' War, in which little Prussia had to contend against what might well have seemed the overpowering coalition of France, Austria, Russia, and even Sweden. Within a year from his entry into Dresden, Frederick was defeated with terrible loss by the Austrians at Kolin (June 18, 1757). England was his only ally, and in a few weeks more the English army in Germany, under the Duke of Cumberland, was in the disastrous plight that produced the humiliating Convention of Kloster-Zeven. Frederick was in despair, and both thought and wrote of suicide by poison, or of seeking death on the battle-field. His sister Wilhelmina, the notable Margravine of Bayreuth, was one of his chief confidants in those days of his deepest despondency. She kept up a correspondence with Voltaire, who was always a favourite of hers, and who had had no direct communication with Frederick since the rejection of his overtures to return to Berlin. Frederick had never ceased to take an interest in him, and after Kolin was in a mood to welcome a word of sympathy from his old ally, whose genius he admired beyond all measure to the last. Voltaire himself, as a Frenchman, wished well to the success of his country's arms, and had not forgiven Frederick the affair of Frankfort. His first thought, on hearing of Frederick's reverses, was that now the time had come for taking vengeance on Freytag & Co., at Frankfort, for their maltreatment of his niece. Already he had begun, in his correspondence, to call Frederick "Luc," the name of a mischievous ape who had bitten him at Les Délices. But he could

not help feeling a little pity for Frederick, at death-grips
with that terrible European coalition, and he was not
a little proud to be able to contrast his own pleasant
existence by the Lake of Geneva, with the anxious and
harassed life, to escape from which Frederick was
almost longing for death. In the August after Kolin,
when Frederick was pouring out his sorrow in prose, and
more emphatically in verse, to Wilhelmina and others,
Voltaire enclosed in a letter to her, a note of sympathy to
be forwarded to her brother. Frederick answered it
graciously, and thus was renewed a correspondence
which lasted as long as Voltaire lived. With his usual
eye to his own interests, Voltaire seized the opportunity
to make himself of importance to his government by
becoming a means of communication between Frederick
and the French ministers, with a view to a peace. His
efforts of this kind were interrupted by Frederick's great
victory over the French at Rossbach (November 5, 1757),
but they were resumed some two years later, when Frederick was desirous of an honourable peace. As they were
entirely unsuccessful, a reference to them must suffice.
Apart from politics, the correspondence might have been
very much as in the days of old : on the one hand verses
from Frederick with laudations of Voltaire's genius, on
the other assurances of Voltaire's affection for Frederick
(against whom he was launching sarcasms in his letters
to his French friends), with philosophizing and moralizing
on both sides. But Voltaire imparted into the correspondence an occasional acrimony, by harping on
Frederick's later treatment of him, on the causes of his
departure from Berlin, and the incidents of his detention

at Frankfort. Nothing, however, that Voltaire could say extracted a syllable of apology or regret from Frederick. Here is a solitary, but adequate, sample of his replies to Voltaire's reproaches. " I will not enter upon a review of the past. You certainly behaved very badly to me. Your conduct would not have been tolerated by any philosopher. I forgave you, and I even wish to forget it all. But you had to do with a fool, in love with your fine genius, and if you had been any one else's guest you would not have extricated yourself so easily. Bear in mind what I say, and let me hear no more of that niece with whom you bore me. She has not her uncle's merits to compensate for her faults. We speak of Molière's old woman "—to whom the great dramatist read his plays before they were acted, forecasting from their effect on her what would be their effect on the audience;—" but no one will ever speak of the niece of Voltaire." For amenities of this kind Voltaire avenged himself, in secret, by writing the scathing account of Frederick at home, in the "Vie privée," apparently dashed off in 1759, but not published, and then surreptitiously, until after its writer's death.

In 1757, with the attempt of Damien on the life of Louis XV., the terrified king was stimulated by remorse, and by her enemies in the ministry, to think seriously of parting with the Pompadour. But the Pompadour triumphed, and displacing her former *protégé*, Bernis, had her new *protégé*, Choiseul, made Minister of Foreign Affairs in his stead. She had been always more or less favourable to Voltaire, and Choiseul was well affected to the *Philosophes* in general, and to Voltaire in particular. With such friends at Court, Voltaire thought that he might safely have a domicile in France, and towards the end of 1758 he negotiated for the purchase of Ferney, the home which of all others is most associated with his name. Of Les Délices he had only a tenancy for life, with the option of retiring from it when he pleased, but he bought the fee-simple of the château and demesne of Ferney, on French soil, three and a half miles from Geneva, and on the northern shore of the lake. If things went wrong with him in France, he could retire to Les Délices in Genevese territory, and if the Genevese were troublesome, he could retire to France and Ferney. But Ferney became his home after he had rebuilt the château, and when for the old and ugly parish church, which shut out the view, and which he pulled down, he had substituted a new one, with the famous inscription, " Deo erexit Voltaire." He also purchased for life the tumbledown château of Tournay, close to Geneva, acquiring with it the right to call himself Comte de Tournay, a title by which Frederick, quizzing him, sometimes addressed him when writing to him. The house at Lausanne, to which, as winter-quarters, he had migrated from Monrion, he got rid of, and he surrendered Les Délices in 1765. At Tournay he built a theatre, and at Ferney, to which was attached a considerable acreage of cultivable ground, he was soon busily planting, gardening, and farming. His yearly income was now between £4,000 and £5,000 of our money, perhaps equivalent to three times as much now. " You are the only man in France," the Cardinal de Bernis said to him once, " that lives like a *grand Seigneur* "—so many who

were born *grand Seigneurs* being deeply in debt, some
of them to Voltaire himself, who is supposed to have
saved, and profitably invested, half his income, year after
year.   But literature was not neglected by the busy and
bustling country gentleman.   One of the tasks which
occupied him at Les Délices, and which he finished at
Ferney, was his "History of Peter the Great," undertaken at the invitation, in 1757, of the Czarina Elizabeth,
who, with Maria Theresa and the Pompadour (for Louis
XV. was a cipher in the business), had concerted the coalition against Frederick.   Elizabeth took care that Voltaire
should have whatever material he needed, and the
Russian archives could supply, and he worked at the
task with his usual diligence.   Many years before, in the
preface to the first edition of his "Charles XII.," Voltaire had spoken of the Swedish king's rival, Peter, as
" much the greater man " of the two, and now he proved
this in detail, in his own bright and animated way.
The "History of the Empire of Russia under Peter the
Great " is not so attractive as his " History of Charles
XII.," but far transcends it in genuine interest.   The
first instalment of it was given to the world in 1759, the
year which also witnessed the publication of "Candide."
Voltaire found, too, time and inclination to succour a
descendant of one of the great writers of the age of Louis
XIV.   A nephew of Corneille was, with his family, in
a state of destitution.   Voltaire heard good accounts
of his eldest daughter, Marie, a girl of seventeen, who
could scarcely read and write.   He sent for her, and,
with Madame Denis, undertook her education, taking
care that she went to mass every day, whither he bore

her company, partly as squire of the parish, partly lest
her friends and his enemies in Paris should accuse him
of corrupting her religious principles. To provide her
with a dowry, he issued proposals for a new edition of
Corneille, with a commentary by himself. Among the
subscribers were the chief potentates and personages of
Europe, the heads of the coalition against Frederick
and William Pitt—Frederick's chief ally, the Chatham
of after-years—many making payment in advance, so
that Voltaire had not to wait for the issue of the
work, in 1764, to provide a dowry when the young
lady was married, in 1763, to a young officer in the
French army. His kindness to her is only one of many
exhibitions of beneficence which redound to Voltaire's
credit.

It was in the earlier years of his settlement at Geneva,
that Voltaire resolved on carrying on no longer a fitful
and episodical, but a persistent and systematic, warfare
against what he called " superstition," and unfurled the
banner which displayed the memorable apostrophe,
Écrasez l'Infâme—" Crush the Infamous one." The
Infamous one, which his allies were bidden crush, was
superstition, calling itself Christian, which demanded
unquestioning obedience from all men, whether in Paris,
in Vienna, or at Geneva, visiting disobedience with secular punishment in this world, whenever possible, and with
threats of everlasting torture in the other. "I wish you,"
he wrote to D'Alembert on June 23, 1760, "to crush
the Infamous one : that is the great point. She," for he
makes the object of his hatred feminine, "must be reduced
to the condition in which she is in England," where the

Church was strictly subordinated to the state, and a thinker, as the history of English Deism testified, could write as he pleased on theology and religion, so long as he avoided such ribaldry as Woolston's. "You can bring this about if you choose," he added; "it is the greatest service that can be rendered to the human race." The outrages on spiritual freedom which produced this declaration of war against an enemy who had harassed him all his life, were perpetrated in 1759. Of one of them Voltaire was himself the victim. He had written, and even printed, years before, a poem on the Law of Nature ("La Loi Naturelle"), an inoffensive title, which, when the piece fell in the course of time under the ban of orthodox bigots in Paris, appears to have been turned by the printer into what would be to them the more suspiciously suggestive one of "The Religion of Nature." In this poem Voltaire promulgated, with emphasis, his favourite theory of ethics, which some of the evolutionists of our day would doubtless condemn as savouring of an antiquated theistic superstition. It was that the sentiment of right and wrong had been implanted in us by the Creator. This is, for Voltaire, "the true light which lighteth every man that cometh into the world."

"Nature," Voltaire sang in eloquent verse, "has furnished with salutary hand whatever in life is necessary to man. . . . The God who made me did not make me in vain. He placed the seal of his divinity on the brow of every mortal. I cannot but know what has been ordained by my master. He has given me his law since he has given me existence. . . . A morality, uniform in all places, speaks in the name of that God to ages without end. It is the law of Trajan, of Socrates, and it is yours. - Of this everlasting worship Nature is the apostle. Common sense receives it, and it is protected by vengeful remorse, whose awful voice makes itself everywhere heard. . . . That law supreme, in China, in Japan, inspired Zoroaster, illuminated Solon. From one end of the world to the other it speaks, it exclaims : 'Adore a God, be just and cherish thy fatherland !' Never in his inmost heart did parricide or calumniator say : 'How beautiful, how pleasant it is to ruin the innocent, to destroy the form which gave us birth ! O just, O perfect God, how attractive is crime.' This, ye mortals, be assured, is what would be said were there not a terrible, a universal law, which is respected by crime even while rebelling against it."

And it was a poem in this harmless strain which, after so many years of effort spent by Voltaire in enriching the higher literature of his country, was, in obedience to a formal decree of the Parliament of Paris, burned with the usual indignities, by the public executioner, just as if it were obscenity or blasphemy. Voltaire's wrath at so transcendent an insult, offered him in the face of France by a body of dull and bigoted Jansenist lawyers, was increased by the sentence of death passed soon afterward on the "Encyclopédie." In March, 1757, the Government prohibited, under severe penalties, the sale of any of the volumes already issued of this monumental work, and of any that might be issued. The Jansenists were just recovering from a cruel persecution by the Jesuits, and now they themselves became persecutors. Some members of the Parliament of Paris were even beginning to hint that not only heterodox books, but their authors, should be burned ! With Pompadour and Choiseul protecting the *Philosophes*, this prohibition of the "Encyclopédie" may seem surprising. But under

the strange *régime* then existing in France, where Parliaments could be at once prosecutors and judges, the
Government had sometimes to curb the *Philosophes* lest
worse befell them at the hands of such bodies as the
Parliament of Paris.   The state of things shown is illustrated by the well-known story told of Diderot.   He
received a message from the amiable and tolerant Malesherbes, the minister who had charge of the book-printing
and bookselling of Paris, warning him that next day his
papers would be seized   Diderot knew not where to hide
them safely at so short a notice.   "Send them to me," said
Malesherbes.   Sent they were, and when the storm was
over, they were returned duly to the harassed philosopher.
The suspension of the "Encyclopédie" was as if an army,
well equipped, and full of spirit and courage, had been
suddenly disbanded, and the troops sent to their homes
in the middle of a successful campaign.   Voltaire had
now not merely his own grievances to avenge, but the
wrong done to the band of *Philosophes* who looked up
to him as their leader.   He began by satirizing, in his
own inimitable way, contributors to the organ of the
Jesuits, the *Journal de Trévoux*, and, passing from them,
Fréron, of the *Année Littéraire*, a declared enemy of the
Philosophes—whom he · brought upon the stage and
savagely caricatured as Frélon ("Wasp") in "L'Ecossaise,"
played triumphantly at Paris, July 26, 1760.   On one unfortunate, Le Franc de Pompignan, who succeeded Maupertuis (deceased) in the Academy, and who in his address
when he was received, said some sharp things of the
Philosophes, Voltaire showered malicious pleasantry until
his victim fled from Paris to his provincial home.

These were shots at stray soldiers of the garrison, but Voltaire was preparing to bring his heavy artillery into play, and open fire on the walls of the citadel itself, by direct attacks on Christianity. To this extreme he was being led by Jesuit and Jansenist repression of milder forms of dissent from the established theology. Protestantism, out of England, he found to be quite as tyrannical as Romanism. At his own door the authorities of Geneva not only sentenced Rousseau's " Émile " to be " burned with infamy," but issued an order for its author's arrest. These things were done in the name of Christianity, and French fanaticism was perpetrating outrages much fouler than the burning of heterodox literature. For Voltaire life had been a long warfare, but never before had he combated in so just and sacred a cause as when he now became the defender of the Calas, and their fellow-victims of a baleful and cruel " superstition."

CHAPTER XI.

THE scene of the Calas tragedy was Toulouse, noted even among French cities of the South, for its papal fanaticism, the Massacre of St. Bartholomew being yearly celebrated by its population with great enthusiasm. In 1761 a few Protestant families lingered on in it, the members of which were prohibited from entering the professions of law and medicine, and from pursuing many minor avocations. The head of one of these families, Jean Calas, a draper, in his sixty-fourth year, had been in business in Toulouse for forty years, and was not only of irreproachable character, but of very mild and amiable disposition. His family consisted of two daughters and four sons, the youngest of whom, Donat, a boy of fifteen, was at the time of the tragedy an apprentice at Nismes. One of these sons, Louis, had been converted to Romanism, without any opposition from his father, who behaved even more liberally to him than to the other sons. The other two sons, Pierre, a young man of twenty-five, and Marc Antoine, the eldest, aged twenty-eight, lived with their parents. Marc

Antoine was an ambitious, and, at the time of the tragedy, a disappointed and gloomy, young man. He had studied for the local bar, and hoped, though a Protestant, to be admitted, since apparently it was not uncommon for an easy-going priest to give without inquiry a certificate of orthodoxy to applicants. The priest to whom he applied was about to give it, but being informed by a servant of the young man's Protestantism, refused it unless he could produce from his confessor an attestation of his Catholicism. To gratify his ambition, Marc Antoine had not hesitated to practise a little temporary deception, but he could not desert to Catholicism, and he openly avowed that such was his decision. This disappointment was aggravated by others of a business kind, and, naturally melancholy, he became more and more morose. Such was his condition, when after supper on the night of October 13, 1761, his younger brother Pierre, escorting to the door a young man, a guest, found him dead in the shop, in the rooms above which the family lived. He had hung himself. An alarm was raised. Pierre and the guest rushed out of the house ; the former to fetch a doctor, and a crowd was soon collected before the door. A magistrate and some police were soon on the spot. While the crowd was wondering at, and speculating about, the cause of the catastrophe, a voice was heard exclaiming that the ill-fated young man had been strangled by his Huguenot family because he had turned Roman Catholic. Magistrate, populace, and clergy took up the cry, and the Calas, father and mother, with their

son Pierre, having been forthwith arrested and imprisoned, were at once found guilty by the public
opinion of Toulouse. Marc Antoine received, as a
martyr to Huguenot fanaticism, a public funeral
according to the rites of the Romish Church. After
something not worthy to be called a trial, the
Parliament of Toulouse (like other French parliaments,
a body of lawyers not elected by the people) on appeal,
condemned the father, Jean Calas, to be tortured, in
order to extract from him a confession of guilt, before
being broken on the wheel, after which his body was to
be burned, and the ashes scattered to the winds. The
poor old man bore without flinching the excruciating
torture to which he was subjected. At the foot of the
scaffold, a priest told off to exhort him at the last,
besought him for a confession of his guilt, only to
receive the reply, "What! do you also believe it possible
for a father to murder his son?" Among his last words
were, "I die innocent." Jean Calas was thus judicially
murdered on March 10, 1762. The month before,
a Huguenot pastor had been hung at Toulouse for
having preached to, baptized, and married, members of
his communion.

When Voltaire first heard of the Calas tragedy he
had no doubt that the judicial version of it was correct.
Although, of course, he condemned with all his heart
and soul the revocation of the Edict of Nantes, he had
no special love for Huguenots, holding them to be
given over to a "superstition" of their own, and
he saw Protestantism at Geneva as ready to persecute
as Jesuitism or Jansenism was in Paris. That a

Toulouse Huguenot should put a son to death rather than see him turn Roman Catholic, was only another proof of the evils of "fanaticism." But when a respectable merchant, coming from Toulouse to Geneva, told him the true story of the tragedy, Voltaire's equanimity became the liveliest curiosity, and he resolved to probe the matter to the bottom. The friends in high places to whom he first applied, such as the Cardinal de Bernis and the Duc de Richelieu, made, at Voltaire's pressing instance, some inquiries at Toulouse, and being of course informed by the authorities that Calas deserved his fate, they threw cold water on the ardour of Voltaire's curiosity. But Voltaire was not satisfied. Hearing that the youngest of the Calas, Donat, was at Geneva, whither he was followed by his brother Pierre, who had found Marc Antoine dead, and who, if murder there had been, must have been one of his brother's murderers, he examined and cross-examined them both. He even had Pierre watched for months without finding anything suspicious in his demeanour and conduct. He sought out bankers and others who knew the Calas family intimately, and testified to the impossibility of their perpetration of such a crime. He procured inquiries by competent investigators in Toulouse itself. He spared no time, trouble, and money to arrive at the truth. At the first blush it seemed incredible that an innocent man should have been condemned to death as a parricide by such a court as the Parliament of Toulouse. At last the conclusion was forced on him that a great judicial crime had been committed. "I am as certain," he said, "of the

innocence of that family as I am of my own existence."

Then he went to work with an energy and thorough-
ness all his own. The Minister in Paris who had
official charge of the affairs of the Reformed Churches,
found himself besieged by persons of rank and influence
—the Pompadour herself was brought to bear on him—
pleading on behalf of the Calas. More effective still,
Voltaire set his own powerful pen in motion, and issued
pamphlet after pamphlet in which the story of the Calas
was told, sometimes with pathetic simplicity in the words
of the members of the family itself. Public opinion
already counted for something in France, and the
iniquity of the proceedings which had issued in the
cruel torture and death of the innocent Jean Calas
provoked general indignation at home and abroad.
To the subscription promoted for the support of the
Calas family, and the costly proceedings for their rehabilitation, contributions were made even in England by
the young Queen Charlotte, by the Primate, by bishops,
noblemen, and gentlemen; and on the Continent by the
Empress of Russia, German princes, and the Protestant
communities throughout Europe. One of the greatest
obstacles to a revision of the sentence was the dogged
inertia of the Parliament of Toulouse, which long
refused to communicate the records of the legal proceedings in the case. Nor was it without difficulty that
Voltaire overcame the repugnance of Madame Calas
herself to appeal against the sentence which had sent
her husband to death, and the reversal of which she
could not believe to be possible. He induced her,

however, to proceed to Paris, where his friends were made hers, and her demeanour, as well as her sad fate, procured her many more. At last the French Council of State ordered a new trial in Paris, and this issued, March 9, 1765, in a judgment, which the Parliament of Toulouse had to accept, affirming the innocence of Jean Calas and every member of his family. The rehabilitation of the Calas made Voltaire the happiest of men, and procured him grateful admirers among many former foes. Protestants throughout Europe were specially thankful to him, and it seemed as if for a time he—as his friend, the unbelieving Frederick, had been—was to be regarded as a Protestant champion.

But Voltaire cared as little for the theology of Protestantism as for that of Romanism. It is significant that in the very year of the execution of Jean Calas, Voltaire for the first time directly assailed the documents on which Judaism and Christianity are based, by sending forth the "Sermon des Cinquante," in which the seminal facts in the narratives of the Old and New Testaments were dealt with contemptuously, as absurd, often ridiculous, and sometimes pernicious, fictions. Thenceforward to the close of his life, followed the issue, from the same workshop, of books and pamphlets with the same object. They were of all degrees of elaborateness, from a brief dialogue to the bulky "Dictionnaire Philosophique," the first slender form of which belongs to the year 1764. In no case was the authorship avowed. In almost every case it was emphatically disavowed, with a hardihood of continuous falsehood as unparalleled as the warfare in which Voltaire was engaged. In many cases pseudonyms were used, and once, to say nothing of the free use made in this way of French prelates and pastors, the Archbishop of Canterbury himself was made to figure as the author of a heterodox deliverance. Every resource of an almost inexhaustible ingenuity was brought into play to aid the circulation of these productions, which, whenever they caught sight of them, the authorities in France and Switzerland always confiscated, and often had publicly burned. For smuggling into Paris first copies of dangerous productions to be distributed among his friends, and for securing his correspondence with them from being opened by the Post Office authorities, he pressed indirectly into his service the French Government itself. One of his most devoted disciples in Paris was a certain Damilaville, the head clerk in a department of the French Treasury, who had officially the right to frank for postal purposes all letters and documents sent from his office, by using the seal of the Controller-General, the French Chancellor of the Exchequer. He cheerfully placed this privilege at the disposal of Voltaire and his friends, and thus copies of Voltaire's anti-religious publications were safely transmitted to Paris for circulation among the faithful, to be reprinted surreptitiously by any bold bookseller willing to risk against certain gain possible detection and punishment. Much illicit printing went on under Voltaire's direction in Geneva itself, and a great deal more in Holland, whence the obnoxious matter, for which no copyright was payable, might be smuggled into France and other countries. From the proximity of Geneva,

the free-thinking of some of its denizens, and the
religious Calvinism of others, Voltaire delighted in
circulating his printed heterodoxy there. An ingenious
stratagem practised by him on the Genevan authorities, is
worth chronicling as intensely characteristic of Voltaire.
They received a communication from him, gravely informing them that there would be received, on a certain day,
by a certain bookseller in Geneva, a parcel containing
publications printed at Amsterdam, among which were
copies of the " Dictionnaire Philosophique." He thought
it his duty, he said, to give this information, in case the
Council might wish to act in the interests of public peace
and order. The local police duly seized the parcel, but
the information was a mere blind. At that very time
a much larger consignment of the same perilous stuff was
crossing the frontier of the republic at a different point,
to be deposited in the shop of another bookseller, who
doubtless found plenty of customers for its contents.
The authorities, indignant when they discovered the trick,
had the " Dictionnaire Philosophique " burned by the
public executioner, a punishment with which it had
previously been visited by the Parliament of Paris. One
device of Voltaire's for carrying on his propagandism
in Calvinistic Geneva, was to give his pamphlets
orthodox titles—Sermons by the Reverend So-and-So,
Address of the Pastors of Geneva, &c., &c.—and then
prefix to their improper contents some pages of orthodox
lucubration, so as to lead on the innocent reader.
Amateur confederates, with colporteurs whom he hired,
thrust his pamphlets among the goods exposed for sale
in shops, slipped them under front doors, dropped them

on the seats of the public promenades, and the benches of workshops. Voltaire even went the length of having them bound like catechisms, and substituting them for the real thing in places where children were catechized. A Genevese worshipper would sometimes take up in church a book lettered as, and looking like, the Psalms, only to find that it was a copy of the one-volume edition of the "Dictionnaire Philosophique." Such was the strategy to which Voltaire stooped in his war against "L'Infâme," but, presumably, only after he had parted with Les Délices, and, being domiciled at Ferney on French soil, was, though so near a neighbour, beyond the jurisdiction of the Geneva authorities.

Voltaire's strenuous and successful intervention on behalf of the Calas made him popular in France, as an irrepressible and invincible champion of oppressed inno- cence. Many who shrank, or would have shrunk, from the perusal of his heterodox writings, looked up to him with respectful regard. Thenceforth, victims among his countrymen and country-women, of "superstition," backed by the law, or of much that was vicious in French jurisprudence and legal procedure, turned to Ferney for aid and deliverance. Sirven, a respectable land-surveyor in Languedoc, was the Protestant father of a weak-minded daughter, who became a Roman Catholic and the inmate of a convent. There she went quite out of her mind, and thence, after a good deal of harsh treatment, she was sent home again. Her insanity was as well known to the friends of the family as the affectionate care bestowed on her by her parents. One day, or rather night, she wandered from home, and her dead body was found in a well into which she had thrown herself. Then the cry was raised that the ill-fated girl had been made away with by her family—father, mother, and two sisters —because she had become a Roman Catholic. An order for their arrest was issued, and, acting on the advice of friends, they fled from France. This was sufficient for the local judiciary to pronounce them guilty. In March, 1764, Sirven and his sexagenarian wife were declared guilty of the murder of their daughter, and sentenced to be hung, while the two daughters, as accomplices, were banished for life from the district. Meanwhile, Sirven, though stripped of all he possessed, had escaped the fate of Jean Calas, and was gaining a livelihood at Geneva. The family implored Voltaire to take up their case, and he did not require much asking. He threw himself into it with the zeal and energy which had rehabilitated the Calas : appealing to Paris, issuing pamphlets, feeing lawyers, and raising a handsome subscription for the Sirven family. Yet so slow and cumbrous was in such cases the French judicial procedure, that not until January, 1772, eight years after the passing of the sentence, was it revoked by the Parliament of Toulouse, which, enlightened by the *dénouement* of the Calas tragedy, condemned the "Court below" to pay all the costs of the original prosecution ; and this, according to Voltaire, was something unexampled.

Among several other atrocities perpetrated in those days of triumphant bigotry, acting in the name of the law, was one which not only deeply interested, but personally affected, Voltaire. It was not due to the bigotry of the fervid South, but to that of the cooler

North—Abbeville in Normandy being the scene of the new
tragedy. One night in August, 1765, a wooden crucifix,
on the bridge at Abbeville, was mutilated, and another
in a cemetery was covered with filth, the same profane
hands having, it was naturally thought, been at work in
both instances. The people and clergy of Abbeville
were horror-struck. They followed in procession the
Bishop of Amiens, who came, in penitential costume,
to the very places where the desecrations had been
committed, and went through the appropriate expiatory
performances. Meanwhile, a young gentleman of good
connections, Gaillard d'Etallonde, was arrested on
suspicion. No evidence of his guilt was adduced, but
a number of witnesses testified that he and two young
friends of his, one of them the Chevalier de la Barre, had
been seen doing, and heard saying, various impious things.
The three young men had been known to remain erect,
and keep their hats on their heads, while the Host was
being borne past them in the street, and the Chevalier
de la Barre had even declared on the occasion that he
saw no sense in worshipping a God of dough. He and
the third friend, a certain Moisnel, followed D'Etallonde
into prison. Without any legal warrant, the official
prosecutor insisted, and successfully, on joining in the
indictment with these offences, for which there was
some evidence against the accused, another charge
of desecrating the crucifixes, for which there was none.
Before the trial D'Etallonde had escaped, and, in
point of fact, the condemnation of La Barre became
the one chief object of the prosecution. In the course
of his examination he admitted that he had, with

D'Etallonde, sung ditties in which Mary Magdalene was treated irreverently. Still more noticeable, in reply to the charge of indulging in "impious language," he said that he was guilty of nothing worse than "reciting some verses which he might have remembered of the 'Pucelle d'Orléans,' a work attributed to the Sieur de Voltaire, and of the 'Épitre à Uranie'" (see *antè* p. 41). The contents of his library were brought in evidence against him, and in it was the one-volume edition of the "Dictionnaire Philosophique," which, in spite of Voltaire's emphatic and reiterated denials, was known by all the world to be his handiwork. The local tribunal condemned La Barre to death by decapitation. The Parliament of Paris was appealed to, but confirmed the sentence. It was carried out on July 1, 1766, after he had been severely tortured to extract from him a confession that it was he who had mutilated the cross on the bridge. He denied it to the last. On the scaffold he behaved with composure and fortitude. With his corpse was burned the "Dictionnaire Philosophique."

The fate of La Barre created the profoundest indignation in France, and out of it. There was no question here of homicide of any kind, but simply of an *escapade*, which, even if he had been guilty of it, and this is doubtful, would have been adequately punished in one so young by a shorter or longer imprisonment. Voltaire's indignation at this foul and cruel victory of "superstition" was unbounded. But it was not followed, for the time at least, by the explosion of passionate protest that might have been expected from him. For once

Voltaire himself was cowed. The rhetorical Tartuffe (for it appears that he was not even a bigot), whose declamations induced fifteen out of twenty-five of the judges in Paris to confirm the sentence of the Abbeville tribunal, had spoken largely and loudly of the responsibility of the *Philosophes* for such "horrible manifestations of impiety" as that with which the poor young La Barre had been charged. Moreover, in the legal proceedings which issued in his execution, irreligious writings of Voltaire had been proved to form part of La Barre's familiar reading, and this fact had been represented as a strong indication of the guilt for which he suffered death. No one could tell what fate might be in store for Voltaire himself, whose responsibility for La Barre's crime was proclaimed in the Parliament of Paris. In Choiseul and Richelieu he had friends at Court, but the King, who was supreme, had never relented towards him, and had refused to annul or mitigate La Barre's ferocious sentence. In his fright Voltaire turned to Frederick, who some three years before had obtained the peace of Hubertsburg, which left him in possession of Silesia, and who was now repairing the material damage done to Prussia by that terrible Seven Years' War. Would he, Voltaire asked him, allow a colony of *Philosophes* to settle in his territory of Cleves, where they might hurl missiles at the *Infâme* without fear of molestation from French governments and parliaments of Paris? Frederick graciously, and even cordially, granted the request; but the scheme came to nothing. The other French *Philosophes* preferred Paris, pleasant and cultivated, with all its risks and dangers, to exile at Cleves, the capital of a province which seems to have been regarded as a Prussian Bœotia. Not one of them would join him, so Voltaire had to reconcile himself to his fate, and remain, if somewhat in fear and trembling, at Ferney. And be it noted, that while sanctioning the migration and emigration to Cleves, Frederick read Voltaire a little lecture on the discretion which he expected the *Philosophes* to exhibit there.

" I offer an asylum to *Philosophes*," he wrote to Voltaire, "on condition that they behave like wise men, and that they show themselves as pacific as the fine title with which they decorate themselves assumes them to be. For all the truths collectively which they announce are not as valuable as tranquillity, the one blessing enjoyable by man on this atom of an earth. For my part, being a reasoner devoid of enthusiasm, I wish men to be reasonable, and, above all, to be tranquil. We know the crimes, the commission of which has been caused by religious fanaticism : let us beware of introducing fanaticism into philosophy."

Indeed, though Frederick's contempt for the *Infâme* was quite equal to Voltaire's detestation of it, and he writes of it sometimes in language of unsurpassable coarseness, he is frequently found trying to restrain Voltaire's vehemence of attack on it, and throwing cold water on his hope of founding a new and pure religion. Frederick had not much faith in human nature or in human progress. At the time of the projected settlement of *Philosophes* at Cleves, it is thus again that he writes to Voltaire :—

" I congratulate you on your good opinion of mankind. As for me, who through the duties of my position am very well acquainted with that species of featherless biped, I predict that neither you nor all the philosophers in the world will ever cure the human race of the superstition to which it cleaves. . . . You think, because the Quakers and the Socinians have established a simple religion, that, by simplifying it still more, we can rear a new belief on that foundation. But I recur to what I have already said, and am almost convinced that if the flock should become considerable in numbers, it would beget in a short time some new superstition, unless minds devoid of fear and weakness were alone selected to compose it. Such are not commonly found. Nevertheless, I believe that the voice of reason, by dint of raising itself against fanaticism, will succeed in making the human race of the future more tolerant than it is to-day, and that is a considerable gain. . . . I commend you to the holy keeping of Epicurus, of Aristippus, of Locke, of Gassendi, of Bayle, and of all those minds purified from prejudices, who became through their immortal genius cherubim attached to the ark of truth.—FÉDÉRIC." Then comes a postscript : " If you will send us some of the books of which you speak, you will confer pleasure on those that place their hope in him who is to deliver his people from the yoke of imposture."

Voltaire was at the time in familiar correspondence with another European potentate, quite as much of a free-thinker and an admirer of his works as Frederick, and reigning over dominions far vaster than the Prussian kingdom. This was the Czarina, Catherine II., who, after having made away with her husband, the Czar, Peter III., reigned in his stead over the Russian Empire. Catherine had fed on Voltaire's writings. She opened a correspondence with him, as a man for whose genius and way of thinking she had the highest admiration, and as a leader of opinion in civilized Europe, whose good word was well worth having. She wrote to him, which would please him, of her legislative tolerance of all religions throughout her vast empire, of her resolute subordination of the Church to the State, as well as of

her appreciation of whatever came dropping from his
pen. She subscribed handsomely to such funds as
those which he raised for the Calas and Sirven families,
and she sent himself imperial gifts, among them magnifi-
cent furs to protect him from the severe cold of the Swiss
winters. Voltaire's letters to Catherine were, as may be
easily supposed, full of enthusiasm and gratitude. She
was " the Star of the North," and, through her religious
toleration, put to shame the government of his own
country, with its pretences to the highest civilization.
When the war of 1768 broke out between Russia and
Turkey, Catherine wrote to him regular accounts of the
victories of her arms, and he, the apostle of peace and
denouncer of military carnage, welcomed ecstatically the
reports of her successes. He hated the Turk as a barbarian
and a Mahometan fanatic, and as the oppressor of the
Greeks, whom he looked to Catherine to liberate and
aid in reviving their ancient glory. Catherine did not
greatly share his enthusiasm for the liberation and resusci-
tation of Greece. " The Greeks, the Spartans," she writes
to him once, " have greatly degenerated ; they love rapine
more than freedom." But she evidently enjoyed his
appeals to her to make an end of the Turkish rule in
Europe. " I would give all that I have in the world,"
he wrote to her, "to see your Imperial Majesty on the
throne of Mustapha. His palace is wretched enough,
his gardens, too ; you would soon have made that
dungeon the most delicious place on earth." And at
one time it seemed as if Catherine could, if she
resolved on it, have made an end of Mustapha, and
settled the " Eastern question " of her day by taking

possession of Constantinople. But, as has happened more than once in the nineteenth century, Austria stopped the way. A war between Austria and Russia would have brought Frederick into the field, since he was bound by treaty engagements to support Catherine. Then France and England could scarcely have kept out of the fray, and there would have been, what Frederick feared above all things, another general European war. Voltaire, in his eagerness, not to say ignorance, wrote to Frederick, imploring him to unite with Austria and Russia in partitioning Turkey. Frederick did not deign to reply. Turkey lay far out of his beat, and a very acceptable acquisition of territory much nearer home was possible. He united cheerfully with Austria and Russia to partition not Turkey, but—Poland.

Voltaire's projected colony of philosophers at Cleves having come to nothing, he began to turn his attention to the formation of an industrial colony at Ferney, where he had already been reclaiming waste land, and making to blossom like the rose what, when he became its owner, was a wilderness tenanted by a score or two of poverty-stricken peasants. Over and above the pleasure, in his case considerable, of creating and fostering a thriving industrial community, he was impelled to the enterprise by his own circumstances, and assisted in it by those of his neighbours at Geneva. Of his large income he saved, it is computed, every year a half, and profitable investments for his savings were becoming scarce. The exigencies of French finance, and the unscrupulous proceedings of its administrators, impoverished the creditors of the State. Voltaire's debtors among *grands Seigneurs* at home, and potentates abroad, were falling in arrear with the payment of the interest due to him for his loans to them. If he invested his money in industrial enterprises at Ferney, he would have his debtors close at hand, under his eye and under his thumb, and whatever profit accrued to him would be his own, since, thanks to Choiseul and the Pompadour, he had obtained from the King an exemption of his domain from the heavy taxation with which France in general was burdened. A supply of skilled labour would be furnished by the civic broils of Geneva. The city of Calvin was then governed by an oligarchy, opposition to whose domination appears to have been roused by Jean Jacques Rousseau's "Contrat Social," the effects of which on the little Swiss republic prefigured those, far more portentous, that helped to shatter the great French monarchy. The *bourgeoisie* of Geneva protested against the despotism of the oligarchy, but resisted the claims of the working-classes to be admitted with them to a share in the government. Voltaire tried, but without success, to mediate between the combatants in this triangular duel. At last it came to rioting, even to bloodshed, and the *plebs* went to the wall. To such of them as were driven from Geneva, Voltaire offered a refuge and means of employment at Ferney, and many accepted the offer. The majority were watchmakers, but some of them were weavers, and a little manufactory of silks and laces was soon established at Ferney. One of the first products of this enterprise was a pair of silk stockings sent by Voltaire to the wife of his ministerial protector, the Duc de Choiseul. The raw material for them was derived from silkworms raised by Voltaire, and the stockings, he declared, were made by himself and by a young Calas, who was finding a home at Ferney. But the watchmaking, for which Geneva had long been renowned, was the staple industry of Ferney, and Voltaire hoped to see it drive Geneva out of the field. He pushed the wares of his *protégés* as energetically as if he had been all his life a manufacturer of watches, and he now employed influence on their behalf which an ordinary watchmaker had not. The watches sent out from Ferney were of every class, cheap and costly, plain and richly ornamented, and in all cases good timekeepers. Voltaire actually issued a circular to the French envoys at foreign courts, appealing to their patriotism, their loyalty, and even to their orthodoxy, to order for themselves, or to recommend to dealers, watches made on French soil, whose makers had been " placed under the patronage of the King by the Duc de Choiseul "—and he was Minister of Foreign Affairs. " They deserve," Voltaire gravely added, " the patronage of your Excellency all the more that they greatly respect the Catholic religion," —perfect toleration for which he had taught his Protestant *protégés*, fresh from bigoted and Calvinistic Geneva. Of course he appealed in their behalf to Catherine. She ordered rather vaguely some thousands of roubles' worth of watches, and received a consignment valued at not much less than 40,000 livres—£1,600. On this Voltaire delicately hinted that as her Imperial Majesty was carrying on an expensive war, she might make a payment of half the amount then, and the remainder six months afterwards. Catherine, however, insisted on paying the whole sum at once, informing her thoughtful French friend that to her such a sum was a trifle, and requesting him not to judge of her finances by the ruinous condition of those of other states of Europe, a hit at the deplorable state of the French exchequer. The Czarina had told him that she was entering into commercial relations with the Emperor of China, whereupon Voltaire suggested that the Ferney watches might thus find their way into the Celestial Empire; and her Majesty graciously encouraged the project. With such a "promoter," the watch industry of Ferney throve apace, and in a few years its products were to be found in demand in many cities and countries, from Paris to Constantinople, from Morocco to America. Before Voltaire's death, little Ferney exported annually manufactured articles to the value of £40,000, and had 1,200 inhabitants. Voltaire reaped a fair return from the capital which he invested in advances of money to his colonists, and in building domiciles for them. He charged from 4 to 5 per cent. interest on loans, and from 5 to 7 per cent. on the value of his houses, to be paid so long as his niece Madame Denis lived; and when one of his houses changed hands, he was entitled to receive a twelfth of its value by way of fine. The result was that the domain at Ferney, which he bought for 100,000 livres—£4,000,—was sold by that lady after his death for 230,000 livres — £9,200—more than double the original price.

Voltaire's multiform activity during the decade glanced at in this chapter, from his sixty-eighth to his seventy-eighth year, was one of great and varied literary productiveness, some results of which have been already mentioned. In 1763 was issued the conclusion of his "History of Russia under Peter the Great," a work which first instructed the civilized world as to the development of the great empire, with the military strength of which Frederick had been made painfully conscious during the Seven Years' War, a struggle closed successfully for him mainly by the death of the Czarina Elizabeth, his implacable foe, and by the accession of his fervent admirer the Czar Peter III. The year 1765 witnessed the completion of the "Essai sur les Mœurs," by having prefixed to it a "Discours préliminaire," a sort of introduction to the philosophy of history, which was dedicated to his new imperial friend, Catherine II. His intention in composing the "Essai," by far the greatest of Voltaire's historical works, was, as already hinted, to write history on a new plan, to substitute for the "old almanack," which it had usually become, a narrative which would illustrate whatever progress mankind had made from savagery and barbarism to civilization, exhibiting with its spiritual, ethical, and intellectual development, that of art and industry. It was to have embraced only the period from Charlemagne to Louis XIV., and instalments of such a narrative were issued from time to time; but the plan of the work expanded as he proceeded, and in its completed form it may be regarded as more or less a panoramic sketch of universal history. Voltaire began with disquisitions on geology, anthropology, and man in his prehistoric condition—most of which are now quite out of date. But in the chapter "on the knowledge of the soul" attained by primitive man, he

gives the same theory of its genesis which is found in the
writings of our chief contemporary apostle of evolution.

"By what steps could men have been led to imagine a metaphysical in our physical being? Certainly men exclusively occupied
with their wants did not know enough of them to delude themselves
as if they were philosophers. In course of time there were formed
societies slightly civilized, in which a few men had leisure for reflection. It must have happened that a man, feeling keenly the death of
his father, or of his brother, or of his wife, saw in a dream the person
whom he regretted. Two or three dreams of this kind would alarm
a whole tribe. Here is one who is dead appearing to the living,
and, nevertheless, the dead person eaten by the worms is always in
the same place. It was then something which was in him that is
moving through the air. It is his soul, his shade, his manes; it is
a slight image of himself. Such is the natural reasoning of ignorance when it begins to reason."

As a whole, the work astonishes by the vastness of Voltaire's reading, the results of which are given in his terse,
lucid, graceful style, with a running commentary of acute
and often pregnant remark. He was not an erudite man,
yet he writes as if he had skimmed all that was known in
his time of the past of humanity and the world. What
repels most in the flowing narrative, is Voltaire's refusal
in general to see that any good thing can come out
of Nazareth. The cruel persecutions of Christians by
Christians, the destruction of human life by wars of
religion, the greed of popes, prelates, and priests, the
evils of monasticism, are dwelt on in detail; but scarcely
a word is said of the vast contributions made by Christianity to the spiritual and material progress of the human
race. Yet there are exceptions to be made to this state-

ment. If the Crusaders are represented as actuated only by a love of plunder, Voltaire does ample justice to Louis IX., although he was a saint, and says of him that "it is not given to man to carry virtue further than he did." Then again, in the midst of sarcasms flung at the successors of St. Peter in the see of Rome, such a passage as the following arrests attention :—

"Perhaps the man who in the rude times which we call the Middle Ages deserved most of the human race, was Pope Alexander III. It was he who, in a council, abolished serfdom as far as he could. It was the same pope who in Venice triumphed, by his sagacity, over the violence of the Emperor Frederick Barbarossa, and who forced Henry II., king of England, to ask pardon of God and man for the murder of Thomas à Beckett. He resuscitated the rights of peoples, and repressed crime in kings."

So, too, his sallies against monasticism are relieved by such an admission as the following: "They," the Benedictines, "were studious. By them alone, as copyists, were books preserved. In short, during those barbarous ages, when peoples were so wretched, it was a great consolation that in cloisters could be found a secure refuge against tyranny." After telling, with no excessive sympathy, the story of Joan of Arc, Voltaire speaks of her as one who "would have had altars raised to her in heroic times, when men erected them to their deliverers." In an unheroic time, her life and work were doomed to be made, by Voltaire himself, the theme of a ribald burlesque! At the close of the "Essai," looking back on the history of man as related in his book of marvellous range, Voltaire makes the far from cheerful reflection : "Once more it must be admitted that in a general way the whole of this history is a collection of crimes, of follies, and of disasters, among which we have seen a few virtues, a few happy ages, just as in savage deserts human habitations are discovered here and there."

During the decade of Voltaire's biography under review, he threw off more than a dozen dramas, tragedies, comedies, and even operas. But none of them, claim mention, except, perhaps, "Le Dépositaire," because in this agreeable comedy the friend of Voltaire's boyhood, Ninon de l'Enclos, was pleasantly introduced, and because, in the two young men who are the principal characters—one devout, austere, and repulsive, the other a free-thinker and free-liver, but attractive—he is surmised to have, in some measure, reproduced the Voltaire and his Jansenist brother Armand (then long deceased), of early years. Some of these dramas were unacted because they were thought in Paris not attractive enough for the stage, but among them was one which never could, or should, have been acted on any public stage. This was "Saul," a prose drama, in which the Biblical story of Saul and David is travestied with mordant wit, its principal personages talking like eighteenth-century Frenchmen and Frenchwomen in a style irresistibly provoking the laughter of the profane. Many were the literary forms adopted by Voltaire in waging his war against *L'Infâme:* among them treatise grave and gay, sprightly dialogue, and amusing tale; but "Saul" was his first and last use of the drama to make both ridiculous and detestable the sacred writings of that Jewish nationality, which, collectively and individually, in its past and in its present, was the unceasing object of his relentless satire.

It was during the same decade that, the issue of the
" Encyclopédie " in detached volumes being suspended,
Voltaire sent forth in instalments his "Questions sur
l'Encyclopédie," afterwards incorporated in, and forming
the bulk of, the " Dictionnaire Philosophique," which is
the work of Voltaire probably most often dipped into.
In it all of Voltaire's wit and reading—and the range
of the latter was marvellous—were brought to bear on
the *Infâme*, and the metaphysical and ethical theories
affiliated to it. Compared with the battering-ram of his
model Bayle, Voltaire's attack on the citadel of orthodoxy
is that of modern ordnance. Numerous articles, moreover,
on non-controversial topics, full of information as well as
of *esprit*, contribute to make much of the " Dictionnaire
Philosophique " very pleasant reading. Then, among
graver treatises, are the " Philosophe Ignorant," and the
" Profession de Foi des Théistes," in which Voltaire
reiterated his exposition of the limitations of human
knowledge, while that of his own theistic metaphysics
and ethics is accompanied by lively summaries of, and
sceptical comments on, philosophical systems ancient and
modern.

The freedom of thought and "emancipation from
prejudice," for which Voltaire had been fighting all his
life, and which he had powerfully aided in extending,
were now producing results from which even he recoiled.
The theism which he preached, had ceased to satisfy
some of the *Philosophes* and their allies. It was no
longer merely the fool who said in his heart that there is
no God ; a man of genius like Diderot was proclaiming
it from the housetop. It was thus that Horace Walpole

wrote from Paris to the poet Gray (November 19, 1765): " The *savants*—I beg their pardon, the *Philosophes*—are insupportable, superficial, overbearing, and fanatic. They preach incessantly, and their avowed doctrine is atheism ; you would not believe how openly. Don't wonder, therefore, if I should return a Jesuit. Voltaire himself does not satisfy them. One of their lady-devotees said of him, '*Il est bigot; c'est un déiste.*'" In 1770 the reading and thinking world was startled by the publication of the Baron d'Holbach's " Système de la Nature," in which God was banished from a self-subsistent, self-sustaining, and self-developing universe. Voltaire and Frederick took alarm. Their first thought was the effect which the work would have in discrediting the *Philosophes*, who had been content to assail the *Infâme*. "The book," Voltaire wrote, "has made all the *Philosophes* execrable in the eyes of the King and of the whole Court. Through this fatal work, philosophy is lost for ever in the eyes of all magistrates and fathers of families. They feel how dangerous to society atheism may be." Frederick, as well as Voltaire, took up the pen to refute Holbach's book (in the composition of which Diderot is surmised to have had a considerable share), and they combated atheism not only for its effects on society, but as in itself irrational and untrue. The King's disquisition is printed in his philosophical works; that of Voltaire is the article " Dieu " in the " Dictionnaire Philosophique." The weightiest of the arguments adduced by both, and borrowed, one fancies, from Frederick by Voltaire, is superadded to the usual one for the existence of a God deduced from the evident marks of design throughout the Universe. Holbach maintained that matter and movement by themselves had produced all phenomena, mind included. No! said Frederick—

"Man is a reasonable being produced by nature. Nature, then, must be infinitely more intelligent than he, or else she would be in the position of having communicated to him perfections which she herself did not possess. If thought is a result of our organization, it is certain that Nature, enormously more organized than man, who is an imperceptible fraction of the great whole, must possess intelligence of the highest degree of perfection."

So, in other words, Voltaire expresses the same idea :—

"The author of the 'Système' maintains that matter, acting blindly and without premeditation (*sans choix*) produces animals possessing intelligence. To produce without intelligence entities which possess it! Is that conceivable? Is such a system supported by the slightest probability?"

Parenthetically, it is noticeable, Holbach's assertion that life can be evolved by lifeless matter, was based upon a belief that animalcules, visible through the microscope in a mixture of flour and water which had been isolated for some time, were produced by the mixture. Voltaire calls this assertion "unheard-of nonsense" (*sottise inouïe*), but it was reserved for our own generation to know that the possibility of spontaneous generation has not yet been proved.

Voltaire's theistic faith, in its antagonism to the atheism fashionable in his later years, has, indeed, been too little noticed, and consequently the orthodox have been left to regard him as a mere scoffer, denier, and destroyer. He neglected no means of inculcating his theism, championing it not only in grave dissertations like the article "Dieu," which has just been cited, but in one of those attractive fictions which remain the most generally popular of all his writings. In his "History of Jenni," written about the time of the appearance of the "System of Nature," he aimed at showing the evil results to social morality which would flow from the general acceptance of the atheism which at the same time he combated as unphilosophical. Several of the characters in the story are English, and real personages, acquaintances of Voltaire during his exile in England : Lord Peterborough, Lady Hervey, Dr. Mead the physician, flitting through it in a shadowy way. The father of Jenni, who is of the masculine not the feminine gender, Mr. Freind, is Voltaire's ideal Englishman, the most devout, amiable, and tolerant of theists, only mildly contemptuous of the *Infâme.* Unfortunately for him, his son Jenni, a youth of good disposition, has become the associate of, and been corrupted by, a band of clever young atheists and debauchees, male and female, who have taught him that there is no life beyond the grave, and that the whole duty of man is to eat and drink to-day, since to-morrow he dies for ever. In the course of a rake's progress, Jenni, having killed a creditor who demanded payment of a debt, is in imminent danger of being hung. Still *han* worse, a young, beautiful, and virtuous maiden, a Miss Primrose, with whom Jenni had sense enough left to fall in love, is poisoned by a lady rejoicing in the singular name of Clive-Hart, a Delilah, who belongs to Jenni's atheistic set, and who, without being faithful to him, is jealous of his new love. Jenni and Miss, or Mrs., Clive-

Hart being, both of them, in danger of the gallows, sail
for North America, accompanied by three of their dissolute young gentlemen friends, among them a Mr. Birton.
Such are the fruits of atheism. Mr. Freind, and the
supposed biographer of Jenni, follow the fugitives, who
are enjoying themselves in Maryland. After a number
of adventures, the whole party, pursuers and pursued,
embark for England, with the exception of the Clive-
Hart, who, as the consequence of a fray between her
companions and some North American Indians, has
been captured by them, and, beautiful but sinful
atheist, been eaten. On board the vessel, Mr. Freind
and the unbelieving Birton engage in a long discussion
on atheism and theism, listened to by an attentive
audience, and reported by Voltaire in that dialogue-form
of which he was so consummate a master. His dialogues
indeed, full of thought and wit, are, with their dramatic
vivacity and candid presentation of both sides of a number of interesting questions, to be regarded as among the
happiest of his productions, much more attractive to
modern English readers than his once far-famed dramas.
Mr. Freind begins by indicating, in the old familiar
fashion, that everything in the universe, from the star to
the meanest weed, bears testimony to a Supreme Being,

"*Birton.* And where is this being? If there be one, why does
he hide himself? Has any one ever seen him? Ought a benefactor
to conceal himself from those to whom he does good?

"*Freind.* Did you ever see Christopher Wren who built St.
Paul's? Nevertheless, that edifice, it is evident, is the work of a
very skilful architect.

"*Birton.* Everybody easily understands that Wren built, at a

great cost, that vast edifice in which Burgess sends us to sleep. ——
We know perfectly why and how our fathers built that structure ;
but, I ask you, why, and how, should, and could, a God have created
this universe out of nothing? You know the old maxim of the
whole of antiquity, out of nothing nothing can come. This is a
truth which nobody ever doubted. Your Bible itself says expressly
that your God made heaven and earth, although heaven, that is to
say, all the stars collectively, is as superior to the earth as the earth
is to the tiniest grain of sand. But the Bible has nowhere said that
God made heaven and earth out of nothing at all. According to
the Bible itself, chaos existed before the earth : therefore matter was
as eternal as your God.

"*Freind.* I have, I think, proved to you that there exists a
supreme intelligence, an eternal power to whom we owe our
transitory life. I did not promise to explain to you the why and
the how. God has given me reason enough to understand that he
exists, but not enough to know if matter has been from all eternity
subjected to him, or if he gave it birth in time. What signifies to
you the eternity or the creation of matter, provided you recognize a
God, the master of matter and of yourself? You ask me where God
is. I know nothing, and ought to know nothing about it ; I know
that he is ; I know that he is our master ; that he is the maker of
everything, and that we ought to expect everything from his goodness.

"*Birton.* From his goodness ! You are laughing at me. You ——
told me to make use of my eyes. Make use of your own. Cast but
a single glance at the whole earth, and then judge whether your
God is good."

"And now," says the narrator, "Mr. Freind felt that
this was the main point of the discussion, and that
Birton was preparing for a strenuous assault on him.
He saw that a breathing-time was needed for the
audience to listen, and for himself to speak. He com-
mended himself to God." The other members of the
party promenaded the deck, and after tea the discussion

was resumed.　Birton began his indictment against the paternal affection of the supposed deity for his supposed children, with a catalogue of the hardships suffered by the inhabitants of northern regions, the scourges to which man is exposed in the finest climates, the destruction of human life by volcanoes, the diseases which poison his existence, the cruelties inflicted by the Spanish conquerors of America on the civilized nations whom they found there, and so forth.

"If there existed a god so powerful and so good, he would not have placed evil on the earth; he would not have doomed his creatures to pain and crime.　If he was not able to prevent evil, he is impotent; if he was able and did not will it, he is barbarous."

From this dilemma Freind thus tries to escape :—

"I am very far from saying, like some reasoners, that private evil is universal good.　That is too ridiculous an exaggeration.　I admit with sorrow that there is much moral and much physical evil, but since the existence of God is certain, it is also very certain that all these evils cannot hinder God from existing.　He cannot be malignant, for what interest could he have in being so?　There are evils which are horrible—well, my friends, do not let us increase their number.　It is impossible that God should not be good, but men are perverse.　They make a detestable use of the freedom which that great Being gave them and was bound to give them, a freedom to do what they will to do, and without which they would be mere machines formed by a malignant being to be shattered by him."

If there is crime on the earth, there has been, and there is, virtue, from Socrates to the Man of Ross. When Birton asks if God has delivered his laws to us, Freind replies :—

"Yes, by the voice of conscience. Is it not the fact that, if you had killed your parents, conscience would shatter you with pangs of remorse as horrible as they are involuntary? Is not this fact felt and acknowledged by the whole universe? And so, in a less degree, is it with lesser crimes. In another world God may punish what is not punished, and reward what is not rewarded in this world. To believe this to be impossible is to do away with all restraint on vice and crime. An atheist, poor and violent, would be a fool if, certain of impunity, he did not murder you to rob you of your money. Believe in a good God and be good."

Logic and rhetoric which would not have convinced Diderot and David Hume, converted Jenni and Birton. They believed. Miss Primrose was not dead, and Jenni married her. A suitable wife was found for Birton. The two reprobates, reformed by being converted from atheism to theism, are, at the end of the story, "the best men in England," and with their spouses no doubt "lived happy ever after." Here atheism seems to be combated mainly because injurious to society, and from the point of view of Voltaire's celebrated saying, "*S'il n'y avait pas un dieu, il faudrait l'inventer.*" Yet Voltaire's theism was one not only of the head, but of the heart. Looking at the heavens and the earth, from the galaxy to the worm, he recognized everywhere the handiwork of a Deity, and sometimes, both in prose and verse, he breaks forth into almost Psalmist-like praises of the wisdom and beneficence of the Creator, and thanks Him for the existence which has allowed the sons of men to contemplate the grandeur and beauty of creation.

CHAPTER XII.

(1772–78.)

VOLTAIRE was now in his seventy-eighth year, and, according to his own account, suffering from a number of maladies, any one of which would have sufficed to carry off an ordinary man. But while representing himself at the point of death, and really ill now and then, he was, as ever, indefatigably active with his pen. During his later years he spent much of his time in bed, living temperately on coffee and broiled eggs, and busily reading and dictating; the quantity of work which he got through being marvellous. The general indignation which, thanks to him, had been aroused by the iniquitous treatment of the Calas, the Sirvens, and other victims of bigotry, appears to have prevented any more prosecutions and persecutions of the kind from which they had suffered. But French juris-prudence and legal procedure had so many vices, that victims of one kind or another were never wanting, and Voltaire, in his bed, was always on the alert to take up his pen in defence of the judicially oppressed. Some-times, as in the case of the Calas, he was too late to do more than to save the family of the victim of a judicial murder from the fate in which the sentence had involved them, and to rehabilitate the memory of the victim himself. The French parliaments in Paris and the provinces were often hurried to unjust decisions by popular clamour, and an iniquitous sentence, sometimes of death, was pronounced, or carried out, before a sufficient interval elapsed for intervention or appeal. At the time of the Calas tragedy, Frederick indicated one great deficiency in French legal procedure, the execution of sentences of death pronounced by parliaments of lawyers, without the direct knowledge and sanction of the sovereign. One case out of many was that of the Montbaillis of St. Omer, a decent couple, engaged with the husband's aged mother in the manufacture of tobacco for the farmers-general. The mother was given to drinking, and one morning she was found dead. As it happened, her death was a misfortune for her son, since it rendered him liable to lose an employment which had been conferred on the three collectively. But the populace of St. Omer rushed to the conclusion that she had been murdered by her son and daughter-in-law, and the magistrates yielded weakly to their clamour. Without forrmal accusers, without a tittle of evidence against them, husband and wife were sentenced to death, the husband to be tortured before being broken on the wheel, the wife to be hung. The husband died protesting his innocence, the wife, *ha* being *enceinte,* was respited. Voltaire took the matter up, though here the *Infâme* had no share in the iniquity. —— Through his influence the case was re-heard, the murdered husband pronounced innocent, and the wife acquitted.

Then there was the case of the brave but im-
petuous Lally, who had planned the extrusion of the
English from India, and, as commander-in-chief of the
French forces there, had fought gallantly for that end,
with the result that it was the French who were driven
from their Indian possessions, and that Lally was taken
prisoner and sent to England. Released on parole,
and returning to France, he was sacrificed to the vindictive clamour of the shareholders of the French East
India Company, which the victories of the English in
India had reduced to inanition. Lally was condemned
to death by the Parliament of Paris. In 1766, gagged
and drawn on a hurdle to the Place de Grève, he was
beheaded, and all his property was confiscated. Lally
(originally, it is said, a Mullally) was the son of an Irish
Jacobite who had taken refuge in France and entered
the French army. Lally, when quite a boy, joined his
father's regiment. He distinguished himself at Fontenoy,
and was made a colonel, rising afterwards to be a lieu-
tenant-general. It was Lally who suggested the abortive
expedition against England in 1746 to support the young
Pretender, which Richelieu was to have commanded,
with the intention of distributing on his arrival the manifesto written by Voltaire, who then became acquainted
with Lally. In his "Précis de l'Histoire de Louis
Quinze," Voltaire, when telling the story of the contest
between French and English in India, told also that of
the ill-fated Lally, executed because he had failed, though
when he did fail, it was under circumstances which made
success impossible. He left his memory to be vindicated
by a son of fifteen, who became known in the French

Revolution, and out of it, as Lally-Tolendal. The task was a long one, and in discharging it he was sedulously aided by the patriarch of Ferney. It was only episodically that Voltaire, in his history of Louis XV., had dealt with the English conquests in India and the story of the ill-fated Lally. With the keen interest which he took in everything great or memorable, especially of his own time, as well as incited by pity for Lally and sympathy with Lally's son, he prosecuted researches into the history of India near and remote. The result was the " Fragments Historiques sur l'Inde, sur le Général Lalli, et plusieurs autres sujets," published in 1773. The story of Lally was re-told in detail, with that of the struggle of French and English for supremacy in India. But under the modest title of " Fragments," Voltaire gave, in his own succinct and animated way, a sketch of India and its inhabitants from early ages to his own, with one of Brahminism and the sacred books of the Hindus. And all this time he was fighting the battle of oppressed communities such as the serfs of Mount-Jura—for serfdom still lingered in France—and with these particular serfs he sympathized the more keenly because their oppressors were monks. His own Pays de Gex, of which his domain of Ferney formed a part, suffered from exactions of farmers-general, and against these Voltaire did battle with his pen for years, with ultimate success. Time, too, had to be devoted to his own private affairs, to the management of a large and scattered revenue, much of it derived from loans, the payment of the interest on which needed vigilant looking after, to fostering his colony of Ferney, to speculations in ships and merchandize sent to India from Cadiz by the mercantile house there with which he had a very long and profitable connection. Whatever of interest was published in Paris and elsewhere he read, and with a voluminous correspondence to carry on—he speaks at one time of writing twenty letters a day—among his correspondents being Frederick and Catherine, German princes and French statesmen, *Philosophes* like D'Alembert—he had always a couple or more of tragedies on hand, and some treatise or pamphlet against the *Infâme*, and the iniquities of French criminal jurisprudence. Still the wonder grows how an octogenarian, and he often an invalid, could at one and the same time do so much and do it so well.

Louis XV. died in May, 1774, not at all regretted by his people, or by the titular gentleman of his bed-chamber at Ferney, who wrote on him, however, an insincere panegyric, which was read at a sitting of the French Academy. Like the rest of the world, Voltaire welcomed the accession of Louis XVI. as the dawn of a hopeful era for France and the *Philosophes*, and great was his joy at the accession of the wise and reforming Turgot to the virtual controller-generalship of finances. Turgot was an admirer of Voltaire, and there was a friendly exchange of letters between them, the patriarch saluting each of the minister's reforms, and the minister sympathetically aiding Voltaire in his efforts for the benefit of the Pays de Gex. Turgot, however, was dismissed in 1776, and Voltaire had to console himself as best he could on seeing him succeeded by Necker, also a reformer and a Protestant.

It was about this time that a new and bright star

appeared in the domestic firmament of Ferney in the person of a Mademoiselle de Varicourt, young, beautiful, graceful, amiable, and intelligent, who accompanied her brothers, *protégés* of Voltaire's, on a visit to Ferney. He was much taken with her brightness and innocence, and so, fortunately, was Madame Denis, still, after a brief intermission some seven years before (due to her violence of temper), at the head of her too fond and indulgent uncle's household. The damsel's family were poor, and she was destined to be a nun. She had no particular liking for the vocation, and Voltaire was only too happy to snatch such a brand from the burning. Madame Denis cheerfully accepted her as a companion, and Voltaire adopted her, christening her *Belle et Bonne*, and finding delight in her pretty, engaging, and caressing ways. He was not, however, long to monopolize the innocent pleasure of her society. Another visitor at Ferney was a young Marquis de Villette, a *roué*, but very wealthy. Fortunately for himself, he not only fell in love with Belle et Bonne, but had the good sense to marry the maiden, whose sole dower was beauty and goodness. Voltaire being delighted with the match, they were married at Ferney in the autumn of 1777, and there they seem to have passed the winter of 1777-8. The Marquis de Villette had an Hotel in Paris where they were to reside, and one can imagine their appeals to their host at Ferney to become their guest. Madame Denis, too, wearied of Ferney where, during the winter, there were few visitors, longed for the excitement and dissipations of Paris, and urged him to a migration. In truth, Voltaire needed no great persuasion to

undertake the journey. He, too, longed to revisit his
still beloved Paris, and the death of Louis XV. had
removed the one main obstacle to the fulfilment of the
wish. Friends in Paris pressed him to come, one of
their pleas being that his presence there would do much
for the arrangements connected with the production of
his new tragedy, "Irène," and he accepted eagerly this
excuse for the visit. He would stay only six weeks, and
then return to them, he assured his colonists at Ferney,
who were sorrow-struck when they heard that he had
decided on leaving them. Preceded by his niece,
Madame Denis, who was accompanied by Belle et
Bonne and her husband, Voltaire left Ferney for Paris
on February 5, 1778. Wherever he paused on the
journey, he was received with acclamations, such as
might have greeted a popular sovereign making a
triumphal progress, and persons of distinction along the
route hastened to pay their homage to him. At one inn
where he passed the night, young enthusiasts donned
waiters' attire that they might attend on him at supper,
and feast their eyes in gazing on the great man. Voltaire, who was accompanied by his secretary and factotum, Wagnière, reached Paris on the afternoon of the
10th of February, and proceeded to the mansion of the
Villettes, whose guest he was to be. The news of his
arrival flew like wild-fire through Paris and to Versailles.
With general joy at the event, there was alarm on the
part of the devout, who began to search the official
registers to discover some trace of an order against his
return ; but Voltaire knew that none such had ever
been issued, and that he could still call himself a gentle-

man-in-ordinary of the royal bed-chamber. Soon a crowd
of visitors, including most of the persons of distinction
then in Paris, filled the *salon* of the Villettes, to pay
their respects to the new-comer, who received them in
his dressing-gown and night-cap, and had the right
word to say to each. Among them were old friends
and new—Richelieu and the octogenarian Madame du
Deffand, D'Alembert and Diderot, Turgot and Franklin.
Franklin, then in Paris as the representative of the
revolted American colonists, brought his grandson, a
youth of seventeen, to receive the blessings of the
patriarch, who, with hands uplifted over his head,
bade him remember the two words, "God and
Liberty."

In his leisure moments Voltaire was diligently polishing
"Irène," and distributing the parts. But the excitement
of the early days of his stay was too much for him. He
began to spit blood, and was confined to bed on the
night of the first public performance of "Irène" at the
Comédie Française, March 16, 1778. All Paris, and
much of Versailles, were there. Marie Antoinette came
with her court, and the Comte d'Artois, afterwards
Charles X. The Queen, indeed, wished Voltaire to
present himself at Versailles, but the devout Louis XVI.
would not hear of it, and expressed himself displeased
that Voltaire should have come to Paris without his permission. Messengers were despatched to tell Voltaire of
the fortunes of the piece as the performance proceeded,
and at its close his friends came to his bedside to congratulate him on its success, one due more to its authorship than to the merits of the piece. From his sick-bed

Voltaire rose once more full of life and spirit, and a fortnight after the first representation of " Irène," there came
for him a day of triumph, such as probably no French
subject had ever before enjoyed. In the afternoon of
Monday the 30th of March, he discarded the dressing-
gown and night-cap, and donned the famous peruke of
Ferney, and the elaborate costume which he wore on
great occasions. Then he drove to a meeting of the
French Academy at the Louvre, through a crowd of
acclaiming spectators, so dense that the carriage could
only with difficulty penetrate it. The Academy honoured
him as it had never honoured a foreign sovereign who
visited it, its members (only the bishops and other ecclesiastics among them being absent) coming in a body to
receive him. During the sitting they elected him
"director" for the ensuing three months; by his acceptance of the office he pledging himself to delay for that
period his return to Ferney. Soon after the close of the
sitting he re-entered his carriage to drive to the Comédie
Française, where it was known he was to witness the
sixth representation of his own " Irène." The crowd,
which collected along his route to the Louvre, had now
increased enormously, and shouted " Vive Voltaire " as
the carriage slowly pierced its way through the immense
mass. Some jumped upon the wheels of his carriage to
get a better view of him, and some pulled hairs from the
fur cloak which the Empress Catherine had given him,
to be preserved like the relics of a saint. At the theatre
he took his seat in the box belonging to the gentlemen
of the royal bed-chamber, between his niece and Belle
et Bonne. He wished to sit behind them, but the cries

of the pit forced him to the front of the box, and com-
pelled him to wear a crown of laurel, which he had
modestly removed when placed on his head by one of
the actors just after he had entered. By this time the
closely-packed house was wildly excited by the presence
of the idol of the moment. It was with difficulty that
the performance of "Irène" could be begun, and it
was applauded without being listened to. When at last
the curtain fell, the enthusiastic hand-clappings and
stamping began again. Behind the curtain the actors
improvised a demonstration of their own. The bust of
Voltaire was brought from the lobby and placed on its
pedestal, actors and actresses grouped themselves in a
semi-circle round it, with garlands in their hands, the
soldiers who had figured in "Irène" formed a back-
ground, and the curtain rose. An actor stepped forward
and crowned the bust. The whole house shouted for
Voltaire, who appeared, with tears in his eyes, and, over-
come with emotion, bowed till his head touched the
front of the box. Then the Madame Vestris of that day
who played *Irène*, came forward and recited a few improvised verses eulogistic of the hero of the evening. They
were received with frantic enthusiasm, and had to be
repeated. One actress proceeded to kiss the bust, and
her comrades followed her example. Marie Antoinette
and the Comte d'Artois had come from Versailles that
evening to the opera, but the Count left it for the
Comédie Française, where he was one of the leaders of
the applause. Little could he have foreseen that, fifty-
two years afterwards, he was to be hurled from the throne
of France through his subservience to the very *Infâme*,

the great assailant of which he was delighting to honour
on that spring night of 1778.

All this excitement told on the frame of a man of
eighty-four, who had not long before been prostrate on a
sick bed. Voltaire himself felt that a return to Ferney
would be best for him, and to that prudent course he
was energetically urged by Tronchin, the chief of his two
Paris physicians. Tronchin, who was previously his
physician at Geneva, had now for some time been settled
in Paris. He was a man of imperious disposition, and
evidently with very little heart. Before Voltaire's arrival
in Paris there had been a coolness between them : Voltaire the man he never seems to have liked, his intellectual sympathies being much more with the semi-orthodox
party at Geneva than with an audacious assailant of the
Infâme, and it will be seen, before long, that, therefore,
his illustrious patient's memory suffered injury at his
hands. But undoubtedly when he urged a speedy return
to Ferney he gave Voltaire the best possible advice, and
such sensible friends as D'Alembert wished that he would
take it. On the other hand, there were undoubtedly
sincere friends of Voltaire's who thought that he would
not be happy again out of Paris, and above all his niece,
the flaunting, flirting, selfish Madame Denis, was for
having him remain in the great city, in comparison with
which Ferney had become more than ever to her
insufferably dull. Except for his health's sake, Voltaire
himself was loth to leave Paris, where he was caressed
and flattered. At last, drawn this way and that, he resolved
upon a compromise. He would buy a house in the Rue
de Richelieu for the joint lives of himself and his niece.

During four months of the year he would occupy it, and
the other eight he would spend at Ferney. Meanwhile
he went about, and two of his movements deserve
recording. One was a visit to the Academy of Sciences,
at which Franklin was to be present. The usual crowd
accompanied him as he went along on foot, and some
one in it, to whom his fame seems to have been unknown, asking what it was all about, he received the
memorable reply : " It is M. de Voltaire. He is the
defender of the unfortunate and oppressed ; it was he
who saved the Calas and the Sirvens." " In the streets,"
the not very sympathetic Madame du Deffand wrote to
her cynical friend Horace Walpole, " he is followed by
the populace, who call him the man of the Calas
(*l'homme aux Calas*). It is only the Court which will
not join in the enthusiasm about him." At the Academy
of Sciences Voltaire and Franklin shook hands, but the
spectators were not satisfied, and they were told to
embrace each other in the French fashion, upon which
they kissed each other's cheeks. According to John
Adams, one of the founders of the American Republic,
who was present, the cry immediately spread through the
whole kingdom (!) " How charming it was to see Solon
and Sophocles embrace ! " This was in the first week
of April ; in the last week of the month he attended a
sitting of the French Academy, and delivered, with
the energy of a man of thirty, a vehement address
on a scheme which he had formed for the compilation
of a new French dictionary, to be undertaken by the
Academy itself. Each of the letters of the alphabet was
to be assigned to a member, and Voltaire offered to

execute the letter A. Before long the scheme was formally approved by the Academy, but Voltaire saw that many of the members were lukewarm, and resolved to stimulate them, if possible, by composing an elaborate dissertation on the necessity for such a work.

By this time he ought to have been on his way to Ferney. But a new and powerful motive had, unfortunately for him, interfered to prevent the journey. Rightly or wrongly, he had been informed that though he would not be expelled from Paris, yet that if he left it, an order would be issued forbidding his return. His visit to Paris had not been one altogether of triumph. The King, displeased with his return, would not give him the slightest countenance. From more than one pulpit his presence in Paris was protested against. An ex-Jesuit abbé thundered in the pulpit of the château of Versailles itself against Voltaire, without directly naming him, and with a distinct reference to the scene at the Comédie Française, vented his indignation at the spectacle of preachers of irreligion receiving crowns instead of punishment. "We are accused of intolerance," said this reverend gentleman. "Ah! do they not know that charity has its fits of passion, and zeal its feeling of vengeance?" To those of his friends who urged that such diatribes ought to hasten his departure, Voltaire replied that, on the contrary, they ought to defer it. It would never do to have it said that a *Philosophe* had been put to flight by the homilies of an ex-Jesuit abbé. One hold the French ecclesiastics had over Voltaire. They could refuse an impenitent *Philosophe* burial in consecrated ground, as they had refused it to Vol-

taire's early friend, Adrienne Lecouvreur, the brilliant
actress, and there were then no cemeteries in France
that were not consecrated. When he came to Paris,
feeling at his age the uncertainty of life, he feared that if
he died there, his remains might be thrown into the
kennel, and during the first serious illness of his visit, he
asked the advice of the prudent D'Alembert, who advised
him to make a kind of peace or truce with the Church.
It was not the first time that Voltaire had made an
attempt of the kind, once at least with an unnecessary
flagrancy that scandalized D'Alembert himself. In Paris
Voltaire took the advice. of his *philosophe*-friend, and
signed a declaration to the effect that he had made his
confession to a certain Abbé Gaultier (who had been an
importunate visitor) and that "if God disposes of me, I
die in the Catholic religion in which I was born, hoping
that the divine mercy will deign to pardon my faults, and
if I have ever scandalized the Church, I ask pardon of
God and of it." This statement made a good deal of
noise in Paris, not of a kind complimentary to the
penitent. His factotum Wagnière, who was a Protestant,
was very indignant at it, and at the way in which clerics
were pestering his master. A few days afterwards he
persuaded Voltaire to give him something in writing
with which he could confront the enemy in case of his
master's death. The result was the following brief confession of faith, in Voltaire's own handwriting : "I die,
adoring God, loving my friends, not hating my enemies,
and detesting superstition." The retractation given to
the Abbé Gaultier, was not satisfactory to him, and
moreover the *curé* of St. Sulpice, Voltaire's parish for

the nonce, who regarded the abbé as an interloper, made his appearance on the scene with offers of spiritual service. But Voltaire was well again and evaded both *abbé* and *curé*. A certain personage was once sick, and wished to be a saint. We all know how his mood changed as soon as he was convalescent.

When Voltaire set himself to the ten or twelve hours' labour of composing the disquisition in support of his project of a new French dictionary, he drank imprudently a number of cups of coffee, partly as a stimulus, and partly to keep himself awake. For the latter object they were only too successful. A long fit of sleeplessness supervened, just when a return of his painful strangury made sleep more than ever desirable. He appears to have been thus attacked about the 12th of May, and the sequel must be pieced together out of various and sometimes conflicting accounts leading up to the last scene of all, the incidents of which have been the subject-matter of much controversy. Feeling extremely ill, he retired to his bed, where he became very feverish. Probably because Tronchin would have said, " Did I not tell you how it would be if you rejected my advice, and prevented him from returning to Ferney?" the Swiss physician was not at once called in, as he ought to have been. Madame Denis sent, however, for an apothecary who supplied some liquid said to be very acrid, the administration of which to the patient brought on violent pains. The Duc de Richelieu, who called to see him in the evening, recommended a preparation of opium which he had himself used during attacks of gout, and after having taken some of it, Voltaire appears to have procured more opium from the apothecary, and to have swallowed it in large doses. It is now that Tronchin re-appears on the scene, to find the poor old gentleman in a state of violent febrile and mental exaltation. What Tronchin said of him at the time must be carefully noted, for much has been made by Voltaire's enemies of this physician's account of his last days. " Voltaire is very ill," Tronchin wrote to his brother at Geneva; "if he dies gaily as he promised I shall be much mistaken;" and then follows a malignant prediction that Voltaire would die the death of a coward. Whether as a coward or not, Voltaire was soon to die. His stomach, we are told, was paralyzed by the quantity of opium which he had taken, and rejected any nourishment, liquid or solid. The delirium which preceded his last days was not continuous. " I conversed with him," La Harpe says, "for a quarter of an hour, and he spoke almost as usual, but with some difficulty and very slowly." A fortnight or so after the commencement of the fatal illness, the dying man was roused from his torpor by some glad tidings which beautifully brightened his waning existence. Whole days were fleeting on without a word from him, or any sign of wakeful and sentient consciousness, when on the 26th of May the news was brought to him that the younger Lally was at last successful, and that the Council of State had cancelled the iniquitous sentence on his father, pronounced and carried out fifteen years before. Voltaire had exerted himself strenuously to procure the reversal of the sentence, and among the last words which he may be said to have written were these, which he dictated when welcoming the announcement:

"The dying man revives on hearing this great news. He embraces very tenderly M. de Lally. He sees that the King is the defender of justice. He will die happy."

The end came on May 30, 1778. The Abbé Gaultier and the *curé* of Saint Sulpice arrived with a retractation, hoping that Voltaire would sign it, and then receive the last sacraments. The retractation was not to be signed ; the sacraments were not to be received. According to La Harpe's account, which appears to be the most trustworthy of any, when the two priests entered the sickroom, their presence was announced to him. It was some time before he understood what was said. At last he replied, "Assure them of my respect." The *curé* of Saint Sulpice came near him and said : "M. de Voltaire, your life is about to end. Do you acknowledge the divinity of Jesus Christ ? " The dying man twice repeated the words, " Jesus Christ! Jesus Christ!" then he stretched out his hand as it were to push back the *curé*, saying, " Let me die in peace." "You see he is not in his senses," the *curé* said to the *abbé*, and both of them left the room. His nurse came towards the bed, and pointing to the two priests as they departed, Voltaire exclaimed in a rather loud voice, "I am dead." But he lingered on for hours, breathing his last a little after eleven at night. The alleged reply of Voltaire to the *curé's* question, just given, "In God's name do not talk to me of that man" ("Au nom de dieu, ne me parlez pas de cet homme là ! ") is, it has been seen, very different from that reported by La Harpe.

The accounts of Voltaire's death, as one of agonized remorse, given by his enemies, or rather perhaps by prejudiced if ardent believers in the creed which he attacked, are mainly mythical. The only authority that can now be, with the slightest show of reason, appealed to in their support, is that of Tronchin. It has, however, been seen with what malignity he predicted for his patient an unhappy death, and it is evident that he would have only been too glad to be able to announce the fulfilment of his inhuman prophecy. But, as it happened, Tronchin was not with Voltaire at the time, or even on the day of his death. Some days before it, he found his patient in a state of delirious excitement, full of the project of the Academy's dictionary, and enraged at the unwillingness of several of his colleagues to co-operate with him in the task. Describing, in a rather goody letter, written June 27, 1778, nearly a month after his patient's death, and addressed to the quasi-orthodox Charles Bonnet at Geneva, no friend or admirer of Voltaire, who had laughed (in print) at some of his theories, Tronchin slides from a report of Voltaire's expressions of indignation at the sluggards of the Academy, to speaking of "the drugs and the follies," which, before he himself was called in, "hastened his death, and which threw him into a state of despair and of the most frightful insanity." Undoubtedly, too, in a letter to Tronchin, written during Voltaire's illness by the friendly D'Alembert, occur the following somewhat significant sentences : "What it is of most importance for you to do at present is to tranquillize him, if it is possible, as to his condition real or supposed. Yesterday I spent some time with him. He appeared to me very much alarmed not only by that condition, but by the disagreeable consequences which it might involve."

But Tronchin's statements in regard to an episode of delirious frenzy, and D'Alembert's partial confirmation of them, have nothing to do with Voltaire's last moments. D'Alembert, in a letter to Frederick, written after Voltaire's death, thus recorded the impression made on him by the dying man. Having described the stupefying effects of the opium, which left his head clear only for brief intervals, D'Alembert, who saw him during one of them, proceeds :—

" He recognized me and even spoke to me some friendly words. But the moment after, he fell back into his state of stupor, for he was almost always dying. He awoke only to complain, and to say, that 'he had come to Paris to die.'" " Throughout his illness," D'Alembert adds, " he exhibited, to the extent which his condition permitted, much tranquillity of mind, although he seemed to regret life. I saw him again the day before his death, and to some friendly words of mine he replied, pressing my hand, ' You are my consolation.' The state in which he was gave me so much pain, and he had such difficulty in expressing himself, even in monosyllables, that I had not strength to continue contemplating the spectacle which he presented. The sight of that great man dying affected me so profoundly, and so vivid an impression of it has remained with me, that it will never be effaced. It was an object which suggested to me the saddest reflections on the nothingness of life, and of glory, and on the woful condition of humankind."

The heads of the French Church, supported by the King, refused the deceased *Philosophe* burial in consecrated ground. Letters were even sent to the Bishop of Annecy, in whose diocese Ferney was, enjoining him to prohibit the *curé* thereof from giving Voltaire's remains Christian burial. Voltaire's nephew, the Abbé Mignot, son of the sister whose death he lamented when an exile in

England, held a ruined abbey at Scellières, in Champagne,
near the village of Romilli—a hundred miles or so from
Paris—where there were also a church and a monastery.
In hot haste the Abbé Mignot huried off thither, and
showing the prior of the monastery Voltaire's profession
of faith, and a government order sanctioning the removal
of his remains to Ferney, procured their burial in the
church, on the understanding that this was only their
temporary resting-place on the way to Ferney. The
abbé had not been much too quick, for on the day of
the interment the bishop of the diocese wrote to the
prior, forbidding the burial without consulting himself.
There was even some talk of having the body exhumed.
At Romilli, however, it was allowed to rest until 1791,
when it was conveyed in a sarcophagus to Paris, and
received there with immense revolutionary enthusiasm.
With great pomp—Belle et Bonne, accompanied by a
little daughter and two female members of the Calas
family, figuring in the procession—it was taken to and
deposited in the Pantheon. But at the return of the
Bourbons to Paris in April, 1814, a party of French
royalist and Roman Catholic zealots, there is reason to
believe, regarding the Pantheon, which had become a
church, as desecrated by being the resting-place of Voltaire
and Rousseau, at dead of night extracted their remains
from their leaden coffins, and buried them at two in the
morning in a piece of waste ground opposite Bercy. In
1864, during the Third Empire, Voltaire's sarcophagus
was opened by order of the Government, and found to be
empty.

Voltaire, by his will, made Madame Denis his chief

legatee, and she thus inherited an income of £3,500, in life-annuities, another, from permanent investments, of half that sum, and more than £10,000 in ready money. She married a respectable nobody, twenty years younger than herself, and sold Ferney to the Marquis de Villette, who let it to an Englishman. Villette became with 1789 an ardent revolutionist, and it was he who first suggested the translation of Voltaire's remains to Paris. His revolutionary ardour cooled with the massacres of September, against which, as deputy of the Oise, he protested, and he voted against the execution of Louis XVI. He escaped the guillotine by dying in July, 1793. Belle et Bonne, left a widow at thirty-six, led a happy life, alternating between her Château of Villette and a house in Paris, where, until her death, she received visits from distinguished foreigners curious to see a lady who had been the friend and favourite of Voltaire. Among these visitors soon after the Restoration of 1815, was Lady Morgan, who, in her book on France, represents her as still Bonne though no longer Belle, and as the centre of a brilliant circle. Lady Morgan described her house in Paris as being a sort of Temple to Voltaire, in which were set out all sorts of memorials and relics of her benefactor, copies of his works, MS. letters, his writing-desk, the rich *robe-de-chambre* in which he had received his visitors in the *salon* of her husband's Hotel, and the very wreath with which he had been crowned on the great night of his appearance at the Comédie Française to witness the performance of his own "Irène." She had watched by the dying Voltaire's bedside, and this was her report to Lady Morgan : "To his last

moment everything he said and did breathed the
benevolence and goodness of his character. All announced in him tranquillity, peace, resignation, except
a little movement of ill-humour which he showed to the
curé of Saint Sulpice, when he begged him to withdraw
and said, 'Let me die in peace.'" Belle et Bonne
herself survived until 1822.

A hundred years after Voltaire's death, its first
centenary was celebrated with great enthusiasm throughout the France of the Third Republic. By 1878, and to
an extent that would have satisfied Voltaire himself, to
whose influence the change was largely due, the Church
in France had been subordinated to the State, and shorn
of its old power of persecuting thinkers during life, and
insulting their remains after death. Editions upon
editions of Voltaire's works had been issued in France
since the Restoration, and in spite of attacks upon him
as a free-thinker by Roman Catholic writers of renown,
while the literary leaders of the advanced republicans
depreciated him on the very plausible ground of his
alleged lack of sympathy with "the people," his
countrymen felt and acknowledged that to him, in the
first instance, was due much of the liberty which so
many revolutions had procured them. The chief French
panegyric or the occasion of Voltaire's centenary was
pronounced by Victor Hugo, who, when a royalist, had
disparaged him, and who now spoke of him as completing
the work begun by the founder of Christianity. "Jesus
wept; Voltaire smiled"—and so forth. From the
rhapsodies of Voltaire's countrymen let us turn to the
words of truth and soberness spoken, ten years earlier,

by a man of science belonging to a nation which had no special reason for doing honour to the memory of Voltaire, the maligner of the memory of its greatest king. A hundred and five years after Voltaire quitted Berlin for ever, the Prussians celebrated, in the last week of January, 1868, the 156th anniversary of the birth of Frederick the Great. At the celebration of it by the Berlin Academy of Science—through his attack on whose President, Voltaire deprived himself of an enviable home in Prussia—its secretary, a distinguished man of science, Du Bois Reymond, delivered before it an address on Voltaire's scientific work, to which, as has been already hinted, he did generous justice. "When we compare," he said in the course of this address, "the immeasurable fame of Voltaire during the eighteenth century—a fame which at last raised him to be a genuine power—with the slight appreciation of him during the first half of the present century, there is presented a two-fold problem of high interest in the history of literature and culture. We have to investigate the reason for the change, and from the stand-point of to-day to place anew on a firm footing the genuine worth and totality of the influence exerted by this extraordinary man. That his poetry is antiquated, that his theory of art is very limited, that his philosophy is shallow, that the weaknesses of his character have been published to the world, all this will not explain why most of us came to regard him as so un-important, and with such indifference. Paradoxical as it may sound, the real cause of this may be that we are all, more or less, Voltairians—Voltairians without knowing it, and without being called such. For we are such only as regards that which was eternally true in Voltairism, and it is only (as Voltaire himself has finely remarked) the adherents of a disputed doctrine who are named after its original author. We have been so thoroughly imbued by him, that the ideal benefits for which he strove throughout a long life, with unwearied zeal, with passionate devotion, with every weapon of the intellect, above all, with his terrible mockery—that toleration, spiritual freedom, human dignity, justice, have become, as it were, an element of our natural life, like the air we breathe, on which we bestow a thought only when we are deprived of it. In one word, whatever once, as it flowed from Voltaire's pen, was the most audacious Thinking, is a common-place to-day." Such a testimony by an eminent modern German to the value of the famous Frenchman's achievements, may fitly close this unavoidably imperfect sketch of Voltaire's prolonged and complex career.

THE END.

INDEX.

BIBLIOGRAPHY.

BY

JOHN P. ANDERSON

(British Museum).

[*This list of the works of Voltaire is far from being complete, many of his minor works being omitted. It has also been found necessary to give only the first edition of the separate works in the original.*]

I. WORKS.

Œuvres de M. Arouet de Voltaire. La Haye, 1728, 12mo.

This is the first edition of the works of Voltaire, and contains the *Œdipe, Le Ballet de la Sottise*, a *Sonnet* and two *Couplets* (not by Voltaire), *Hérode et Mariamne, Le Mauvais Ménage* (by Legrand and Dominique), *La Henriade* and its *Critique*.

Among numerous other editions may be mentioned, Amsterdam, 1732, 8vo, 2 vols.; Amsterdam, 1736, 12mo, 4 vols.; Amsterdam, 1738-39, 4 vols.; Londres, 1746, 12mo, 6 vols.; Dresde, 1748, 8vo, 8 vols.; Dresde, 1756, 12mo, 5 vols.; Genève, 1757-76, 8vo, 43 vols.; Amsterdam, 1764, 12mo, 18 vols.; Lausanne, 1770-80, 8vo, 57 vols.; Liège, 1771-77, 12mo, 30 vols.; Genève, 1775, 8vo, 40 vols.; Kehl, 1785-1801, 8vo, 72 vols.; Paris, 1792-1800, 8vo, 55 vols.; Paris, 1800-20, 18mo, 63 vols.; Paris, 1817-20, 12mo, 56 vols.; Paris, 1819-23, 8vo, 66 vols.; Paris, 1823-27, 8vo, 72 vols.; Paris, 1824-32, 8vo, 97 vols.; Paris, 1829-34, 8vo, 70 vols.; Paris, 1852, 8vo, 13 vols.; Paris, 1877-85, 8vo, 52 vols.

The Works of Mr. de Voltaire. Translated from the French. With notes, historical and critical. By Dr. Smollett and others. Vol. 1-25. London, 1761-65, 12mo.

The second and remaining vols. bear the name of Dr. T. Francklin, in addition to that of Dr. Smollett, on the title-page. Neither of these appear to have taken any part in the translation.

The Works of Mr. de Voltaire, translated from the French, with notes, historical, critical, and explanatory, by T. Francklin, T. Smollett, and others. A new edition. 38 vols. London, 1778-81, 12mo.

Works translated from the French, with notes, critical and explanatory, by William Campbell, J. Johnson, and others. Under the direction of W. Kenrick. 14 vols. London, 1779-80, 8vo.

II. SMALLER COLLECTIONS.

The Dance ; Pythagoras ; Plato's Dream : [the last two translated from Voltaire] and other poems. By S. Baruh. London, 1825, 12mo.

Le dernier volume des Œuvres de Voltaire. Contes, Comédies, etc. Paris, 1862, 8vo.

Dialogues et Entretiens philosophiques par Voltaire. 2 vols. Paris, 1820, 18mo.

Dictionnaire historique des événements remarquables, etc. Paris, 1824, 8vo.

Élite de Poésies Fugitives. 5 vols. Londres, 1764-1770, 12mo.

L'Esprit de M. de Voltaire. [Paris] 1759, 8vo.

Esprit de Voltaire, etc. Paris, 1855, 18mo.

Extraits de Voltaire. Lectures littéraires, philosophiques et morales, etc. Paris, 1886, 18mo.

Le Joli Recueil, ou l'Histoire de la Querelle Littéraire où les auteurs s'amusent en amusant le public. 2 pts. Genève, 1760-61, 8vo.

Mélanges de Littérature et de Morale. 2 vols. Paris, 1833, 8vo.

Mélanges de Littérature pour servir de supplément à le dernier édition des Œuvres de M. de Voltaire. —, 1768, 12mo.

Mélanges de Littérature, d'Histoire, de Philosophie, etc. [Paris] 1761, 8vo.

Troisième Suite des Mélanges de Poésies, de Littérature, d'Histoire et de Philosophie. [Paris, 1761] 8vo.

Nouveaux Mélanges, Philosophiques, Historiques, Critiques, etc. 19 pts. [Geneva] 1765-1776, 8vo.

——Dialogues and Essays, Literary and Philosophical. Glasgow, 1764, 12mo.

——Miscellanies ; Philosophical, Literary, Historical, etc. Translated by J. Perry. London, 1779, 8vo.

——Philosophical, Literary, and Historical Pieces. Translated by W. S. Kenrick. London, 1780, 8vo.

Mélanges de Philosophie, par Voltaire. 5 vols. Paris, 1837, 8vo.

Mélanges de Poésies et de pièces fugitives de divers genres en vers. 2 vols. Lausanne, 1772, 8vo.

Mélanges de Politique et de Législation. Paris, 1836, 8vo.

Mélanges historiques. 4 vols. Paris, 1822, 18mo.

Œuvres badines de Voltaire. Paris, 1820, 18mo.

Œuvres Choisies de M. de Voltaire. 5 vols. —, 1756, 12mo.

Œuvres Choisies de M. de Voltaire. Avignon, 1761, 8vo.

Œuvres Choisies de Voltaire. 33 vols. Paris, 1838, 8vo.

Œuvres Choisies de Voltaire, publiées avec prefaces, notes, et variantes, par George Bengesco, etc. Paris, 1887, etc., 8vo.

Œuvres de Voltaire. Nouvelle édition avec des notes et des observations critiques par M. Palissot. 55 vols. Paris, 1792, etc., 8vo.

Œuvres de Voltaire. 21 vols. Paris, 1817, 12mo.

Œuvres Melées d'un auteur célèbre qui s'est retiré de France. Berlin, 1753, 8vo.

Opuscules poétiques, ou le plus charmant des recueils, contenant plusieurs pièces fugitives de M. de Voltaire, qui n'ont pas encore vu le jour. Amsterdam [1773], 24mo.

Ouvrages Classiques de l'élégant poète M. Arouet, fameux sous le nom de Voltaire. Nouvelle édition. Tom. 1. Oxford, 1771, 8vo.

Les Pensées de M. de Voltaire. 2 pts. —, 1765, 12mo.

Pensées et Maximes de Voltaire, recueillies par René Périn. 2 vols. Paris, 1821, 18mo.

Pensées Philosophiques de M. de Voltaire, ou Tableau Encyclopédique des Connaissances humaines, contenant l'esprit, principes, maximes, etc., de Voltaire. —, 1766, 8vo.

Pensées, Remarques et Observations de Voltaire. Ouvrage posthume. Paris [1802], 8vo.

Pièces inédites de Voltaire, imprimées d'après les manuscrits originaux, pour faire suite aux différentes éditions publiées jusqu'à ce jour. Paris, 1820, 8vo.

Pièces Nouvelles de M. de Voltaire. Amsterdam, 1769, 8vo.

Pièces recueillies de MM. de Voltaire et Piron, etc. —, 1744, 8vo.

La Philosophie de Voltaire, avec une introduction et des notes, par Ern. Bersot. Paris, 1848, 18mo.

La Philosophie et le Fanatisme, par Voltaire. Paris, 1876, 18mo.

Poétique de M. de Voltaire, ou Observations recueillies de ses ouvrages concernant la versification Française, etc. Genève, 1766, 8vo.

Le Portefeuille Trouvé, ou Tablettes d'un Curieux. 2 vols. Genève, 1757, 12mo.

Premier, Second, Troisième, etc. — Dixième Recueil de Nouvelles Pièces Fugitives de M. de Voltaire. 10 vols. Genève, 1762-1775, 8vo.

Recueil de divers traités sur l'éloquence et la poésie, par Fénelon, de Sillery . . . et Voltaire. 2 vols. Amsterdam, 1731, 12mo.

Recueil de Pièces en vers et en prose. Amsterdam, 1750, 12mo.

Recueil de Pièces fugitives en prose et en vers. [Paris] 1740, 8vo.

Recueil de Pièces fugitives. 12 vols. Berlin, 1766, 8vo.

Recueil d'Épîtres, Satires, Contes, Odes et Pièces fugitives du poète philosophe, etc. Londres, 1771, 8vo.

Résumé de l'Histoire Générale, par Voltaire. Paris, 1826, 18mo.

Rhétorique et Poétique de Voltaire, etc. Paris, 1828, 8vo.

Le Trésor du Parnasse, ou le plus joli des Recueils. 6 vols. Londres, 1762-1770, 12mo.

Voltaire. Édition publiée par M. Touquet. 15 vols. Paris, 1820, 12mo.

Voltaire en un volume, par J. B. Gouriet. Paris, 1821, 12mo.

Voltaire. Œuvres Choisies. Édition de Centénaire, 30 Mai, 1878. Paris, 1878, 8vo.

Voltaire. Œuvres Choisies. Paris [1889], 8vo.

Voltaire Chrétien. Preuves tirées de ses ouvrages, suivies de pièces religieuses et morales du même auteur. Paris, 1820, 18mo.

Voltairiana, or Recueil choisi des bon mots, plaisanteries, sarcasmes, etc., de Voltaire, etc. Paris, 1819, 8vo.

Voltairiana; selected and translated by Mary Julia Young. 4 vols. London, 1805, 12mo.

III. DRAMATIC WORKS.

Le Théâtre de M. de Voltaire. Nouvelle édition qui contient un recueil complet de toutes les pièces de théâtre qui l'auteur a données jusqu' ici. 4 vols. Amsterdam, 1753, 16mo.

Ouvrages Dramatiques avec les pièces relatives à chacun. 4 vols. [Geneva] 1756, 8vo.

Supplément aux Œuvres Dramatiques de Voltaire. Genève, 1763, 8vo.

Œuvres de Théâtre de M. de Voltaire. 5 vols. Paris, 1764, 12mo.

Œuvres de Théâtre. 6 vols. Paris, 1767, 4to.

Le Théâtre de M. de Voltaire. 6 vols. Amsterdam, 1768-70, 16mo.

Théâtre Complet de M. de Voltaire. 8 vols. Lausanne, 1772, 8vo.

Les Chefs-d'Œuvre dramatiques de M. de Voltaire. 3 vols. Genève, 1778, 12mo.

Théâtre de Voltaire augmenté de deux pièces qui ne se trouvent pas dans les éditions précédentes. 10 vols. Londres, 1782, 18mo.

——Another edition. 8 vols. Amsterdam, 1782, 18mo.

Œuvres de Théâtre. 8 vols. Neufchâtel, 1783, 8vo.

Théâtre Complet de M. de Voltaire conforme à la dernière édition. 9 vols. Caen, 1788, 12mo.

Théâtre de Voltaire. 12 vols. Paris [1801], 18mo.

Théâtre de Voltaire. 5 vols. Paris [1803], 32mo.

Chefs-d'Œuvre dramatiques de Voltaire. 4 vols. Paris, 1808, 18mo.

Théâtre Choisi de Voltaire. 3 vols. Paris, 1823, 18mo.

Chefs-d'Œuvre dramatiques de Voltaire. 6 vols. Paris, 1824, 32mo.

Théâtre Choisi de Voltaire. 7 vols. Paris, 1831-32, 8vo.

Chefs-d'Œuvre Dramatique de Voltaire. 4 vols. Paris, 1838, 18mo.

Théâtre de Voltaire. Paris, 1842, 12mo.

Chefs-d'Œuvre Dramatiques de Voltaire. Paris, 1847, 8vo.
Théâtre Choisi de Voltaire. Paris, 1849, 12mo.
Théâtre de Voltaire. Paris, 1854, 8vo.
Théâtre Choisi de Voltaire. Paris, 1870, 18mo.
Théâtre Complet de Voltaire. Paris, 1873, 8vo.
Théâtre de Voltaire. Paris [1874], 18mo.
Théâtre de Voltaire. Paris, 1875, 18mo.
Théâtre Choisi de Voltaire. Paris, 1876, 12mo.

———

Adélaïde du Guesclin, tragédie représentée pour la première fois le 18 Janvier 1734, etc. Paris, 1765, 8vo.
Alzïre ou les Américains, tragédie représentée pour la première fois à Paris, le 27 Janvier 1736. Paris, 1736, 8vo.
——Alzira : a tragedy [translated from Voltaire by A. Hill]. London, 1736, 8vo.
——Another edition. Dublin, 1736, 8vo.
——Another edition. [London, 1760] 8vo.
——Another edition. London, 1779, 8vo.
——Another edition. London, 1791, 8vo.
In vol. vii. of "Bell's British Theatre."
Le Brutus de M. de Voltaire. Avec un discours sur la tragédie. Paris, 1731, 8vo.
——Discourse on Tragedy, etc. London, 1731, 8vo.
Le Caffé ou L'Écossaise, comédie par M. Hume, traduite en Français. Londres, 1760, 12mo.
——The Coffee-House ; or fair fugitive. A comedy of five acts, written by Mr. Voltaire [entitled "Le Café, ou l'Écossaise."]. London, 1760, 8vo.
Charlot, ou la Comtesse de Givri. Pièce dramatique, etc. Genève, 1767, 8vo.
Le Comte de Boursoufle, ou les Agréments du Droit d'Aînesse, comédie. Paris [1826], 32mo.
This is *L'Échange* under another title.
Le Comte de Boursoufle, ou Mademoiselle de la Cochonnière : comédie-bouffe en trois actes et en prose, etc. Paris, 1862, 12mo.
This is a new version of *L'Échange*.
Le Dépositaire : comédie en vers et en cinq actes. Genève, 1772, 8vo.
Don Pèdre, roi de Castille, tragédie et autres pièces. [Geneva] 1775, 8vo.
Le Droit du Seigneur : comédie en vers. Genève, 1763, 8vo.
Le Duc d'Alençon, ou les Frères Ennemis, tragédie. Paris, 1821, 8vo.
Le Duc de Foix, tragédie. Paris, 1752, 8vo.
L'Échange, ou quand est-ce qu'on me marie ? Comédie en deux actes. Vienne, 1761, 8vo.
L'Écueil du Sage, comédie. Vienne, 1764, 8vo.
L'Enfant Prodigue : comédie en vers dissillabes représentée sur le théâtre de la Comédie-Française, le 10 Octobre, 1736. Paris, 1738, 8vo.
——The Prodigal. [A prose translation of "L'Enfant Prodigue."] [London, 1750 ?] 8vo.

L'Euvieux: comédie en trois actes et en vers, etc. Paris, 1834, 8vo.

Ériphile, tragédie de M. de Voltaire, représentée par les comédiens ordinaires du roi, le vendredi 7 Mars 1732. Paris, 1779, 8vo.

La Femme qui a raison : comédie en trois actes, en vers. Genève, 1759, 12mo.

Les Guèbres ou la Tolérance : tragédie par M. D * * * M * * *. [Geneva] 1769, 8vo.

Hérode et Mariamne, tragédie. Paris, 1725, 8vo.

L'Indiscret, comédie. Paris, 1725, 8vo.

Irène, tragédie représentée pour la première fois, le 16 Mars 1778. Paris, 1779, 8vo.

Les Loix de Minos ou Astérie; tragédie en cinq actes. Genève, 1773, 8vo.

Mahomet, tragédie, représentée sur le théâtre de la Comédie-Française, le 9 Août, 1742. Bruxelles, 1742, 8vo.
Unauthorised edition.

——Le Fanatisme ou Mahomet le Prophète, tragédie. Amsterdam, 1743, 8vo.
First authorised edition.

——Mahomet the Impostor. A tragedy [adapted from the French of Voltaire] by J. Miller. London, 1744, 8vo.
Numerous editions.

La Mérope Française avec quelques petites pièces de Littérature. Paris, 1744, 8vo.

——Merope ; a tragedy. Translated from the French of M. de Voltaire by J. Theobald, etc. [London, 1744], 8vo.

——Merope. A tragedy [adapted from Voltaire] by Aaron Hill. London, 1749, 8vo.
Numerous editions.

La Mort de César, tragédie. Nouvelle édition, corrigée et augmentée par l'Auteur. Londres, 1736, 8vo.
An unauthorised edition was printed the previous year at Amsterdam.

Nanine, comédie en trois actes, en vers de dix syllabes. Paris, 1749, 8vo.

Octave et le jeune Pompée ou le Triumvirat, avec des remarques sur les proscriptions. Amsterdam, 1767, 8vo.

Œdipe, tragédie en cinq actes, etc. Paris, 1719, 8vo.

Olimpie, tragédie nouvelle de M. de Voltaire, suivie de Remarques historiques. Francfort, 1763, 8vo.

Oreste, tragédie. Paris, 1750, 8vo.

L'Orphelin de la Chine, tragédie représentée pour la première fois à Paris, le 20 Août, 1755. Paris, 1755, 12mo.

——The Orphan of China : a tragedy translated from the French of M. de Voltaire. London, 1756, 8vo.
Numerous editions.

Les Pélopides ou Atrée et Thieste, tragédie. Genève, 1772, 8vo.

La Princesse de Navarre, comédie-ballet. [Paris, 1745] 8vo.

La Prude ou la Gardeuse de Cassette, comédie en cinq actes, en vers, de dix syllabes. Paris, 1759, 8vo.

Rome Sauvée, tragédie. Berlin, 1752, 12mo.

——Rome Preserv'd : a tragedy. Translated from the French of M. de Voltaire. London, 1760, 8vo.

Saül, tragédie tirée de l'écriture
sainte. —, 1755, 8vo.
——Saul: a drama. Translated
from the French of M. de
Voltaire. By Oliver Martext,
of Arden. London, 1820, 8vo.
Les Scythes, tragédie. Nouvelle
édition, corrigée et augmentée
sur celle de Genève. Paris,
1767, 8vo.
La Tragédie de Sémiramis et quelques autres pièces de Littérature. Paris, 1749, 8vo.
——Semiramis: a tragedy. Translated from the French of M. de
Voltaire. London, 1760, 8vo.
——Another edition. Dublin,
1760, 12mo.
Socrate, ouvrage dramatique
traduit de l'Anglais de feu
M. Tompson. Amsterdam,
1759, 12mo.
——Socrates, a tragedy of three
acts, translated from the
French of Monsieur de Voltaire.
London, 1760, 12mo.
Sophonisbe, tragédie de Mairet
réparée à neuf. Paris, 1770,
8vo.
Tancred, tragédie en vers croisés
et en cinq actes, etc. Paris,
1761, 8vo.
——Almida, a tragedy. [Altered
from Voltaire's "Tancrède."]
By a lady [Mrs. Celisia].
London, 1771, 8vo.
Le Temple de la Gloire, fête
donnée à Versailles le 27
Novembre 1745. [Paris, 1745]
8vo.
Fragment de Thérèse. [Paris,
1830] 8vo.
Zayre, tragédie. Rouen, 1733,
8vo.
—— The Tragedy of Zara.
[Adapted from Voltaire's Zaire

by Aaron Hill.] London,
1736, 8vo.
Numerous editions.
——Zaire. A dramatic poem.
In five acts. Translated from
the French tragedy into
English rhyme verse by A.
Wallace. Worthing, 1854,
8vo.
Zulime, tragédie en cinq actes.
Genève, 1761, 8vo.

IV. POETRY.

Mélanges de Poésies, etc. 2 vols.
Lausanne, 1772, 8vo.
——Nouvelle édition considér-
ablement augmentée, etc. 2
vols. [Paris] 1773, 12mo.
Voltaire Poéte. Nouvelle édition,
etc. 15 vols. Paris, 1798, 8vo.
Poésies de Voltaire. 5 vols.
Paris, 1823, 8vo.

La Bataille de Fontenoy. Poème.
Paris, 1745, 4to.
La Begueule, conte moral. 1772,
8vo.
Les Cabales, œuvre pacifique.
—, 1772, 8vo.
Le Cantique des · Cantiques en
vers. Paris, 1759, 8vo.
Ce qui plait aux dames, conte.
Paris, 1764, 8vo.
Les Chevaux et les Ânes ou
Étrennes aux Sots. [—, 1761]
8vo.
Contes de Guillaume Vadé.
[Geneva] 1764, 8vo.
Contes et Poésies diverses. À
La Haye, 1777, 18mo.
Contes et Poésies diverses.
Londres, 1780, 18mo.
Only three copies printed on
vellum, one of which is in the
British Museum Library.

Contes en vers, satires et poésies mêlées de Voltaire. Paris [1800], 18mo.

Contes en vers, satires et poésies mêlées. Paris, 1808, 8vo.

Contes en vers, satires et poésies mêlées. Paris, 1822, 18mo.

Contes, satires, épitres, poésies diverses, etc. Paris, 1841, 12mo.

Poëmes sur le Désastre de Lisbonne et sur la Loi Naturelle, avec des préfaces, des notes, etc. Genève [1756], 8vo.

Poëmes sur la Religion Naturelle et sur la Destruction de Lisbonne. —, 1756, 8vo.

Dialogue de Pégase et du Vieillard. [Geneva, 1774] 8vo.

Le Dimanche ou les Filles de Minée. Poëme adressé par M. de Voltaire, sous le nom de M. de la Visclède, à Madame Harnanche. Londres, 1775, 8vo.

[Discours en vers sur l'Homme.] Épitres sur le Bonheur, la Liberté, et l'Envie. Amsterdam, 1738, 8vo.

These are the first three of the seven "Discours en vers sur l'Homme."

——Epistles translated from the French, or happiness, liberty, and envy. By W. Gordon. London, 1738, 8vo.

——Three epistles in the ethic way. From the French—viz., 1, Happiness; 2, Freedom of will; 3, Envy. London, 1738, 8vo.

A free imitation of Voltaire's "Discours sur l'Homme"; entirely different from Gordon's translation.

Discours en vers sur les Événements de l'Année 1744. Paris, 1744, 8vo.

Épitre de M. de V*** en arrivant dans sa terre près du Lac de

Genève, eu Mars 1755. [—, 1755!] 4to.

Épitre de M. de Voltaire à Mdlle. Clairon. [—, 1761] 8vo.

Epitre de M. de Voltaire à Madame Denis sur l'Agriculture. [—, 1761] 8vo.

Épitre à l'Auteur du livre des Trois Imposteurs. [—, 1769] 8vo.

Épitre au Roi de la Chine sur son Recueil de Vers qu'il a fait imprimer. [—, 1770] 8vo.

Épitre à Horace. [—, 1772] 8vo.

Épitre à un Homme. [Geneva, 1776] 8vo.

Épitres, Satires, Contes, Odes et pièces fugitives du poète philosophe, dont plusieurs n'ont point encore paru, etc. Londres, 1771, 8vo.

Épitres, Stances et Odes. 2 vols. Paris, 1823, 32mo.

Épitres, Satires, Épigrammes de Voltaire, suivis de fragments de la Pucelle. Paris, 1874, 8vo.

La Guerre Civile de Genève, ou les Amours de Robert Covelle. Poëme héroïque. Besançon, 1768, 8vo.

——The Civil War of Geneva; or, the Amours of Robert Covelle, an heroic poem. Translated from the French, by T. Teres. London, 1769, 12mo.

La Ligue ou Henri le Grand. [La Henriade.] Poëme épique. Genève, 1723, 8vo.

La Henriade appeared for the first time under this title.

——La Henriade. Londres, 1728, 4to.

——The Henriade of M. de Voltaire. London, 1729, 8vo.

"No. 1 of the Herculean Labour," by Ozell.

——Henriade, an epick poem translated from the French into English blank verse; to which are now added the argument to each canto, and large notes, historical and critical [by J. Lockman]. London, 1732, 8vo.

——Another edition. London, 1797, 4to.

——Another edition. Translated by D. French, Esq. London, 1807, 8vo.

——Translation of the ninth canto of Voltaire's Henriad. [London] 1812, 16mo.

——Another edition. Translated by C. L. Jones. Mobile, 1834, 12mo.

——The Henriad. [Translated into English verse.] London, 1854, 8vo.

Pp. 377-526 of Captain R. G. Macgregor's " Indian Leisure."

Jean qui pleure et Jean qui rit. Lausanne, 1772, 8vo.

Le Marseillais et le Lion. —, 1768, 8vo.

Le Mondain. [—, 1736 ?] 12mo.

Nouvelle Épitre au Roi par M. de Voltaire. Presentée à Sa Majesté au camp devant Fribourg le 1 Novembre 1744. [Paris, 1744] 4to.

Le Pauvre Diable. Paris, 1758 [1760], 4to.

Poëmes, Épitres et autres Poésies. Genève, 1777, 18mo.

Poëmes, Épitres et autres Poésies. Londres, 1779, 18mo.

Poëmes et Discours en vers de Voltaire. Paris, 1800, 18mo.

Précis de l'Ecclésiaste en vers. Paris, 1759, 8vo.

La Pucelle d'Orléans, poëme héroï-comique, etc. Louvain, 1755, 12mo.

——La Pucelle, or The Maid of Orleans, translated from the French. London, 1781, 4to.

——The Maid of Orleans. Cantos 1 to 5 in English verse. London, 1785, 4to.

——La Pucelle. From the French. The first, second, third, fourth, and fifth cantos. 2 pts. London, 1789, 4to.

——La Pucelle, or the Maid of Orleans, with the author's preface and original notes. (By Lady Charleville.) 2 vols. [Dublin] 1796-97, 8vo. Privately printed.

——The Maid of Orleans, or La Pucelle of Voltaire. Translated into English verse ; with notes by W. H. Ireland. 2 vols. London, 1822, 8vo. Suppressed.

La Religion Naturelle. Poëme en quatre parties. Genève, 1756, 12mo.

La Russe à Paris. [—, 1760] 4to.

Les Sistèmes. [—, 1772] 8vo.

La Tactique. Pièce de vers. [—, 1773 ?] 8vo.

Le Temple du Goust. [Rouen] 1733, 8vo.

——The Temple of Taste. London, 1734, 8vo.

Le Temple de l'Amitié et le Temple du Goût. [Rouen] 1733, 12mo.

Les Trois Empereurs en Sorbonne. —, 1768, 8vo.

La Vanité, par un frère de la doctrine chrétienne. [—, 1760] 4to.

V. HISTORICAL WORKS.

Annales de l'Empire depuis Charlemagne, etc. 2 vols. Bâle, 1753, 12mo.

——Annals of the Empire from the time of Charlemagne, etc. 2 vols. Loudon, 1755, 12mo.

——Annals of the Empire; from the reign of Charlemagne. Translated from the French of Voltaire constituting a part of a complete edition in English of the works of that writer by D. Williams, H. Downman, etc. London, 1781, 8vo.

Essay sur l'Histoire Générale et sur les Mœurs et l'Esprit des Nations, depuis Charlemagne jusqu' à nos jours. 7 vols. [Geneva] 1756, 8vo.

——The General History and State of Europe. 3 vols. Edinburgh, 1758, 8vo.

——An Essay on Universal History; the manners and Spirit of Nations from Charlemagne to Louis XIV. 3 vols. Edinburgh, 1758, 12mo.

——An Essay on Universal History. Translated, with additional notes and chronological tables, by M. Nugent. The third edition, revised. 4 vols. Dublin, 1759, 12mo.

——Another edition. 5 vols. London, 1761, 12mo.

——Another edition. 3 vols. London, 1777, 12mo.

——Another edition. 6 vols. London, 1825, 12mo.

Abrégé de l'Histoire Universelle, depuis Charlemagne jusqu' à Charles V. 3 vols. La Haye, 1753, 12mo.

——The general history and state of Europe from the time of Charlemain to Charles V. With a preliminary view of the Oriental empires. [Translated from the "Abrégé de l'Histoire Universelle.] London, 1754, 8vo.

Histoire de Charles XII., roi de Suède. 2 vols. Basle, 1731, 12mo.

——The History of Charles XII., King of Sweden, translated from the French, etc. 2 pts. London, 1732, 8vo.

——Second edition, corrected. London, 1732, 8vo.

——Third edition. London, 1732, 8vo.

——Fifth edition. 2 pts. London, 1733, 12mo.

——Seventh edition. 2 pts. London, 1740, 12mo.

——The History of Charles XII., King of Sweden, etc. [Translated from the French of Voltaire. By Andrew Henderson ?] London, 1734, 4to.

——Another edition. London, 1739, 12mo.

——Another edition. Glasgow, 1750, 12mo.

——Another edition. A new translation from the last Paris edition. London [1802 ?], 12mo.

——Another edition. Morpeth, 1808, 8vo.

——The history, life, and campaigns of Charles the Twelfth. London, 1853, 8vo.

Vol. i., Biography. The Universal Library.

——Another edition. Edinburgh, 1873, 8vo.

Histoire de la Guerre de 1741. 2 pts. Amsterdam, 1755, 12mo.

——The history of the war of seventeen hundred and forty-one. In 2 parts. London, 1756, 8vo.

——Second edition. In 2 parts. 1756, 8vo.

——Second edition. Carefully revised, etc. Dublin, 1756, 12mo.

——Another edition. [London] 1756, 12mo.

Histoire de l'Empire de Russie sous Pierre le Grand. 2 tom. Genève, 1759-63, 8vo.

——The History of the Russian Empire under Peter the Great. 2 vols. Loudon, 1763, 8vo.

Histoire du Parlement de Paris, par M. L'Abbé Big. 2 vols. Amsterdam, 1769, 8vo.

La Philosophie de l'Histoire. Genève, 1765, 8vo.
This work became in 1769 the Introduction to the "Essai sur les Mœurs" in the quarto edition of the works.

——The Philosophy of History. London, 1766, 8vo.

——Another edition. London, 1822, 8vo.

Le Siècle de Louis XIV., publié par M. de Francheville, etc. 2 vols. Berlin, 1751, 12mo.

——An essay on the age of Louis XIV., by Mr. de Voltaire, being his introduction to the work. Translated from the French by Mr. Lockman. London, 1739, 8vo.

——The Age of Louis XIV. 2 vols. Dublin, 1752, 12mo.

——New edition, corrected by Mr. Chambaud. 2 vols. London, 1753, 12mo.

——The Age of Louis XIV., to which is added an Abstract of the Age of Louis XV., with notes, critical and explanatory, by R. Griffith. 3 vols. London, 1779, 8vo.

Supplément au Siècle de Louis XIV., Catalina, tragédie, et autres pièces du même auteur. Dresde, 1753, 8vo.

Précis du Siècle de Louis XV. Servant de suite au Siècle de Louis XIV. du même auteur. 2 vols. Genève, 1769, 12mo.

——The Age of Louis XV. Being the sequel of the Age of Louis XIV. Translated from the French of M. de Voltaire. 2 vols. London, 1770, 12mo.

——Another edition. 2 vols. London, 1774, 12mo.

VI. PHILOSOPHICAL WORKS.

Dictionnaire Philosophique Portatif. Londres, 1764, 8vo.

——The Philosophical Dictionary for the pocket. Translated, with notes, etc. London, 1765, 8vo.

——Another edition. London [1767], 12mo.

——Philosophical Dictionary; or the opinions of modern philosophers on metaphysical, moral, and political subjects. 4 vols. London, 1786, 12mo.

——Another edition. London, 1796, 12mo.

——Another edition. 2 vols. Edinburgh, 1807, 12mo.

——Another edition. 6 vols. London, 1824, 12mo.

——Another edition. New York, 1835, 12mo.

——Another edition. 2 vols. London, 1843, 12mo.

——Another edition. 2 vols. Boston, 1852, 8vo.

Questions sur l'Encyclopédie par des Amateurs. 9 vols. [Geneva] 1770-72, 8vo.

VII. ROMANCES, TALES, Etc.

Recueil des Romans de M. de Voltaire, contenant Babouc, Memnon, Micromégas, Le Songe de Platon, Les Voyages de Scarmentado, Zadig et Candide. 2 vols. [Paris] 1764, 12mo.

Recueil de Romans Moraux et Philosophiques. 2 vols. .Neufchâtel, 1771, 12mo.

Romans et Contes Philosophiques. 2 vols. Londres, 1775, 12mo. Numerous other editions.

Romances, Tales, and smaller pieces. 2 vols. London, 1794, 8vo.

——Another edition. Romances, Novels, and Tales. 2 vols. London, 1806, 8vo.

The Philosophical Tales, Romances, and Satires of M. de Voltaire. London, 1871, 8vo.

Voltaire's Romances. Translated from the French. A new edition. With numerous illustrations. New York, 1885, 8vo.

Jeannot and Colin—Zadig—Micromegas, etc. (*Leigh Hunt's Classic Tales*, vol. ii.) London, 1807, 12mo.

———

Babouc, or the World as it goes. By Voltaire. To which are added letters concerning his disgrace at the Prussian Court. With his letter to his niece on that occasion, etc. London, 1754, 8vo.
Babouc, ou le Monde Comme il va, first appeared in tom. viii. of the Œuvres de Voltaire, published at Dresden in 1748.

——Another edition. Dublin, 1754, 12mo.

Candide ou l'Optimisme. Traduit

de l'Allemand de M. le docteur Ralph. [Geneva] 1759, 12mo.

——Candid : or, All for the Best. London, 1759, 12mo.

——Another edition. Edinburgh, 1773, 12mo.

——The History of Candid ; or, All for the Best. Translated from the French of M. Voltaire. Cooke's edition. London [1796], 12mo.

——Voltaire's Candide; or, The Optimist, etc. With an introduction by H. Morley. London, 1884, 8vo.
Part of "Morley's Universal Library."

Histoire de Jenni, ou le Sage et l'Athée, par M. Sherloc. Traduit par M. de la Caille. Londres, 1775, 8vo.

——Young James ; or, the Sage and the Atheist. London, 1776, 8vo.

The History of the voyages of Scarmentado : a satire ; translated from the French. London, 1757, 8vo.
The "Histoire des Voyages de Scarmentado" appeared in 1756 in tom. v. of Voltaire's *Œuvres*.

L'Homme aux quarante écus. [Geneva] 1768, 8vo.

——The Man of Forty Crowns. London, 1769, 8vo.

L'Ingénu, histoire véritable tirée des manuscrits du Père Quesnel. Utrecht, 1767, 8vo.

——The Pupil of Nature; a true history, found amongst the papers of Father Quesnel. Translated from the original French [entitled "L'Ingénu," also called "Le Huron"] of M. de Voltaire. London, 1771, 12mo.

——The Sincere Huron, a true history. Translated from the

French by F. Ashmore. London, 1786, 8vo.

——Another edition, London, 1801, 12mo.

Les Lettres d'Amabed, etc. Traduites par l'abbé Tamponet. [Geneva, 1769] 8vo.

Le Micromégas de M. de Voltaire. Londres [1752], 12mo.

——Micromegas: acomicromance. Translated from the French. London, 1753, 12mo.

The Ears of Lord Chesterfield and Parson Goodman. Translated by J. Knight. Bern, 1786, 12mo.

Printed in 1775 in the 17th part of the "Nouveaux Mélanges," pp. 333-362.

——Lord Chesterfield's Ears, a true story. Translated from the French. London, 1826, 8vo.

La Princesse de Babilone. [Geneva], 1768, 8vo.

——The Princess of Babylon. London, 1769, 8vo.

Le Taureau Blanc, traduit du Syriaque par Dom Calmet. [Geneva] 1774, 8vo.

——The White Bull; an oriental history, from an ancient Syriac manuscript, communicated by Mr. Voltaire. The whole faithfully done into English [by J. Betham]. 2 vols. London, 1774, 8vo. ·

——Le Taureau Blanc; or, the White Bull. Second edition. London, 1774, 8vo.

[Zadig] Memnon, histoireorientale. Londres, 1747, 8vo.

Zadig first appeared with the above title.

——Zadig; or, the Book of Fate. Translated from the French. London, 1749, 12mo.

——Another edition. Translated

by F. Ashmore. London, 1780, 8vo.

——Another edition. London, 1794, 12mo.

——Select Pieces; Zadig; Letter from a Turk on Titles of Honour, etc. London, 1754, 12mo.

——Another edition. Zadig and Astarte. Translated by C. Bayley. London, 1810, 12mo.

——Another edition. London, 1837, 4to.

——Zadig; or the Book of Fate. A Tale from the French. (Hazlitt's "Romancist and Novelist's Library," vol. iv.) London, 1841, 8vo.

—— ——The Hermit; an Oriental Tale. [Translation of a chapter in "Zadig."] London, 1779, 12mo.

VIII. MISCELLANEOUS, Etc.

L'A.B.C. Dialogue Curieux, traduit de l'Anglais de Monsieur Huet. Londres, 1762 [1768], 8vo.

Les Adorateurs ou les louanges de Dieu. Ouvrage unique de M. Imhof. Traduit du Latin. Berlin, 1769, 8vo.

Anecdote sur Bélisaire. Seconde anecdote sur Bélisaire. [—, 1767] 8vo.

Anecdotes sur Fréron, écrites par nn homme de lettres à un magistrat qui voulait être instruit des mœurs de cet homme. [Geneva, 1770] 8vo.

Appel à toutes les nations de l'Europe des jugements d'un Ecrivain Anglais, ou manifeste au sujet des honneurs du pavilion entre les théâtres de Londres et de Paris. [Paris] 1761, 8vo.

Arbitrage entre M. de Voltaire et M. de Foncemagne. [Geneva, 1764] 8vo.

Avis au public sur les parricides imputés aux Calas et aux Sirven., [Geneva, 1766] 8vo.

Balance Egale. [Geneva, 1762] 12mo.

La Bible en fin expliquée par plusieurs Aumôniers de S. M. L. R. D. P. (Sa Majesté le Roi de Prusse). 2 vols. Londres, 1776, 8vo.

La Canonisation de Saint Cucufin. [Geneva, 1768 ?] 8vo.

Catéchisme de l'honnête homme ou dialogue entre un caloyer et un homme de bien, etc. [Geneva, 1758, *i.e.*, 1763] 12mo.

Un Chrétien contre six Juifs. La Haye, 1777, 8vo.

Cinquième Homélie prononcée à Londres le Jour de Paques dans une assemblée particulière. [Geneva, 1769] 8vo.

Les Colimaçons du Révérend Père L'Escarbotier, par la Grace de Dieu capucin indigne, prédicateur ordinaire et cuisinier du grand couvent de la ville de Clermont en Auvergne,. au Révérend Père Elie, carme chaussé, etc. [Geneva] 1768, 8vo.

Collection d'Anciens Évangiles ou Monuments du premier siècle du Christianisme, extraits de Fabricius, Grabius, et autres savants, par l'Abbé B * * * (Bigex). Londres, 1769, 8vo.

Commentaire historique sur les Œuvres de l'auteur de la

Henriade, etc., avec les pièces originales et les preuves. Basle, 1776, 8vo.

Commentaire sur le Livre des Délits et des Peines [by the Marquis de Beccaria], par un avocat de Province. [Geneva] 1766, 8vo.

——An Essay on ·Crimes and Punishments, translated from the Italian : with a Commentary attributed to Mons. de Voltaire. Translated from the French. London, 1766, 8vo. Numerous editions.

Commentaire sur l'esprit des lois de Montesquieu. [Geneva, 1777 ?] 1778, 8vo.

Conseils à M. Racine sur son poëme de la Religion, par un amateur des belles-lettres. [—, 1742] 8vo.

Conseils raisonnables à Monsieur Bergier pour la Défense du Christianisme, etc. [Geneva, 1768] 8vo.

Conversation de M. L'Intendant des Menus en exercice avec M. L'Abbé * * * [Paris ?, 1761] 12mo.

——The dispute between Mademoiselle Clairon, a celebrated actress at Paris, and the fathers of the church, etc. London, 1768, 8vo.

Le Cri des Nations. [Geneva] 1769, 8vo.

Le Cri du Sang innocent. [Geneva] 1775, 8vo.

Critical essays on dramatic poetry. [Extracts from various works of Voltaire ; translated.] Glasgow, 1761, 12mo.

Défense de Louis XIV. [Geneva, 1769] 8vo.

Défense de Milord Bollingbroke,

par le docteur Good Natur'd Vellvisher. Traduit de l'anglais [or rather written by Voltaire]. —, 1752, 8vo.

——A Defence of Lord Bollingbroke's Letters on the Study and Use of History. Translated from the French. London, 1753, 8vo.

——Miscellaneous observations on the Works of Lord Bolingbroke; on the several answers to them, and Mons. Voltaire's Defence of his Lordship, etc. London, 1755, 8vo.

La Défense de mon oncle. [Geneva, 1767] 8vo.

——Defence of my Uncle, from the French. London, 1768, 8vo.

Dialogue du Douteur et de l'Adorateur, par M. L'Abbé de Tilladet. [Geneva, 1766 ?] 8vo.

Dialogues Chrétiens ou préservatif contre l'Encyclopédie. Genève, 1760, 8vo.

Diatribe à l'auteur des Éphémérides. [Geneva] 1775, 8vo.

Diatribe du Docteur Akakia, médicin du pape. — Decrét de l'Inquisition et Rapport des Professeurs de Rome au sujet d'un prétendu Président. Rome, 1753, 8vo.

Dieu et les Hommes. Œuvre théologique, mais raisonnable, par le Docteur Obern. Tradnit par Jacques Aimon. [Geneva] 1769, 8vo.

Le Dîner du Comte de Boulainvilliers, par M. St. Hiaciute [Geneva] 1728 [1767], 8vo.

Discours de M. Belleguier, ancien avocat, sur le texte proposé par l'Université de Paris, pour le sujet des prix de l'Année 1773. [Geneva, 1773] 8vo.

Discours prononcés dans l'Académie Française le lundi 9 Mai 1746, à la Réception de M. de Voltaire. Paris, 1746, 4to.

Dissertation sur les principales Tragédies anciennes et modernes qui ont paru sur le sujet d'Electre et en particulier sur celle de Sophocle, par M. Du Molard. Londres, 1750, 8vo.

Doutes Nouveaux sur le Testament attribué au Cardinal de Richelieu, par M. de Voltaire. Genève, 1765 [1764], 8vo.

Les Droits des Hommes et les Usurpations des Autres. Traduit de l'Italien. Amsterdam, 1768, 8vo.

Éléments de la Philosophie de Newton, mis à la portée de tout le monde. Amsterdam, 1738, 8vo.

——The Elements of Sir I. Newton's Philosophy, translated from the French. Revised and corrected by J. Hanna. London, 1738, 8vo.

——The Metaphysics of Sir I. Newton; or, a comparison between the opinions of Sir I. Newton and Mr. Leibnitz, by M. de Voltaire. Translated from the French by D. E. Baker. London, 1747, 8vo.

Eloge de Louis XV. prononcé dans une Académie, le 25 Mai 1774. [Geneva, 1774] 8vo.

Éloge de M. de Crébillon. Paris, 1762, 8vo.

L'Epitre aux Romains, par le Comte Passeran. Traduite de l'Italien. [Geneva, 1768] 8vo.

L'Équivoque. [Paris, 1771] 8vo.

Essai historique et critique sur

les dissentions des églises de Pologne, par Joseph Bourdillon, etc. Basle, 1767, 8vo.

Essai sur les probabilités en fait de justice. [Geneva, 1772] 8vo.

An essay upon the Civil Wars of France, extracted from curious manuscripts. And also upon the epick poetry of the European nations, etc. London, 1727, 8vo.

The copy in the British Museum was presented to Sir Hans Sloane by Voltaire. This work appeared originally in English, and the essays appeared separately in French in 1728 and 1729.

——Second edition, corrected. London, 1728, 8vo.

——Fourth edition, corrected. To which is now prefixed a discourse on tragedy, etc. 2 parts. London, 1731, 8vo.

——An essay upon the Civil Wars of France. To which is prefixed a short account of the author. By J[onathan] S[wift ?], D.D. Dublin, 1760, 8vo.

An Essay on Taste, by A. Gerard. To which are annexed three dissertations on the subject by M. de Voltaire, M. D'Alembert, and M. de Montesquieu. Edinburgh, 1764, 12mo.

Examen important de milord Bolingbroke, écrit sur la fin de 1736. Nouvelle édition, etc. [Geneva] 1767, 8vo.

The first edition forms part of the "Recueil Necessaire," published at Geneva in 1765 [1766].

——The important Examination of the Holy Scriptures, attributed to Lord Bolingbroke, but written by M. Voltaire, and

first published in 1736. Now first translated from the French. London, 1819, 8vo.

——Another edition. London, 1841, 8vo.

Fragment des Instructions pour le Prince de * * *. Berlin, 1766 [1767], 8vo.

Fragments sur l'Inde, sur le Général Lalli et sur le Comte de Morangiès. [Geneva] 1773, 8vo.

Homélie du Pasteur Bourn, prêchée à Londres, le Jour de la Pentecôte. [Geneva] 1768, 8vo.

Homélies prononcées à Londres en 1765 dans une assemblée particulière. [Geneva] 1767, 8vo.

Les Honnêtetés Littéraires, etc. [Geneva] 1767, 8vo.

Idées Republicaines par un membre d'un corps. [Geneva, 1762 ?] 8vo.

Letters concerning the English nation. London, 1733, 8vo.

This work was afterwards published in French under the title, "Lettres Philosophiques."

——Another edition. Dublin, reprinted, 1733, 12mo.

——Third edition. Glasgow, 1752, 8vo.

——Fourth edition, corrected. Glasgow, 1759, 12mo.

——Another edition. [With an introduction by H. Morley.] London, 1889, 8vo.

Vol. 171 of "Cassell's National Library."

——Lettres Philosophiques. Amsterdam, 1734, 12mo.

Letter to the French Academy, containing an appeal to that society on the merits of Shakspere. London, 1777, 8vo.

Lettre anonime écrite à M. de

Voltaire et la Réponse. [Geneva, 1769] 8vo.

Lettre civile et honnête à l'auteur malhonnête de la critique de l'Histoire Universelle de M. de V***, qui n'a jamais fait d'Histoire Universelle. Le tout au sujet de Mahomet. Genève, 1760, 12mo.

Lettre curieuse de M. Robert Covelle, célèbre citoyen de Genève, à la louange de M. le Professeur Vernet, professeur en théologie de la même ville. Dijon, 1766, 8vo.

Lettre de Charles Gouju à ses frères au sujet des RR. PP. Jésuites. [Geneva, 1761] 8vo.

Lettre de M. de l'Ecluse chirurgien dentiste, seigneur du Tilloy, près Montargis, à M. son curé, etc. [Geneva, 1763] 8vo.

Lettre de Monsieur de Voltaire à M. Hume. Ferney [Geneva], 1766, 8vo.

——A Letter from Mons. de Voltaire to Mr. Hume, on his dispute with M. Rousseau. Translated from the French. London, 1766, 8vo.

Lettre de Voltaire à M. de Machault, Contrôleur-Général, à l'occasion de l'impôt du vingtième (1749). Paris, 1829, 8vo.

Lettre d'un Ecclésiastique sur le prétendu rétablissement des Jésuites dans Paris. [Geneva, 1774] 8vo.

Lettre sur la prétendue Comète. Lausanne, 1773, 8vo.

Lettres à son Altesse Monseigneur le Prince de *** (Brunswick), sur Rabelais et sur d'autres auteurs accusés d'avoir mal

parlé de la religion chrétienne. Amsterdam, 1767, 8vo.

——Letters addressed to the Prince of *** [i.e., Charles William Ferdinand, Duke of Brunswick-Luneburg], containing comments on the writings of the most eminent authors who have been accused of attacking the Christian religion. London, 1768, 8vo.

——Another edition. Glasgow, 1769, 12mo.

Lettres Chinoises, Indiennes et Tartares à M. Pauw, par un Bénédictin. Avec plusieurs autres pièces intéressantes. Paris, 1776, 8vo.

Lettres sur la Nouvelle Héloïse ou Aloisia de Jean Jacques Rousseau. [Geneva] 1761, 8vo.

Lettres sur les Panégiriques, par Irenée Aléthès, etc. [Geneva, 1767] 8vo.

Mandement du Révérendissime père en Dieu Alexis, archevêque de Novgorod la Grande. [—, 1765] 8vo.

Mémoire du Sieur de Voltaire. La Haye, 1739, 8vo.

Mémoires de M. de Voltaire écrits par lui-même. Genève, 1784, 8vo.

——Memoirs of the life of Voltaire, written by himself. Translated from the French. London, 1784, 8vo.

——Life; with notes, illustrative and explanatory. Translated by G. P. Monke. London, 1787, 8vo.

La Méprise d'Arras par M. de Voltaire. Lausanne, 1771, 8vo.

Da la mort de Louis XV. et de la fatalité. [Geneva, 1774] 8vo.

Notes sur la Lettre de Monsieur de Voltaire à Monsieur Hume, par M. L. [Geneva, 1766] 12mo.

Nouvelles probabilités en fait de justice. [Geneva] 1772, 8vo.

De la Paix perpetuelle, par le Docteur Goodheart. [Geneva, 1769] 8vo.

Panégyrique de Saint Louis, Roi de France, prononcé dans la chapelle du Louvre en presence de Messieurs de l'Académie Française, le 25 Août, 1749. Paris, 1749, 4to.

Pensées, Remarques et Observations de Voltaire. Ouvrage posthume. Paris, 1802, 8vo.

Petit Avis à un Jésuite. [Geneva, 1762] 12mo.

Les Peuples aux Parlements. [Geneva, 1771] 8vo.

La Philosophe Ignorant. [Geneva] 1766, 8vo.

——Ignorant Philosopher; with an address upon the Parricides. Glasgow, 1767, 8vo.

Pièces originales concernant la mort des Sieurs Calas et le jugement rendu à Toulouse. [Geneva, 1762] 8vo.

——Original pieces relative to the trial and execution of Mr. John Calas. With a preface, and remarks by M. de Voltaire. *Fr. and Eng.* London, 1762, 8vo.

Histoire d'Elizabeth Canning et de Jean Calas. [Geneva, 1762] 8vo.

——The history of the misfortunes of Jean Calas, a victim to fanaticism; to which is added a letter from M. Calas to his wife and children. London, 1772, 8vo.

——Another edition. Edinburgh, 1776, 8vo.

Plaidoyer pour Genest Ramponeau, cabaretier à la Courtille, prononcé contre Gaudon, entrepreneur d'em théâtre des Bouleverts. Genève, 1760, 8vo.

Précis du Procès de M. le Comte de Morangiès contre la famille Verron. [—, 1773] 8vo.

Le Préservatif ou critique des observations sur les écrits modernes. La Haye, 1738, 12mo.

Le Président de Thou justifié contre les accusations de M. de Buri, auteur d'une Vie de Henri IV. [Geneva] 1766, 8vo.

Prix de la Justice et de l'Humanité, par l'auteur de la Henriade, avec son portrait. Ferney, 1778 [1777], 8vo.

Procès de Claustre. Supplément aux Causes Célèbres. [Geneva, 1769] 8vo.

La Profession du foy des théistes, par le Comte Da... au R. D. Traduit de l'Allemand. [Geneva, 1768] 8vo.

Les Questions de Zapata, traduites par le Sieur Tamponet, docteur en Sorbonne. Leipsik, 1766 [1767], 8vo.

——The Questions of Zapata; translated from the French by a Lady. London [1776], 12mo.

Questions sur les Miracles à M. le Professeur Cl. par un Professeur. [Geneva, 1765] 8vo.

Reflexions philosophiques sur le procès de Mlle. Camp avec des vers sur le Massacre de la Saint Barthélomi. Genève, 1772, 8vo.

Réfutation d'un écrit anonyme contre la Mémoire de fen M. Joseph Saurin, de l'Académie des Sciences, examinateur des livres et préposé au Journal des Savants, lequel écrit anonime se trouve dans le Journal Helvétique du mois d'Octobre 1758. [Geneva, 1758] 8vo.

Relation de la Maladie, de la Confession, de la Mort et de l'Apparition du Jésuite Bertier. [Geneva, 1759] 8vo.

Relation de la Mort du Chevalier de la Barre, par M. Cass*** (Cassen), Avocat au Conseil du Roi. À Monsieur le Marquis de Beccaria. —, 1766 [1768], 8vo.

Rélation du Bannissement des Jésuites de la Chine, etc. Amsterdam, 1768, 8vo.

Remarques pour servir de Supplément a l'Essay sur l'Histoire Générale et sur les Mœurs et l'esprit des nations depuis Charlemagne jusqu'à nos jours. [Geneva] 1763, 8vo.

Remerciment Sincere à un homme charitable. Amsterdam, 1750, 8vo.

Remonstrances du Grenier à Sel. [Geneva, 1771] 8vo.

Réponse à toutes les objections principales qu'on a faites en France contre la philosophie de Newton. —, 1739, 8vo.

Rescrit de l'Empereur de la Chine. [Paris, 1761] 8vo.

Au Roi en son conseil. Pour les sujets du roi qui réclament la liberté de la France contre des moines Bénédictins devenus Chanoines de Saint Claude en Franche-Comté. [Geneva, 1770] 8vo.

Sermon des Cinquante. [Geneva], 1749 [1762?], 8vo.

Sermon du Papa Nicolas Charis-teski, prononcé dans l'église de Sainte-Toleranski, etc. [Geneva, 1771] 8vo.

Sermon du Rabin Akib. [Geneva? 1761] 8vo.

Le Sermon preché à Balo le premier jour de l'an 1768, par Josias Rosette, ministre du Saint Évangile. [Geneva, 1768] 8vo.

Les Singularités de la Nature, par un Académicien de Londres, de Boulogne, de Pétersbourg, de Berlin, etc. Basle, 1768, 8vo.

Supplément du Discours aux Welches avec une lettre du Libraire de l'Année Littéraire à M.V. et la réponse de M.V. à cette lettre. [Paris] 1764, 8vo.

The "Discours aux Welches" was printed in 1764 in the *Contes de Guillaume Vadé.*

Théâtre de Pierre Corneille avec des Commentaires, etc. 12 vols. [Geneva, 1762-63] 8vo.

Thoughts on the pernicious consequences of war. [179—?] 8vo.

Le Tocsin des Rois aux Souverains de l'Europe. —, 1772, 12mo.

——Le Tocsin; an alarm to Kings. London, 1772, 8vo.

Le Tombeau de la Sorbonne. Constantinople, 1753, 12mo.

Tout en Dieu, Commentaire sur Mallebranche. [Geneva] 1769, 8vo.

Traité sur la Tolérance. [Geneva] 1763, 8vo.

——A Treatise on Religious Toleration. Occasioned by the execution of the unfortunate J. Calas for the supposed murder of his son. Translated from the French by the translator of Eloisa. London, 1764, 8vo.

——Another edition. Glasgow, 1765, 12mo.

——Another edition. London, 1820, 12mo.

——A Treatise on Toleration; the Ignorant Philosopher; and a commentary on the Marquis of Becaria's treatise on Crimes and Punishments. Translated from the last Geneva edition of M. de Voltaire, by David Williams. 2 pts. London, 1779, 8vo. ⸜

Vie de Molière avec des Jugements sur ses ouvrages. Paris, 1739, 12mo.

La Voix du Curé sur le procès des Serfs du Mont Jura. [Geneva, 1772] 8vo.

La Voix du Sage et du Peuple. Amsterdam, 1750, 8vo.

IX. LETTERS, Etc.

Ode et Lettres à M. de Voltaire en faveur de la famille du grand Corneille, par M. Le Brun, avec la Réponse de M. de Voltaire. Genève, 1760, 8vo.

Lettres et Réponses de M. Palissot à M. de Voltaire. [—, 1760] 12mo.

Lettres de M. de Voltaire à l'Électeur Palatine et au Roi de Prusse. [Geneva ? 1761] 8vo.

Lettres Secrètes de M. de Voltaire, etc. Genève, 1765, 8vo.

Monsieur de Voltaire peint par lui-même, ou Lettres de cet écrivain dans lesquelles ou verra l'histoire de sa vie, de ses ouvrages, de ses querelles, de ses correspondances, etc. Lausanne, 1766, 12mo.

Lettres de M. de Voltaire à ses amis du Parnasse, avec des

Notes Historiques et Critiques. Genève, 1766, 8vo.

Lettre de Monseigneur l'Évêque d'A*** (Annecy) à M. de V*** avec les réponses, du 11 Avril 1768. [—, 1769] 8vo.

——Genuine Letters between the Archbishop of Anneci and Mons. de Voltaire on the subject of his preaching at the Parish Church of Ferney, etc. London, 1770, 8vo.

Letters to several friends ; translated from the French by the Rev. Dr. Franklin. London, 1770, 12mo.

——Second edition. London, 1773, 12mo.

Historical Memoirs of the author of the Henriade. With some original pieces. To which are added, genuine letters of Mr. de Voltaire taken from his own minutes. Translated from the French [of J. L. Wagnière]. London, 1777, 8vo.

Lettres de M. de Voltaire à M. L'Abbé Moussinot, son trésorier, écrites depuis 1736 jusqu' en 1742, etc. La Haye, 1781, 8vo.

Lettres Curieuses et Intéressantes de M. de Voltaire et de plusieurs autres personnes distinguées, etc. Dublin, 1781, 8vo.

Lettres de M. de Voltaire et de sa célèbre amie, suivies d'un petit poëme, d'une lettre de J. J. Rousseau, etc. Genève, 1782, 12mo.

Mémoires pour servir à l'histoire de M. de Voltaire, dans lesquels on trouvera divers écrits de lui peu connus, sur ses différends avec J. J. Rousseau, etc. 2 pts. Amsterdam, 1785, 12mo.

Frédéric II., Voltaire, Jean-Jacques

. . . avec plusieurs lettres curieuses de M. de Voltaire. Paris, 1789, 8vo.

Correspondance de Voltaire et du Cardinal de Bernis, depuis 1761 jusqu' à 1771, etc. Paris, 1799, 8vo.

Lettres Inédites de Voltaire à Frédéric le Grand, Roi de Prusse, publiées sur les originaux. Paris, 1802, 8vo.

Mon Sejour auprès de Voltaire et Lettres Inédites que m'écrivit cette homme célèbre, etc., par C. A. Collini. Paris, 1807, 8vo.

Supplément au Recueil des Lettres de M. de Voltaire. 2 vols. Paris, 1808, 8vo.

Lettres Inédites de Voltaire adressées à Mme. la Comtesse de Lutzelbourg, etc. Paris, 1812, 8vo.

Choix de Lettres Inédites de Voltaire au Marquis de Vauvenarques. Aix, 1813, 8vo.

Lettres Inédites de Madame la Marquise du Chatelet et Supplément à la Correspondance de Voltaire avec le Roi de Prusse et avec des différentes personnes célèbres. Paris, 1818, 8vo.

Lettres Inédites de Voltaire. Paris, 1818, 8vo.

Lettres Inédites de Buffon, J. J. Rousseau, Voltaire, etc. Paris, 1819, 8vo.

Vie privée de Voltaire et de Madame du Chatelet . . . suivie de cinquante lettres inédites de Voltaire. Paris, 1820, 8vo.

Pièces Inédites de Voltaire, imprimées d'après les manuscrits originaux, pour faire suite aux différentes éditions publiées

jusqu' à ce jour. Paris, 1820, 8vo.

Lettres diverses recueillies en Suisse par le Comte Fédor Golowkin, etc. Genève, 1821, 8vo.

Lettres inédites de Voltaire, de Madame Denys et de Colini, adressées à M. Dupont, etc. Paris, 1821, 8vo.

Lettres inédites de Voltaire à Mademoiselle Quinault, à M. d'Argental, etc. Paris, 1822, 8vo.

Lettres de Voltaire. Paris, 1823, 8vo.

Correspondance inédite de Voltaire avec P. M. Hénnin, etc. Paris, 1825, 8vo.

Lettres inédites de Voltaire. Paris, 1826, 8vo.

Lettres de Voltaire et de J. J. Rousseau à C. J. Panckoucke, éditeur de l'Encyclopédie Méthodique. Paris, 1828, 8vo.

Correspondance inédite de Voltaire avec Frédéric II., le Président de Brosses, etc., avec notes, par Th. Foisset. Paris, 1836, 8vo.

Lettres inédites de Voltaire. [Paris, 1840] 8vo.

Lettres inédites de Voltaire, recueillies par M. de Cayrol et annotées par M. Alphonse François, etc. 2 vols. Paris, 1856, 8vo.

Voltaire à Ferney. Sa correspondance avec la Duchesse de Saxe-Gotha, suivie de lettres et des notes historiques entièrement inédites, recueillies et publiées par MM. Évariste Bavoux et A. F. Paris, 1860, 8vo.

Voltaire. Lettres inédites sur la Tolérance, publiées avec une Introduction et des notes par A.

Coquerel fils, etc. Paris, 1863, 18mo.

Lettres et Billets de Voltaire à l'époque de son retour de Prusse en France, en 1753. Paris, 1867, 8vo.

Lettres de Voltaire à M. le Conseiller Le Bault, publiées et annotées par Ch. de Mandat-Grancey, etc. Paris, 1868, 8vo.

Voltaire. Lettres et Poésies inédites adressées à la Reine de Prusse, à la Princesse Ulrique, à la Margrave de Baireuth, etc. Paris, 1872, 16mo.

Six lettres inédites de Voltaire. Bourg [1874], 8vo.

Voltaire et le pays de Gex. Lettres et documents inédits par A. Vayssière. Bourg, 1876, 8vo.

Lettres et vers de Voltaire adressés à M. de Belmont, directeur des spectacles de Bordeaux. Bordeaux, 1880, 8vo.

Dix Lettres inédites de Voltaire à son neveu De La Houlière, etc. Montpellier, 1885, 8vo.

Voltaire. Lettres et billets inédits publiés d'après les originaux du British Museum avec une introduction et des notes par Georges Bengesco. Paris, 1887, 8vo.

Lettre à M. Rameau. [1738] 8vo.

Lettre de M. de Voltaire à M. L'Abbé Dubos. [—, 1739] 12mo.

Lettre de M. de Voltaire sur son Essai de l'Histoire de Louis XIV. à Milord Harvey, Garde des Sceaux d'Angleterre. —, 1740, 8vo.

Lettre à M. Norberg, chapelain du Roy de Suède Charles XII., auteur de l'Histoire de ce monarque. Londres, 1744, 8vo.

Lettre de M. de V***.* au Révérend

Père de la Tour, principal du Collège de Louis-le-Grand. [Paris] 1746, 4to.

Lettre de M. de V* * * à un de ses élèves. [—, 1756] 8vo.

Lettre de M. de Voltaire au Roi Stanislas. Genève, 1760, 8vo.

Lettre de M. de Voltaire à M. le Duc de la Vallière. [Geneva ? 1760] 8vo.

Lettre de M. de Voltaire à Monsieur * * * (Le Duc de Bouillon). [—, 1761] 8vo.

A letter from Mons. de Voltaire to the author of [the English tragedy of] the Orphan of China [A. Murphy]. London, 1759, 8vo.

Lettre de M. de Voltaire sur plusieurs sujets intéressants, adressée à M. le Marquis Albergati Capacelli, sénateur de Bologne. [Geneva, 1761 ?] 8vo.

Réponse de M. de Voltaire á M. Diodati de Torazzi (Deodati de Tovazzi), auteur du livre de l'Excellence de la langue Italienne. [—, 1761] 8vo.

Lettre de M. de Voltaire, de l'Académie Française, à M. L'Abbé d'Olivet, chancelier de la même Académie. [Paris, 1761] 8vo.

Réponse de M. de Voltaire au Sieur Fez, libraire d'Avignon, du 17 Mai, 1760 (1762). [—, 1762] 8vo.

Lettre de M. de Voltaire à M. d'Alembert. [Paris, 1763] 8vo.

Aux Plaisirs, 27 Janvier 1764. [Geneva, 1764] 8vo.

Lettre de M. de Vol. . . . à M. d'Am. . . . [Paris, 1765] 8vo.

Réponse de M. de Voltaire à M. L'Abbé d'Olivet. [Geneva, 1767] 8vo.

Lettre de M. de Voltaire à M. Élie de Beaumont, avocat au Parlement, du 20 Mars, 1767. [—, 1767 ?] 8vo.

Réponse de M. de Voltaire au Comte de la Touraille. [Paris, 1768] 8vo.

Lettre d'un père à son fils faisant l'auteur et le bel esprit à Paris, suivie d'une lettre de M. de Voltaire. Castres, 1773, 8vo.

Lettre de M. de Voltaire à M. le Curé de Saint-Sulpice. [Paris, 1778] 8vo.

Lettre de Voltaire à l'Abbé Raynal, suivie d'une Lettre du Chancelier d'Aguesseau au Marquis de Torcy. [Paris, 1820 ?] 8vo.

Lettre de Voltaire à M. Seguy, imprimée pour la Société des Bibliophiles Français. Paris, 1826, 8vo.

Lettre de Voltaire relative à son Histoire de Pierre 1er adressée au Comte d'Alion, etc. Paris, 1839, 8vo.

Une Lettre inédite de Voltaire, annotée par Émile Biais, etc. Angoulême, 1880, 8vo.

X. SUPPOSITITIOUS WORKS.

L'Arbre de Science, roman posthume de Voltaire, etc. Paris, 1843, 32mo.

Candide, ou l'Optisme, traduit de l'Allemand de M. le docteur Ralph. Seconde partie. —, 1761, 12mo.

Chinki, histoire Cochinchinoise qui peut servir à d'autres pays. Londres, 1768, 8vo.

Coligni, ou la Saint-Barthélemy, tragédie. Amsterdam, 1740, 8vo.

Lo Connaisseur, comédie en trois

actes et en vers, per M. le Baron de Saint * * * Geneva, 1773, 8vo.

Démocrito prétendu fou, comédie eu trois actes, etc. Paris, 1730, 8vo.

Jean Hennuyer, évêque de Lisieux, drame en trois actes, etc. Genève, 1772, 8vo.

Misogug, ou les Femmes commes elles sont. Histoire Orientale, traduite du Chaldéen. 2 pts. Paris, 1788, 12mo.

La Mort de Caton, tragédie en trois actes, etc. Paris, 1777, 8vo.

L'Odalisque, ouvrage traduit du Turc. Constantinople, 1779, 12mo.

L'Optique, ou le Chinois à Memphis. Essais traduits de l'Égyptien. 2 pts. Londres, 1763, 12mo.

Pièces fugitives des Œuvres Mêlées de M. de Voltaire. La Haye, 1779, 12mo.

Suite de la Pucelle d'Orléans, en sept chants, etc. Berlin, 1791, 18mo.

XI. APPENDIX.

Biography, Criticism, Etc.

[*The Literature upon Voltaire and his Works being so extensive, it has been only possible to make a selection in the following list.*]

Anti-Jacobin. — New Lights on Jacobinism, abstracted from Professor Robison's History of Free Masonry. With an appendix, containing an account of Voltaire's behaviour on his death-bed, etc. Birmingham, 1798, 8vo.

Arouet de Voltaire, François Marie.
— Repentir ; ou, Confession
publique de M. de Voltaire.
Vienne, 1771, 8vo.
——The history of the life and
writings of M. Arruet de
Voltaire, from a collection
published in France, in the
year 1781, etc. 2 pts. London, 1782, 8vo.
——The last hours of a learned
infidel [Voltaire] and an humble
Christian [Poor Joseph] con-
trasted. London, 1798, 12mo.
——The infidel and Christian
philosophers ; or, the last hours
of Voltaire and Addison con-
trasted ; a poem, etc. King-
ston-upon-Hull, 1802, 4to.
——The Contrast ; or, the last
hours . . . of Voltaire and
Wilmot Earl of Rochester.
London [1806 ?], 12mo.
No. 48 of the "Cottage Library,"
etc.
——The Contrast ; or, an account
of the last hours of a learned
infidel [Voltaire] and of a
learned Christian [Dr. Dodd-
ridge]. London [1820], 12mo.
——A brief sketch of the life and
writings of M. de Voltaire, etc.
London [1841], 8vo.
——Recantation of Paine and
Voltaire. The last moments of
Thomas Paine and M. de
Voltaire. London [1863], 12mo.
——Voltaire et Mme. du Châte-
let, révélations d'un serviteur
attaché à leurs personnes, etc.
Paris, 1863, 12mo.
Asch, M. — Shakspere's and
Voltaire's Julius Cæsar com-
pared. Gardelegen [1881], 4to.
Baretti, Giuseppe.—A Disserta-
tion upon the Italian Poetry,

in which are some remarks
on M. Voltaire's Essay on the
Epic Poets. London, 1753, 8vo.
——Discours sur Shakespeare et
sur Monsieur de Voltaire. Londres, 1777, 8vo.
Bénard, V.—Frédéric II. et Vol-
taire. Paris, 1878, 8vo.
Bengescu, Georges. — Voltaire.
Bibliographie de ses œuvres.
4 tom. Paris, 1882-90, 8vo.
Bersot, E.—La Philosophie de
Voltaire, etc. Paris, 1848,
12mo.
Brougham, Henry, *Lord.*—Lives
of Men of Letters and Science,
who flourished in the time of
George III. 2 vols. London,
1845-6, 8vo.
Voltaire, vol. i., pp. 1-142.
Bungener, L. L. F.—Voltaire et
son temps. Études sur le
dix-huitième siècle, etc. 2
tom. Paris, 1851, 12mo.
——Voltaire and his times.
Edinburgh, 1854, 8vo.
Caritat, M. J. A. N., *Marquis de
Condorcet.*—Vie de Voltaire ;
suivie des Mémoires de Voltaire,
écrits par lui-même. [Kehl]
1789, 8vo.
——The Life of Voltaire. To
which are added Memoirs of
Voltaire, written by himself.
Translated from the French.
2 vols. London, 1790, 8vo.
——Another edition. Philadel-
phia, 1792, 12mo.
——Another edition. (*Autobio-
graphy,* etc., vol. 2.) London,
1826, 18mo.
Chaudon, L. M.—Historical and
critical memoirs of the life and
writings of M. de Voltaire, etc.
From the French. London,
1786, 8vo.

Collins, John Churton.—Bolingbroke, a historical study ; and
Voltaire in England. London,
1886, 8vo.

Despreux, S.—Soirées de Ferney ;
ou, confidences de Voltaire, etc.
Paris, 1802, 8vo.

Duvernet, T. I.—La Vie de
Voltaire. Genève, 1787, 12mo.

Espinasse, Francis. — Life and
Times of François Marie Arouet,
calling himself Voltaire. Vol. 1.
London, 1866, 8vo.
No more published.

Findlay, Robert.—A vindication
of the Sacred Books, and of
Josephus, from various mis-
representations and cavils of M.
de Voltaire. Glasgow, 1770, 8vo.

Forbes, Litton.—Voltaire : his
life and times. A lecture
delivered before the Sunday
Lecture Society, November 16th,
1884. London, 1884, 8vo.

Gaberel, Jean.—Voltaire et les
Génévois. Deuxième édition,
revue et corrigée. Paris, 1857,
12mo.

Guyon, C. M.—L'oracle des nouveaux philosophes, pour servir
de suite et d'éclaircissement aux
œuvres de M. de Voltaire.
2 pts. Berne, 1760, 8vo.

Hamley, General Sir Edward.—
Voltaire. [An account of his
life and writings.] London,
1877, 8vo.
Vol. ii. of Mrs. Oliphant's "Foreign
Classics," etc.

Hodenberg, Bodo von, Baron.—
Voltaire und Friedrich II., etc.
Altona, 1871, 8vo.

Horn, Georg.—Voltaire und die
Markgräfin von Baireuth. [With
their correspondence.] Berlin,
1865, 8vo.

——The Margravine of Baireuth
and Voltaire. [Containing their
correspondence.] Translated by
Princess Christian. London,
1888, 8vo.

Houssaye, Arsène.—Philosophers
and Actresses. 2 vols. New
York, 1852, 8vo.
Voltaire, pp. 29-108 ; Voltaire and
Mlle. de Livry, pp. 109-133.

——Le Roi Voltaire, sa jeunesse
—sa cour—ses ministres—son
peuple—ses conquêtes—sa mort
—son dieu—sa dynastie. Paris,
1858, 8vo.

Joseph, ben Jonathan, pseud.—Lettres de quelques Juifs Portugais
et Allemands à Monsieur de
Voltaire, etc. 2 tom. Paris,
1772, 8vo.

——Letters of certain Jews to
Monsieur Voltaire. Translated
by P. Lefanu. 2 vols. Dublin,
1777, 8vo.

Keate, George.—Ferney : an epistle
to Mons. de Voltaire [in verse].
London, 1768, 4to.

La Mottraye, A. de.—Remarques
historiques et critiques sur
l'histoire de Charles XII., etc.
Paris, 1732, 8vo.

——Historical and critical Re-
marks on the History of Charles
XII. Translated from the
French. London, 1732, 8vo.

Lebrocquy, G.—Voltaire peint par
lui-même. Conferences données
à Malines, etc. Bruxelles, 1868,
8vo.

Lepan, É. M. J.—Vie politique,
littéraire et morale de Voltaire,
etc. Paris, 1817, 8vo.

Linguet, S. A. II.—Examen des
ouvrages de M. de Voltaire, etc.
Bruxelles, 1788, 8vo.

——A critical analysis and review

of all M. Voltaire's works. Translated by J. Boardman. London, 1790, 8vo.

Longchamp, S. G.—Mémoires sur Voltaire, et sur ses ouvrages par Longchamp et Wagnièrc, ses secrétaires, etc. 2 tom. Paris, 1826, 8vo.

McCarthy, Justin.—"Con Amore"; or, critical chapters. London, 1868, 8vo.
    Voltaire, pp. 1-34.

Maggiolo, A., *Viscount*.—Voltaire [a biography]. Paris, 1878, 12mo.

Mahrenholtz, R.—Voltaire Studieu, etc. Oppeln, 1880, 8vo.
——Voltaire's Leben und Werke. 2 Bde. Oppeln, 1885, 8vo.

Marchand, J. H. — Nouveau et dernier testament politique de M. de Voltaire. Genève, 1771, 8vo.

Martin, Josiah.—A Letter from one of the people call'd Quakers to Francis de Voltaire, occasioned by his remarks on that people in his Letters concerning the English nation. London, 1741, 8vo.
——Another edition. London, 1749, 12mo.

Maugras, Gaston.—Querelles de Philosophes. Voltaire et J. J. Rousseau. Paris, 1886, 8vo.

Maynard, Abbé. — Voltaire, sa vie et ses œuvres. 2 tom. Paris, 1867, 8vo.

Merivale, Herman. — Historical Studies. London, 1865, 8vo.
    Voltaire, Rousseau, and Goethe, pp. 180-185; appeared originally in the *Edinburgh Review*, vol. 92, 1850.

Mickle, W. J.—Voltaire in the Shades; or, dialogues on the deistical controversy. London, 1770, 8vo.

Montagu, Elizabeth.—An essay on the writings and genius of Shakespear, etc. London, 1769, 8vo.
    Numerous editions.

Morley, John. — Voltaire. [A study.] London, 1870, 8vo.
——Second edition. London, 1870, 8vo.
——Another edition. London, 1886, 8vo.

Nisard, M. É. C.—Les Eunemis de Voltaire, etc. Paris, 1853, 8vo.

Noël, Eugène.—Voltaire, sa vie et ses œuvres. Sa lutte contre Rousseau. Paris, 1878, 12mo.
——Voltaire et Rousseau. Paris [1862?], 12mo.

Paillet, De Warcy, L.—Histoire de la Vie et des Ouvrages de Voltaire, etc. 2 tom. Paris, 1824, 8vo.

Parton, James.—Life of Voltaire. 2 vols. London, 1881, 8vo.

Perey, Lucien, *pseud.* [*i.e.*, Luce Herpin, and Maugras, Gaston]. —La Vie intime de Voltaire aux Délices et à Ferney, 1754-1778, d'après des lettres et des documents inédits. Paris, 1885, 8vo.

Pompery, E. de. —La vie de Voltaire. L'homme et son œuvre. Paris, 1878, 12mo.

Poniatowski, S.—Remarques sur l'Histoire de Charles XII. Paris, 1741, 12mo.
——Remarks on M. de Voltaire's History of Charles XII. London, 1741, 8vo.

Postel, Victor.—Voltaire, philosophe, citoyen, ami du peuple. Paris, 1860, 24mo.

Quérard, J. M. — Bibliographie Voltairienne. Paris, 1842, 8vo.

Rolli, Paul.—Remarks upon M. Voltaire's Essay on the epic poetry of the European nations. London, 1728, 8vo.

Schulthess, Robert. — Friedrich und Voltaire in ihrem persönlichen und litterarischen Wechselverhältnisse. Nordhausen, 1850, 8vo.

Standish, Frank Hall.—The Life of Voltaire, with interesting particulars respecting his death; and anecdotes and characters of his contemporaries. London, 1821, 8vo.

Strauss, D. F.—Voltaire. Sechs Vorträge. Leipzig, 1870, 8vo.

Vayssière, A —Voltaire et le Pays de Gex. Lettres, etc. Bourg, 1876, 8vo.

Venedey, Jacob.—Friedrich der Grösse und Voltaire. Leipzig, 1859, 8vo.

Vinet, Alexander. — History of French Literature in the Eighteenth Century. Translated from the French by the Rev. James Bryce. Edinburgh, 1854, 8vo.

    Voltaire, pp. 254-336.

Wagnière, J. L.—Commentaire historiqne sur les œuvres de l'auteur de la Henriade, etc. Basle, 1776, 8vo.

Wilkins, John H.—Civilisation: a play (founded on Voltaire's Le Huron). London [1853], 12mo.

    In vol. x. of "Lacy's Acting Edition of Plays."

Wilson, John.—Studies of Modern Mind and Character. London, 1881, 8vo.

    Voltaire, pp. 141-192.

Zabuesnig, J. C. von.—Historische Nachrichten von dem Leben und den Schriften des Herrn von Voltaire, etc. 2 Bde. Augsburg, 1777, 8vo.

MAGAZINE ARTICLES, ETC.

Voltaire, François Marie.—Dublin University Magazine, by J. W. Calcraft, vol. 44, 1854, pp. 681-689.—Methodist Quarterly, vol. 48, 1866, pp. 546-560.—Blackwood's Edinburgh Magazine, vol. 111, 1872, pp. 270-290; same article, Littell's Living Age, vol. 113, pp. 131-146.—Fraser's Magazine, vol. 5 N.S., 1872, pp. 678-691.—Quarterly Review, vol. 135, 1873, pp. 331-373; same article, Littell's Living Age, vol. 119, pp. 707-731. —Nineteenth Century, by A. A. Knox, vol. 12, 1882, pp. 613-632.

——*and the Duchesse de Choiseul.* Nation, March 7, 1889, pp. 201, 202.

——*and the Fair Sex.* St. James's Magazine, by Dr. Michelsen, vol. 12, 1865, pp. 213-221.

——*and Frederick the Great.* New Monthly Magazine, vol. 116, 1859, pp. 475-485; same article, Littell's Living Age, vol. 63, pp. 259-267.

——*and the French Revolution.* National Quarterly, by C. W. Super, vol. 38, p. 91, etc.

——*and Geneva.* American Church Review, vol. 10, p. 1, etc.

——*and Gibbon.* New Monthly Magazine, vol. 58, 1840, pp. 558-561.—Tinsley's Magazine, by A. D. Vandam, vol. 19, 1876, pp. 10-15.

——*and his Panegyrists.* Catholic

Voltaire, François Marie.
1865, pp. 347-389.—Cornhill
Magazine, by J. C. Carr, vol.
46, 1882, pp. 452-465, 677-690;
same article, Littell's Living
Age, vol. 158, pp. 500-509.
——*in the Netherlands.* Temple
Bar, by J. C. A. van Sypesteyn,
vol. 50, 1877, pp. 174-188;
same article, Littell's Living
Age, vol. 134, pp. 97-105.
——*in Politics.* Nation, by E. L.
Godkin, vol. 26, 1878, pp. 369,
370.
——*in Switzerland.* Nation, by
A. Laugel, vol. 43, 1886, pp.
412, 413, 452, 453, 518, 519.
——*"Innkeeper for Europe."*
Gentleman's Magazine, by Jas.
Ramsay, July 1890, pp. 22-32.
——*Last Visit to Paris.* Bel-
gravia, by C. Hervey, vol. 54,
1884, pp. 334-341; same article,
Eclectic Magazine, vol. 103, pp.
621-625, and Littell's Living
Age, vol. 163, pp. 117-121.
——*Letters of.* Portfolio, vol. 1,
1809, pp. 316-329.—Littell's
Living Age (from the Athenæum), vol. 51, 1856, pp. 676-683.
——*Life of.* Portfolio, vol. 30,
1823, pp. 4-12.
——*Life and Character of.*
Foreign Review, by T. Carlyle,
vol. 3, 1829, pp. 429-475, reprinted in *Critical and Miscellaneous Essays*, 1839.—Biblical
Repository, vol. 3, 3rd ser.,
1847, pp. 458-483. — Westminster Review, vol. 43, 1845,
pp. 384-430.— Monthly Review,
vol. 108, 1825, pp. 377-385.
——*Life and genius of.* Dublin
University Magazine, vol. 61,
1863, pp. 93-106, 168-187.

Voltaire, François Marie.
——*Morley's Life of.* North
American Review, by T. S.
Perry, vol. 115, 1872, pp. 431-
435.—Nation, by A. Laugel,
vol. 15, 1872, pp. 150-152.—
New Englander, by W. L.
Kingsley, vol. 32, 1873, pp.
561-589.—Christian Observer,
vol. 72, 1872, pp. 186-209.
——*Parton's Life of.* Fortnightly
Review, by G. Saintsbury, vol.
30 N.S., 1881, pp. 149-167;
same article, Eclectic Magazine, vol. 97, pp. 474-486.—
Atlantic Monthly, by J. F.
Clarke, vol. 48, 1881, pp. 260-
273.—Nation, by A. V. Dicey,
vol. 33, 1881, pp. 276-278, 297,
298.—Unitarian Review, vol.
16, p. 293, etc.—Dial (Chicago),
by V. B. Denslow, vol. 2, 1882,
pp. 59-61.—Spectator, April 22,
1882, pp. 533-535
——*a philosopher without philosophy.* Chambers's Edinburgh
Journal, vol. 20 N.S., 1854, pp.
425-427; same article, Eclectic
Magazine, vol. 31, pp. 423, 424.
——*Private Life of.* North
American Review, by A. H.
Everett, vol. 12, 1821, pp. 38-60.
——*Romances of, and their moral.*
Westminster Review, vol. 75,
1861, pp. 363-380; same
article, Littell's Living Age,
vol. 69, pp. 387-397.
——*Romances, Philosophy of.*
Temple Bar, vol. 80, 1887, pp.
91-110.
——*Rousseau, and Goethe.* Edinburgh Review, by H. Merivale,
vol. 92, 1850, pp. 188-220,
reprinted in *Historical Studies*,
1865.
——*Rousseau, and Hume.* New

Voltaire, François Marie.
  Englander, by J. Murdoch,
  vol. 1, 1843, pp. 169-183.
——*School Days of.* Atlantic
  Monthly, by J. Parton, vol. 47,
  1881, pp. 507-517.
——*Strauss's.* Nation, by A. V.
  Dicey, vol. 21, 1875, pp. 215, 216.
——*Study of.* Radical, by J. W.
  Chadwick, vol. 10, 1872, pp.
  274-288.

Voltaire, François Marie.
——*versus Shakespeare.* Knicker-
  bocker, vol. 6, 1835, pp. 319-
  322.
——*Visit to.* Temple Bar, vol.
  64, 1882, pp. 121-131 ; same
  article, Littell's Living Age,
  vol. 152, pp. 290-295.
——*Visit to, by Casanova.* New
  Monthly Magazine, vol. 4, 1822,
  pp. 171-178, 232-237.

XII. CHRONOLOGICAL LIST OF WORKS.

Histoire des Voyages de
  Scarmentado . . . 1756
La Religion Naturelle . 1756
Poëmes sur le Desastre de
  Lisbonne et sur la Loi
  Naturelle . . . 1756
La Prude, comédie . . 1759
La Femme qui a raison,
  comédie 1759
Socrate, tragédie . . 1759
Le Cantique des Cantiques 1759
Candide 1759
Histoire de l'Empire de
  Russie sons Pierre le
  Grand . . . 1759-63
Le Pauvre Diable . . 1760
Le Caffé ou L'Écossaise,
  comédie . . . 1760
Appel à tontes les Nations
  de l'Europe des juge-
  ments d'un Écrivain
  Anglais 1761
Tancred, tragédie . . 1761
Zulime, tragédie . . 1761
L'Echange, comédie . 1761
L'A.B.C. Dialogue Curieuse
                    1762 [1768]
Histoire d'Elizabeth Can-
  ning et de Jean Calas . 1762
Pièces originales concernant
  la mort des Sieurs Calas 1762
Théâtre de Pierre Corneille
  avec des Commentaires 1762-3
Traité sur la Tolérance . 1763
Remarques pour servir de
  Supplément à l'Essay sur
  l'Histoire Générale, etc.. 1763
Olimpie, tragédie . . 1763
Le Droit du Seigneur,
  comédie . . . 1763
Dictionnaire Philosophique 1764
Contes de Guillaume Vadé 1764
Ce qui plait aux dames . 1764
L'Ecueil du Sage, comédie 1764
Doutes Nouveaux sur le
  Testament, etc. 1765 [1764]

La Philosophie de l'Histoire 1765
Adelaïde du Guesclin,
  tragédie. . . . 1765
Commentaire sur le Livre
  des Délits et do Peines
  [by the Marquis de
  Beccaria] . . . 1766
Le Philosophe Ignorant . 1766
Les Questions de Zapata
                    1766 [1767]
Lettres à Son Altesse Mon-
  seigneur le Prince de
  * * * (Brunswick) . . 1767
La Défense de mon Oncle . 1767
Examen important de
  Milord Bolingbroke . 1767
Les Honnêtetés Littéraires 1767
L'Ingénu 1767
Charlot ou la Comtesse de
  Givri 1767
Les Scythes, tragédie . 1767
Octave et le jeune Pompée 1767
La Princesse de Babilone . 1768
L'Homme aux quarante
  écus 1768
Les Singularités de la
  Nature 1768
La Guerre Civile de Genève 1768
Dieu et les Hommes . . 1769
De la Paix Perpetuelle . 1769
Collection d'Anciens Évan-
  giles 1769
Les Lettres d'Amabed . 1769
Histoire du Parlement de
  Paris 1769
Précis du Siècle de Louis
  XV. 1769
Les Guèbres ou la Tolérance,
  tragédie . . . 1769
Sophonisbe, tragédie. . 1770
Questions sur l'Encyclo-
  pédie . . . 1770-72
Épitres, Satires, Contes,
  Odes, etc. . . . 1771
La Begueule . . . 1772
Le Dépositaire, comédie . 1772

THE WALTER SCOTT PRESS, NEWCASTLE-ON-TYNE

THE SCOTT LIBRARY.

Cloth, Uncut Edges, Gilt Top. Price 1s. 6d. per Volume.

London: WALTER SCOTT, LIMITED, 24 Warwick Lane.

THE SCOTT LIBRARY—continued.

London: WALTER SCOTT, LIMITED, 24 Warwick Lane.

THE SCOTT LIBRARY—continued.

London: Walter Scott, Limited, 24 Warwick Lane.

48 STORIES FROM CARLETON. SELECTED, WITH INTRO-
duction, by W. Yeats.

49 JANE EYRE. BY CHARLOTTE BRONTË. EDITED BY
Clement K. Shorter.

50 ELIZABETHAN ENGLAND. EDITED BY LOTHROP
Withington, with a Preface by Dr. Furnivall.

51 THE PROSE WRITINGS OF THOMAS DAVIS. EDITED
by T. W. Rolleston.

52 SPENCE'S ANECDOTES. A SELECTION. EDITED,
with an Introduction and Notes, by John Underhill.

53 MORE'S UTOPIA, AND LIFE OF EDWARD V. EDITED,
with an Introduction, by Maurice Adams.

54 SADI'S GULISTAN, OR FLOWER GARDEN. TRANS.
lated, with an Essay, by James Ross.

55 ENGLISH FAIRY AND FOLK TALES. EDITED BY
E. Sidney Hartland.

56 NORTHERN STUDIES. BY EDMUND GOSSE. WITH
a Note by Ernest Rhys.

57 EARLY REVIEWS OF GREAT WRITERS. EDITED BY
E. Stevenson.

58 ARISTOTLE'S ETHICS. WITH GEORGE HENRY
Lewes's Essay on Aristotle prefixed.

59 LANDOR'S PERICLES AND ASPASIA. EDITED, WITH
an Introduction, by Havelock Ellis.

60 ANNALS OF TACITUS. THOMAS GORDON'S TRANS-
lation. Edited, with an Introduction, by Arthur Galton.

61 ESSAYS OF ELIA. BY CHARLES LAMB. EDITED,
with an Introduction, by Ernest Rhys.

62 BALZAC'S SHORTER STORIES. TRANSLATED BY
William Wilson and the Count Stenbock.

63 COMEDIES OF DE MUSSET. EDITED, WITH AN
Introductory Note, by S. L. Gwynn.

64 CORAL REEFS. BY CHARLES DARWIN. EDITED,
with an Introduction, by Dr. J. W. Williams.

London : WALTER SCOTT, LIMITED, 24 Warwick Lane.

THE SCOTT LIBRARY—continued.

65 SHERIDAN'S PLAYS. EDITED, WITH AN INTRO-
duction, by Rudolf Dircks.

66 OUR VILLAGE. BY MISS MITFORD. EDITED, WITH
an Introduction, by Ernest Rhys.

67 MASTER HUMPHREY'S CLOCK, AND OTHER STORIES.
By Charles Dickens. With Introduction by Frank T. Marzials.

68 TALES FROM WONDERLAND. BY RUDOLPH
Baumbach. Translated by Helen B. Dole.

69 ESSAYS AND PAPERS BY DOUGLAS JERROLD. EDITED
by Walter Jerrold.

70 VINDICATION OF THE RIGHTS OF WOMAN. BY
Mary Wollstonecraft. Introduction by Mrs. E. Robins Pennell.

71 "THE ATHENIAN ORACLE." A SELECTION. EDITED
by John Underhill, with Prefatory Note by Walter Besant.

72 ESSAYS OF SAINTE-BEUVE. TRANSLATED AND
Edited, with an Introduction, by Elizabeth Lee.

73 SELECTIONS FROM PLATO. FROM THE TRANS-
lation of Sydenham and Taylor. Edited by T. W. Rolleston.

74 HEINE'S ITALIAN TRAVEL SKETCHES, ETC. TRANS-
lated by Elizabeth A. Sharp. With an Introduction from the French of
Theophile Gautier.

75 SCHILLER'S MAID OF ORLEANS. TRANSLATED,
with an Introduction, by Major-General Patrick Maxwell.

THE SCOTT LIBRARY may be had in the following Bindings :—
Cloth, uncut edges, gilt top, 1s. 6d. ; Half-Morocco, gilt top, antique ;
Red Roan, gilt edges, etc.

London : WALTER SCOTT, LIMITED, 24 Warwick Lane.

GREAT WRITERS.

A NEW SERIES OF CRITICAL BIOGRAPHIES.

Edited by Professor ERIC S. ROBERTSON, M.A.

A Complete Bibliography to each Volume, by J. P. ANDERSON, British Museum, London.

Cloth, Uncut Edges, Gilt Top.   Price 1/6.

VOLUMES ALREADY ISSUED—

LIFE OF LONGFELLOW. By PROF. ERIC S. ROBERTSON.
"A most readable little work."—*Liverpool Mercury.*

LIFE OF COLERIDGE. By HALL CAINE.
"Brief and vigorous, written throughout with spirit and great literary skill."—*Scotsman.*

LIFE OF DICKENS. By FRANK T. MARZIALS.
"Notwithstanding the mass of matter that has been printed relating to Dickens and his works . . . we should, until we came across this volume, have been at a loss to recommend any popular life of England's most popular novelist as being really satisfactory. The difficulty is removed by Mr. Marzials's little book."—*Athenæum.*

LIFE OF DANTE GABRIEL ROSSETTI. By J. KNIGHT.
"Mr. Knight's picture of the great poet and painter is the fullest and best yet presented to the public."—*The Graphic.*

LIFE OF SAMUEL JOHNSON. By COLONEL F. GRANT.
"Colonel Grant has performed his task with diligence, sound judgment, good taste, and accuracy."—*Illustrated London News.*

LIFE OF DARWIN. By G. T. BETTANY.
"Mr. G. T. Bettany's *Life of Darwin* is a sound and conscientious work.'
—*Saturday Review.*

LIFE OF CHARLOTTE BRONTË. By A. BIRRELL.
"Those who know much of Charlotte Brontë will learn more, and those who know nothing about her will find all that is best worth learning in Mr. Birrell's pleasant book."—*St. James' Gazette.*

LIFE OF THOMAS CARLYLE. By R. GARNETT, LL.D.
"This is an admirable book. Nothing could be more felicitous and fairer than the way in which he takes us through Carlyle's life and works."—*Pall Mall Gazette.*

London : WALTER SCOTT, LIMITED, 24 Warwick Lane.

GREAT WRITERS—continued.

LIFE OF ADAM SMITH. By R. B. HALDANE, M.P.

"Written with a perspicuity seldom exemplified when dealing with economic science."—*Scotsman.*

LIFE OF KEATS. By W. M. ROSSETTI.

"Valuable for the ample information which it contains."—*Cambridge Independent.*

LIFE OF SHELLEY. By WILLIAM SHARP.

"The criticisms . . . entitle this capital monograph to be ranked with the best biographies of Shelley."—*Westminster Review.*

LIFE OF SMOLLETT. By DAVID HANNAY.

"A capable record of a writer who still remains one of the great masters of the English novel."—*Saturday Review.*

LIFE OF GOLDSMITH. By AUSTIN DOBSON.

"The story of his literary and social life in London, with all its humorous and pathetic vicissitudes, is here retold, as none could tell it better."—*Daily News.*

LIFE OF SCOTT. By PROFESSOR YONGE.

"This is a most enjoyable book."—*Aberdeen Free Press.*

LIFE OF BURNS. By PROFESSOR BLACKIE.

"The editor certainly made a hit when he persuaded Blackie to write about Burns."—*Pall Mall Gazette.*

LIFE OF VICTOR HUGO. By FRANK T. MARZIALS.

"Mr. Marzials's volume presents to us, in a more handy form than any English or even French handbook gives, the summary of what is known about the life of the great poet."—*Saturday Review.*

LIFE OF EMERSON. By RICHARD GARNETT, LL.D.

"No record of Emerson's life could be more desirable."—*Saturday Review.*

LIFE OF GOETHE. By JAMES SIME.

"Mr. James Sime's competence as a biographer of Goethe is beyond question."—*Manchester Guardian.*

LIFE OF CONGREVE. By EDMUND GOSSE.

"Mr. Gosse has written an admirable biography."—*Academy.*

LIFE OF BUNYAN. By CANON VENABLES.

"A most intelligent, appreciative, and valuable memoir."—*Scotsman.*

LIFE OF CRABBE. By T. E. KEBBEL.

"No English poet since Shakespeare has observed certain aspects of nature and of human life more closely."—*Athenæum.*

LIFE OF HEINE. By WILLIAM SHARP.

"An admirable monograph . . . more fully written up to the level of recent knowledge and criticism than any other English work."—*Scotsman.*

London : WALTER SCOTT, LIMITED, 24 Warwick Lane.

GREAT WRITERS—continued.

LIFE OF MILL. By W. L. COURTNEY.

"A most sympathetic and discriminating memoir."—*Glasgow Herald.*

LIFE OF SCHILLER. By HENRY W. NEVINSON.

"Presents the poet's life in a neatly rounded picture."—*Scotsman.*

LIFE OF CAPTAIN MARRYAT. By DAVID HANNAY.

"We have nothing but praise for the manner in which Mr. Hannay has done justice to him."—*Saturday Review.*

LIFE OF LESSING. By T. W. ROLLESTON.

"One of the best books of the series."—*Manchester Guardian.*

LIFE OF MILTON. By RICHARD GARNETT, LL.D.

"Has never been more charmingly or adequately told."—*Scottish Leader.*

LIFE OF BALZAC. By FREDERICK WEDMORE.

"Mr. Wedmore's monograph on the greatest of French writers of fiction, whose greatness is to be measured by comparison with his successors, is a piece of careful and critical composition, neat and nice in style."—*Daily News.*

LIFE OF GEORGE ELIOT. By OSCAR BROWNING.

"A book of the character of Mr. Browning's, to stand midway be tween the bulky work of Mr. Cross and the very slight sketch of Miss Blind, was much to be desired, and Mr. Browning has done his work with vivacity, and not without skill."—*Manchester Guardian.*

LIFE OF JANE AUSTEN. By GOLDWIN SMITH.

"Mr. Goldwin Smith has added another to the not inconsiderable roll of eminent men who have found their delight in Miss Austen. . . . His little book upon her, just published by Walter Scott, is certainly a fascinating book to those who already know her and love her well; and we have little doubt that it will prove also a fascinating book to those who have still to make her acquaintance."—*Spectator.*

LIFE OF BROWNING. By WILLIAM SHARP.

"This little volume is a model of excellent English, and in every respect it seems to us what a biography should be."—*Public Opinion.*

LIFE OF BYRON. By HON. RODEN NOEL.

"The Hon. Roden Noel's volume on Byron is decidedly one of the most readable in the excellent 'Great Writers' series."—*Scottish Leader.*

LIFE OF HAWTHORNE. By MONCURE CONWAY.

"It is a delightful *causerie*—pleasant, genial talk about a most interesting man. Easy and conversational as the tone is throughout, no important fact is omitted, no valueless fact is recalled; and it is entirely exempt from platitude and conventionality."—*The Speaker.*

LIFE OF SCHOPENHAUER. By PROFESSOR WALLACE.

"We can speak very highly of this little book of Mr. Wallace's. It is, perhaps, excessively lenient in dealing with the man, and it cannot be said to be at all ferociously critical in dealing with the philosophy."—*Saturday Review.*

London: WALTER SCOTT, LIMITED, 24 Warwick Lane.

GREAT WRITERS—continued.

LIFE OF SHERIDAN. By LLOYD SANDERS.

"To say that Mr. Lloyd Sanders, in this little volume, has produced the best existing memoir of Sheridan, is really to award much fainter praise than the work deserves."—*Manchester Examiner.*

LIFE OF THACKERAY. By HERMAN MERIVALE and F. T. MARZIALS.

"The monograph just published is well worth reading, . . . and the book, with its excellent bibliography, is one which neither the student nor the general reader can well afford to miss."—*Pall Mall Gazette.*

LIFE OF CERVANTES. By H. E. WATTS.

"We can commend this book as a worthy addition to the useful series to which it belongs."—*London Daily Chronicle.*

LIBRARY EDITION OF "GREAT WRITERS," Demy 8vo, 2s. 6d.

London : WALTER SCOTT, LIMITED, 24 Warwick Lane.

THE NOVELTY OF THE SEASON.

SELECTED THREE-VOL. SETS

IN NEW BROCADE BINDING.

6s. per Set, in Shell Case to match.

THE FOLLOWING SETS CAN BE OBTAINED—

POEMS OF

WORDSWORTH.	COLERIDGE.	EARLY ENGLISH
KEATS.	SOUTHEY.	POETRY.
SHELLEY.	COWPER.	CHAUCER.
		SPENSER.
LONGFELLOW.		
WHITTIER.	BORDER BALLADS.	HORACE.
EMERSON.	JACOBITE SONGS.	GREEK ANTHOLOGY.
	OSSIAN.	LANDOR.
HOGG.		
ALLAN RAMSAY.	CAVALIER POETS.	GOLDSMITH.
SCOTTISH MINOR	LOVE LYRICS.	MOORE.
POETS.	HERRICK.	IRISH MINSTRELSY.
SHAKESPEARE.		
BEN JONSON.	CHRISTIAN YEAR.	WOMEN POETS.
MARLOWE.	IMITATION OF	CHILDREN OF POETS.
	CHRIST.	SEA MUSIC.
	HERBERT.	
SONNETS OF THIS		
CENTURY.		PRAED.
SONNETS OF EUROPE.		HUNT AND HOOD.
AMERICAN SONNETS.	AMERICAN HUMOR-	DOBELL.
	OUS VERSE.	
	ENGLISH HUMOROUS	
HEINE.	VERSE.	MEREDITH.
GOETHE.	BALLADES AND	MARSTON.
HUGO.	RONDEAUS.	LOVE LETTERS.

SELECTED TWO-VOLUME SETS

IN NEW BROCADE BINDING.

4s. per Set, in Shell Case to match.

SCOTT (Lady of the Lake, etc.).	BYRON (Don Juan, etc.).
SCOTT (Marmion, etc.).	BYRON (Miscellaneous).
BURNS (Songs).	MILTON (Paradise Lost).
BURNS (Poems).	MILTON (Paradise Regained, etc.).

London : WALTER SCOTT, 24 Warwick Lane, Paternoster Row.

SELECTED THREE-VOL. SETS

IN NEW BROCADE BINDING.

6s. per Set, in Shell Case to match.

O. W. HOLMES SERIES—

Autocrat of the Breakfast-Table.

The Professor at the Break-fast-Table.

The Poet at the Breakfast Table.

LANDOR SERIES—

Landor's Imaginary Conversations.

Pentameron.

Pericles and Aspasia.

THREE ENGLISH ESSAYISTS—

Essays of Elia.

Essays of Leigh Hunt.

Essays of William Hazlitt.

THREE CLASSICAL MORALISTS—

Meditations of Marcus Aurelius.

Teaching of Epictetus.

Morals of Seneca.

WALDEN SERIES—

Thoreau's Walden.

Thoreau's Week.

Thoreau's Essays.

FAMOUS LETTERS—

Letters of Burns.

Letters of Byron.

Letters of Shelley.

LOWELL SERIES—

My Study Windows.

The English Poets.

The Biglow Papers.

London : WALTER SCOTT, 24 Warwick Lane, Paternoster Row.

THE CANTERBURY POETS.

EDITED BY WILLIAM SHARP. IN 1/- MONTHLY VOLUMES.

Cloth, Red Edges	-	1s.	Red Roan, Gilt Edges, 2s. 6d.
Cloth, Uncut Edges	-	1s.	Pad. Morocco, Gilt Edges, 5s.

London: WALTER SCOTT, LIMITED, 24 Warwick Lane.

THE CANTERBURY POETS—continued.

London: WALTER SCOTT, LIMITED, 24 Warwick Lane.

THE

MUSIC OF THE POETS:

A MUSICIANS' BIRTHDAY BOOK.

EDITED BY ELEONORE D'ESTERRE KEELING.

THIS is a unique Birthday Book. Against each date are given the names of musicians whose birthday it is, together with a verse-quotation appropriate to the character of their different compositions or performances. A special feature of the book consists in the reproduction in fac-simile of autographs, and autographic music, of living composers. Three sonnets by Mr. Theodore Watts, on the "Fausts" of Berlioz, Schumann, and Gounod, have been written specially for this volume. It is illustrated with designs of various musical instruments, etc.; autographs of Rubenstein, Dvorák, Grieg, Mackenzie, Villiers Stanford, etc., etc.

"To musical amateurs this will certainly prove the most attractive birthday book ever published."—*Manchester Guardian.*

"One of those happy ideas that seems to have been yearning for fulfilment. . . . The book ought to have a place on every music stand."—*Scottish Leader.*

London: WALTER SCOTT, 24 Warwick Lane, Paternoster Row.